DJ Rising

by Love Maia

LITTLE, BROWN AND COMPANY
New York   Boston

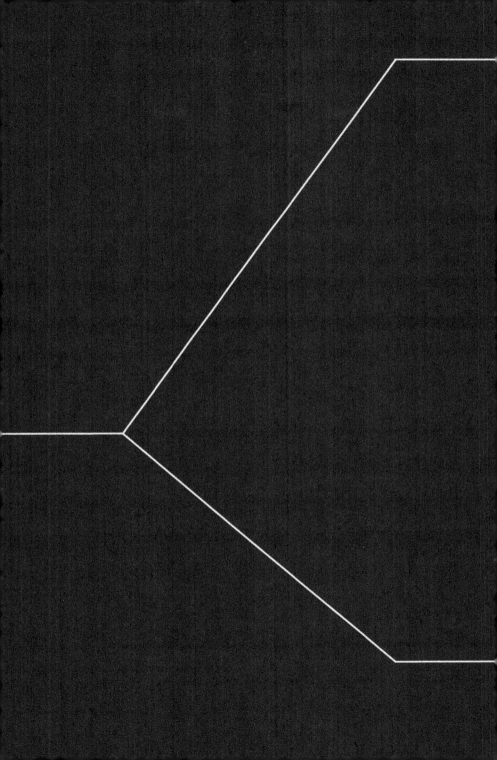

Copyright © 2012 by Love Maia

Little, Brown and Company

Hachette Book Group
237 Park Avenue, New York, NY 10017
Visit our website at www.lb-teens.com

Little, Brown and Company is a division of Hachette Book Group, Inc.
The Little, Brown name and logo are trademarks of Hachette Book Group, Inc.

The publisher is not responsible for websites
(or their content) that are not owned by the publisher.

First Paperback Edition: February 2013
First published in hardcover in February 2012 by Little, Brown and Company

Library of Congress Cataloging-in-Publication Data

Maia, Love.
DJ rising / by Love Maia. — 1st ed.
p. cm.
Summary: Sixteen-year-old Marley Diego-Dylan's career as "DJ Ice" is skyrocketing, but his mother's
heroin addiction keeps dragging him back to earth.
ISBN 978-0-316-12187-3 (hc) / ISBN 978-0-316-12189-7 (pb)
[1. Disc jockeys—Fiction. 2. Success—Fiction. 3. Mothers and sons—Fiction. 4. Drug abuse—Fiction.
5. Death—Fiction. 6. Racially-mixed people—Fiction.] I. Title.
PZ7.M2774Dj 2012
[Fic]—dc22
2010048626

10 9 8 7 6 5 4 3

RRD-H

Printed in the United States of America

For anyone who's ever had a dream.
Never give up.
Anything is possible.

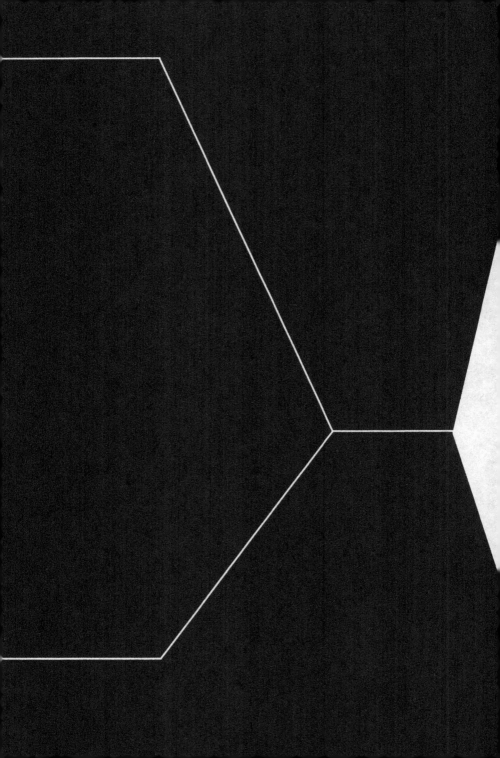

IN THE END

HERE'S HOW I SEE IT. I'M THE STAR DJ AT THE
city's most elite club, Fever. I lounge on a long, red velvet
couch in the VIP Room chatting up friends and flirting
with beautiful girls. I go by the name Lord.

When midnight strikes, it's on to the DJ booth, a huge
room with a floor-to-ceiling window looking out over a
massive dance floor the size of a basketball court.

The vast space below looks hollow and dark,
empty and depressing. But then I start pulling

records, releasing light and color into all the empty spaces. My music circles the room, spreading smiles onto hundreds of faces. The crowd sways to the beat and hollers in approval as I draw them to the floor, making them feel weightless and alive and sucking them farther and farther from their real-world problems.

Every person in Fever falls under my control, giving me sole power over every movement they make, every step, every shift, every turn, every head bob beneath the bright, flashing strobes. The bass line throbs and pulses like a heart-beat, exploding from deep within, then flowing out in a mad, endless rush. I have the power to pump people up, to mellow them out, to make them fall in love. I am everything in this moment, and everything can become anything I want it to be.

Suddenly a fight breaks out in a far corner of the club. The crowd's attention turns and everyone moves in that direction as people pack in tight around the brawlers, craning for a better look. Several bouncers rush in and quickly drag the guys outside, but the flow of energy on the dance floor has shifted and the mood is totally disrupted now. It's up to me to pull the crowd back in.

I needle a new track, smoothing over the tension as rays of sound pour from the speakers, bounce off the walls, and echo in energy. I drop a booming, confident beat that pounds in the shadows, doubling in time, then falling hard, shaking the floorboards below as the two sounds blend together in a hyp-notic mix of electro house.

People dance and cheer at the beauty of my unique mix, the fight long forgotten. Yes! That is the kind of power a DJ has.

A sexy cocktail waitress stops and smiles at me. "Care for a drink, DJ Lord?" she asks with a wink.

"Champagne," I instruct, winking back, cooler than cool, my voice deep and confident, my headphones hanging about my neck like jewelry.

"Cristal, right? Only the best for DJ Lord."

"Of course," I agree. "Only the best for the best."

That's how I see it all going down whenever I picture myself spinning at Fever.

But I've only been there in dreams.

In reality, the closest I've ever gotten to that club is the sidewalk across the street.

Six nights a week, when I'm done busing tables and washing dishes at Spazio's restaurant, I walk the two blocks to Fever and sit on the sidewalk across the street from the club to eat a crust-free tuna fish sandwich and drink a can of cold Mug Root Beer while eagerly taking in every bit of action, every detail that might give me a hint of what's going on inside.

I know there was a fight tonight because I was watching when the massive bouncers in the matching black Fever tees exploded from the front entrance and threw four twenty-something guys out into the street. The guys made their way to the corner, where they continued to go at it until the cops rolled up.

I know the infamous DJ Lord was spinning because I saw him exit a taxi and enter the club, a girl wrapped around each arm. I don't know what the guy likes to drink. Cristal just seemed right, since it's expensive and only important people drink it. There is no one more important in a club than the DJ.

I've never been inside Fever. I'm not old enough to get in. But sitting across the street from the hottest club around keeps my dream alive.

Five years from now I will go to Fever and see the real DJ Lord in action, see what the inside of that place is really like.

That isn't the dream, though. The dream is to bring my own records to Fever and get paid for dropping my own beats on the ones and twos.

Someday it'll be me up in that booth controlling every-body's good time.

Then it won't be about DJ Lord anymore.

It'll be all about DJ Marley.

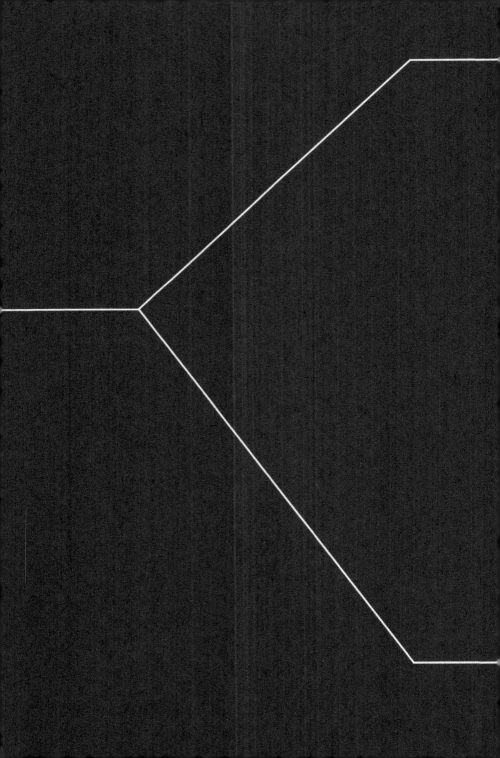

1

SPINNING IN A CLUB IS THE DREAM, BUT REALITY
goes more like this: Go to school, learn, go home, study, go to
work, work, walk to Fever, daydream, go home, study more,
go to bed, get up, repeat.

"Morning, Ma," I mumble sleepily as I pass through the
small front room of our apartment on my way to the kitchen.

My mother doesn't respond, but then she hardly ever does.

I pull the Cookie Crisp down from the cupboard and shuffle to the fridge for milk, still caught in an early-morning
haze, going through the motions, but not really with it yet.

There's no milk. The only things in the fridge are a family-size bag of fried chicken cutlets, a pot of rice and beans, half a stick of butter, and a jar with maybe two scoops of applesauce left in it.

I peer back into the front room and speak to my mother as evenly and patiently as I can. "Ma? What happened to all the milk?"

My mother sits motionless, staring at the television set from her permanent spot, sucked into the cushions on the couch as if she hasn't heard me. Half-moons sink into her cheeks below her vacant brown eyes. She is straight up skin and bones, her olive complexion looking veiny and transparent. Her hair, once long, thick, and shiny black, has gone from luscious Spanish curls to couch-potato gnarl.

My mother's a straight-up junkie, aka a dope fiend, and a hard-core one too. The kind that has no job and spends all the time she isn't doing drugs trying to figure out how to score more. And by dope I mean snow, brown sugar, Dragon, junk, smack. Or as Webster's would define it—heroin.

She was only fourteen when she walked into a clinic with an abnormal weight gain and walked out five months pregnant. Normally it wouldn't make much sense that someone could get to be an entire five months pregnant and not know it. Unless you know my mother.

Afraid to tell her own mother the news, mine ran away from home with tears in her eyes and me in her belly. Her boyfriend, Rodney Dylan, soon to be my father, had dropped out of high school the year before and was living in a studio in the projects when Ma moved in.

Four months later, my parents and a bunch of their friends

got tickets to one of those Bob Marley Day Festivals where people camp by a river for a week and watch bands perform in honor of the late, great Bob Marley. My mother went into labor the very first day. But instead of having her friends take her to the hospital, like a logical person would, she stayed at the festival.

I was born in a first-aid tent at the side of the main stage during a lesser-known Bob Marley song called "Johnny Was." It's about this boy who gets shot down in the street by a stray bullet. His mother weeps over his dead body asking why and crying out that "Johnny was a good man who never did a thing wrong."

My own mother was probably crying out too, her voice muffled by the cheers of the crowd. And then there I was. Marley Johnnywas Diego-Dylan, a baby boy born amid thousands of Bob Marley fans, my ears filling with music as I took my first breaths of weed-laced air.

I grew up dreaming of that music and dreaming of a better life. Now, at sixteen, I dream more than ever. That my pop could still be alive. That my mother could quit using. That one day I won't have to work full-time to make rent and pay bills and buy food.

I dream I have no responsibilities in life except to be a teenager. And I dream that one day I'll escape all this and find a home for my own music like Bob Marley himself must have dreamed of finding a home for his once upon a time.

"Ma," I try again, "I bought two whole gallons of milk yesterday. Who drank it all? Was it your boyfriend?"

No answer. Sometimes I wonder why I even bother.

"I have to get ready for school, but maybe we can talk about this tonight. Okay? Please?"

She acknowledges my words by flipping the channel on the television and focusing her bloodshot eyes on one of those morning shows where the hosts sit around talking endlessly to each other about nothing at all for an entire hour.

My mother wasn't always a heroin addict. She didn't get into the drugs until after my father died, four years ago. At first we were both super depressed. But within a year Ma's depression had pulled her into a downward spiral of heavier and heavier drinking. The drinking became painkillers. The painkillers turned into heroin. She's been using for a year and a half now. Sometimes it feels like I'm just watching her slowly die right in front of me.

I take a quick shower and dress for school in a pair of over-sized skater jeans, a black tee, sneakers, and an Etnies cap. I've got Etnies in black, white, red, and dark gray to cover my tightly shaved head, and today it's all about the black one.

I'm pretty much toothpick-skinny, not the ultimate body type, I suppose, but I grew a ton last year and now stand six-two, which goes over pretty well with the females. I've sort of got the baby face thing going on, but girls seem to dig a young face on a tall dude, so I do all right with it. Plus, I got some decent features from my parents. Being half black and half Puerto Rican has turned into an advantage lately. You don't see that every day.

On the bus, I crank my iPod volume and shuffle through flash cards for the presentation I have to give on Ernest Hemingway in English today. We're only a month into the school year and I'm already about to give my second presentation. I'm a horrible speaker and my first presentation was a total disaster.

But that's okay because this one'll be different. This time I'll be cool, calm, and collected. Hemingway's life will pour from my lips like sweet maple syrup. I glance at the top flash card on which I've written in big, block letters:

ERNEST HEMINGWAY WAS BORN IN 1899 IN CHICAGO, ILLINOIS.

Hemingway.
1899.
Chicago.
Easy.

2

"UM...AND SO...HEMINGWAY WAS ORIGINALLY from Chicago, right? I mean, well, that's where he was born and stuff. I'm not sure how long he stayed, though, or where all else he might've lived when he was growing up. And uh...that's in Illinois. Chicago is, I mean, not Hemingway. Or I guess he was in Illinois too. Born there at least. Um...in...1899."

Or maybe not so easy.

"Uh, and also he served in this war, right? World War One actually. Oh, and um, the Spanish Civil War, he was in that one too. Both of those. Wars, I mean."

"Don't forget to make eye contact with your audience, Marley," Ms. Beckett says, smiling warmly.

Eye contact with my audience? Is she kidding? I'm too busy torturing my audience.

"In 1952, Hemingway wrote a novella called 'The Old Man and the Sea' and it, um, it won him this prize called a Pulitzer. No wait. No. Yeah. Pulitzer. Pulitzer Prize."

Melanie Jergens snaps her gum loudly from her front row desk, and the sound pops in my ears all sudden-like and totally irritating. She's been doing it ever since I started— snapping it on purpose to distract me, just like Brittany Danes is purposely letting out these loud, exasperated sighs. They both give me nasty smirks whenever I do my "eye contact intervals." It's rude, but then that's how the junior Have girls at Ellington Prep are. They go out of their way to be nasty to anyone that isn't them. I try to pick a generic spot to focus on but always end up looking right at Melanie or Brittany. It's impossible not to.

"He also won the Nobel Prize. Uh…that was in 1954…. That's this top book award. Or I mean, that and the Pulitzer both are. Top awards, I mean. Or…um…yeah. Top book awards."

Richie Edwards, Jordan Max, and Steve O'Neill snicker together in the back of the room in that quiet way that only sounds like they're trying to be quiet when in fact they really want you to hear them making fun of you. As usual, our sweet, elderly English teacher, Ms. Beckett, doesn't notice.

"When Hemingway first moved to Cuba…"

My mouth feels dry. My underarms are wet. My left foot itches for some reason. I make another attempt at the eye interval thing, but instead end up looking right at Lea Hall. Lea isn't paying me any mind whatsoever. She's busy writing something down in a fuzzy pink notebook. Probably something about how much she loves some perfect boyfriend or something like that. Probably something about a perfect, unbelievably rich boyfriend who's an older guy attending a perfect college majoring in something perfect.

It would be fair to say that Lea is the most beautiful girl I've ever seen in person. Most guys would say Melanie is hotter, but that's because most guys have no idea what they're talking about. Melanie's too obvious with the low-cut tops and the miniskirts and the tight jeans.

Lea covers up her body more, but you can still tell how hot she is underneath and I like letting my imagination run wild wondering about the stuff I can't see. Her conservative clothes and that brown-eyed, rosy-cheeked, innocent-girl look of hers make me want to walk up and grab her and kiss her like crazy ten times more than I'd want to if she were wearing some slutty outfit. She doesn't wear a ton of makeup either, the way a lot of girls at our school do. She doesn't need to.

I look down at my flash card notes and then out at her again. Jeez, I'm being so obvious and yet she never seems to notice me staring. You'd think she'd feel my eyes burning into her like two hot coals, but she never even looks up.

I watch her curl a few loose strands of blond hair behind one ear and nibble on her pencil. I love it when she does that curl-her-hair-behind-her-ear thing. I picture her sitting alone in the classroom with her hair blowing off her face in a dramatic sexy slow-mo. She winks at me and blows me a slow, sensual fantasyland kiss.

Just then, Richie lets out an enormous burp, bringing me back to reality with a jolt, catching me by surprise, and causing me to spill my flash cards all over the floor. The whole class erupts in laughter as Jordan reaches across Steve's desk to high-five Richie.

"Gentlemen, please," Ms. Beckett finally warns.

Richie leans back in his chair rubbing his stomach and grinning proudly. I kneel and gather my cards into a pile as quickly as possible, picking them up from the floor as the last few chuckles pass through the room. They're totally blowing my concentration. As if I wasn't nervous enough already. But that's how the popular junior Have guys at Ellington are. They're even worse than the girls.

I gaze out again at a sea of bored faces, my flash cards now completely out of order. I hate this class. I hate how alone I feel here.

"In 1952, Ernest Hemingway wrote this novella called 'The Old Man and the Sea' and, um, he got a Pulitzer Prize for it."

"Uh, hello?" Richie shouts. "You already told us that."

I look up in time to see Steve form an index finger and a thumb into an *L* on his forehead, and mouth the word *loser*.

Jordan scratches his nose with his middle finger.

What a bunch of assholes. If I were still at my old school, I'd tell them so as we file out into the hall when the bell rings, but these days I keep my mouth shut. Especially in English, since pretty much all the miserable, stuck-up junior Haves are in my Advanced Lit class and not one of them is worth getting into it with. Not when I've got a scholarship to protect. *Be cool, Marley. Keep it to yourself for now.*

"Interesting speech, Marley," Richie says, slapping me on the shoulder as he passes by.

Richie, Jordan, Steve, and Jason Camp all turn to look at me and crack up laughing as they start down the hall. I don't want to follow them. But we have the same next class on the other side of campus and there's no other way to get to the gym in five minutes. I slip on my phones and crank the volume to block them out, watching them blankly with their scrunched-up faces and their mouths going a mile a minute as I focus on the melody in my ears. Music always gets me through when I'm alone.

I follow them out of the building and that's when I see Charles "Chuckie" Wu and Reginald "Scuzz" Owens heading our way. They approach the Haves first, Scuzz stepping right up to Richie and giving him a stern nod inches from Richie's face. Richie gives a quick nod back before moving out of Scuzz and Chuckie's way. He motions to the other three Haves and they rush off toward the locker room. I break into a grin as I watch it all happen without a single word being exchanged.

Scuzz approaches me next. We grip hands. I turn to Chuckie and we pound fists. I am no longer alone. I've got my boys with me now.

"Your speech must've been pretty bad," Scuzz states matter-of-factly as we head in the direction of the locker room.

"How'd you know?"

"Well, for one thing, those stuck-up Have wimps were making cracks about it when they walked out of the building."

"And for another thing," Chuckie says, "*all* of your speeches suck."

I shrug in reply. He's right. They do.

"Speaking of things that suck..." Scuzz says, raising his eyebrows at each of us.

"Gym," I finish for him. "You're glad you play football so you don't have to go."

"You know this."

"Not all of us can be superstars with a pigskin, Scuzzy," Chuckie says.

Scuzz laughs extra loud as he grips hands with each of us once more before we head on into the locker room. "Lucky for me!"

I can still hear him laughing to himself as the locker room doors shut behind us.

*　　*　　*

Entering the gym locker room is like taking that first step onto a path that will lead you into the fiery depths of hell. When I picture what that hell will be like, I never fail to see my gym teacher, Ms. Tyler, with red horns shooting out of her head and a long, sharp tail whipping back and forth behind her as she greets you with an old, deflated basketball or a dumb-ass badminton racquet.

Sure, it's an exaggeration, but I can't help it. Scuzz is right. Gym sucks. And not only because I'm not the athletic type, even though I'm not. Not because the gym equipment is really old either, because it isn't. This is Ellington Prep after all. Nothing is ever old or deflated here. No, it's the fact that we have yet to learn how to play a single team sport properly that makes gym such a joke.

"'Sup, Transplants?" Chuckie calls out to Will, K.C., and Juan when we meet up with them at our lockers.

"Chillin', you low-down, dirty excuse for a couple of Transplants," Will replies.

Transplants—lower-income students who transferred into the infamous, overprivileged, educationally renowned Ellington Preparatory High School, a wealthy private school that finally integrated itself for the first time last year by adding thirty-three financial-aid students to a student body of a thousand.

I don't remember which of us came up with the name. Probably Chuckie. The rest of the school refers to us by more proper names, like *transfers* or *scholarship students*, but we wanted our own name for ourselves, something that would constantly remind us who we are and where we come from.

If you get an organ transplant, and the transplant takes, it can save your life. That organ will always have originally belonged to someone else, though.

Going to Ellington Prep may not physically save our lives, but it could sure switch up our futures pretty drastically, which could have the same result. Ellington doesn't belong to us, though, not really. It's more like we're using it temporarily; borrowing it from kids with privileged lifestyles who live in homes with things like fireplaces and front yards and washing machines you don't need coins to operate.

We call each other Transplants so we don't forget that as soon as we hear that last bell ring, we'll all be headed right back to our respective hoods.

Haves is the name we came up with for the most popular crowd at Ellington. We call them Haves because they have everything and think they're better than everyone else. But that's also a name we use only with each other. We'd never call them that to their faces. Unlike them, we have respect for other people.

"So how'd your speech go down, Marley?" Will asks.

"Not so good," I answer, opening my locker and tossing my lid on the shelf inside. I yank my T-shirt up over my head and take out the reversible, yellow and blue shirt and gym shorts they make us wear. I put on my shirt, yellow side up. We're playing soccer all this week and I'm on the gold team.

"Richie and them were messing with him," says Chuckie. "Huh, Mar."

I nod. "I don't get why they act like that."

"They act like that because they think they're better than everyone else," Juan says. "Guys like Richie try to get at us because they want to keep us down. Especially you, because you're the only Transplant in that class."

"Swear to God, son," says K.C., "that Richie Edwards is way overdue to get his sorry ass kicked."

"Richie Edwards..." Will repeats, shaking his head all vigorous-like as if he can simply undo Richie's entire existence if he shakes his head hard enough. "How're you gonna be rich and then turn around and have the nerve to call your kid *Richie* anyway?"

"His given name isn't even Richard," Juan points out. "It's Rich. There are rich people out there who actually named their kid Rich. Who does some shit like that?"

"That'd be like if my mama named me *Poor*," says Will.

Everybody cracks up laughing as Chuckie drops an arm across Will's shoulder. "Come on, then, Poor. Let's get out there and see if you're a better goalie than Will is."

We trudge through the locker room and out onto the field for a wannabe game of something that has no right calling itself soccer. Our game has hardly anything to do with organized sports. We kick the ball back and forth with no real direction and not much skill. That's the thing about gym. You dip your toes in several sports, but you never actually learn to swim.

I love having gym outside among the trees, though. I focus on the sun, which shines down in these sleepy rays that kiss the tip of each blade of grass in the field. It warms the school buildings behind us from the outside in and puts me in daydream mode. The music in my head goes perfectly with the sun and the trees and the grass, an upbeat melody with a touch of a melancholy feel to it, but in a way that's so right. I try to picture myself spinning for the Fever crowd, thinking of the type of people that were standing outside the club last night and wondering if they'd dig the mix I'm imagining for them.

If I had to describe Fever in one word, that word would be *unreal*. You feel like you're in this whole other world when you're anywhere near that club. There's always a huge spotlight set up outside on Friday and Saturday nights like it's a movie premiere or something. You can see those white beams of light moving through the sky from everywhere, and the colored bulbs that line the exterior of the building light the crowd in shades of blue, red, yellow, and green. It's like a fantasyland the way the club is all lit up and makes everyone seem really glamorous.

A piercing sound floods my ears as Ms. Tyler blows her whistle like crazy. I don't know why she even bothers. Gym is almost over and neither side has made a single goal. I watch K.C. and Richie struggle to kick the ball in different directions even though they're on the same team. Then I slip back into thoughts of Fever, wondering when it will be my turn to walk beyond those red ropes that hold the line at bay and drop some of my addictive beats on their crowd.

I imagine no longer having to fight the exhaustion of working long shifts after a full day of school just to make enough to keep a roof over Ma and me. I imagine getting paid for my hands to spend all night pulling records instead of getting paid for my hands to spend all night pruning up from hot water and dirty dishes like they do now. I imagine one day being one of the important people who gets to skip the line at Fever and walk right on into the club ahead of the crowd, instead of being the guy who cleans up after those important people. I imagine I am somebody else.

3

"HEY, MA," I CALL OUT AS I WALK THROUGH THE
front door of our apartment after school.

I head straight through the swinging door to the kitchen,
dropping my school pack on the floor and pulling some left-
overs out of the fridge to make for dinner. Most nights I get
something to eat at the restaurant where I work before starting my shift, which saves me money, but I have to make my
mother a proper meal once a day. If I don't cook for her, she
doesn't eat. It's like she forgets or something.

The pot of beans and rice is still sitting on the top shelf

where I left it, but the fridge is otherwise empty save for that half a stick of butter on a paper plate and the practically empty applesauce jar. I peer back into the front room.

"Ma," I say as I hover in the doorway that splits the front room from the kitchen, "what happened to that bag of fried chicken cutlets I cooked up for you a couple nights ago? It was here when I left for school this morning."

My mother pretends she doesn't hear me.

"Ma, please help me out here."

"Frederick," she finally drones, her eyes never lifting from the television screen. "Frederick ate the chicken."

"Aw, Ma. There was a whole economy-size bag's worth in here when I left for school."

"He was real hungry," she says.

"He was real high," I correct her. "He's always high. Thanks to him I only have beans and rice to heat up for your dinner. And no milk."

I go back into the kitchen and light the stove to reheat the beans and rice. Frederick. Figures. There's been a whole string of guys like him around ever since she started using— so-called boyfriends who're really just drug addicts who hang around our apartment and hook up with my mother on a regular basis in exchange for getting her dope and helping her shoot up.

It kills me to let them stay in our apartment. It kills me to let them through the front door. But if I don't, they wander the streets all night and get high in shady-ass drug dens. Ma goes with them when they do, and I simply can't have that.

Frederick is my mother's latest loser boyfriend and he's the biggest loser of them all, which is really saying something.

17

But the good news is he's been around for almost a month now, so his time's about up. No boyfriend has ever lasted more than a month.

"Tell Frederick he needs to buy his own food from now on and stop eating ours," I tell my mother as I pass through the front room on my way to the bathroom, but she ignores me.

I take a three-minute shower. That's all you get in this place before the water runs cold. For me it's enough. Those three minutes alone with the rushing hot water are like therapy. Running my face under the wet heat is like having all my problems sucked inside out and flushed down the drain with the dirt and grime.

By the time six thirty rolls around, my mother's dinner is ready and so am I. It's Friday night and I have plans with friends. The only night off I get from my job is Tuesday, so I usually work on Friday and Saturday nights, but once a month I switch with my buddy Julio and get an actual weekend night off.

My heartbeat quickens in anticipation of getting out of this place and being free for the night. No responsibilities. Nobody to cook for or clean up after, nobody to take care of but myself. My boy's signature honk comes from down on the street a few minutes after seven. I grab my jacket and lock up my bedroom. "I'm headed out for the night, Ma."

My mother's bloodshot eyes never leave the TV screen. I don't even care that I get no response from her. As of this moment, I am officially a teenager for the rest of the night.

4

"MARLEY, MAR! 'SUP, MAN."

"'Sup," I reply with a nod as I slide into the passenger seat of Scuzz's Buick. I lean back and let out a deep breath I swear I've been holding since I first got home from school. That place upstairs may be where I live, but this, this feels like home: like where I'm supposed to be, sitting in an old-school, worn-out, tan leather, bench-style car seat, surrounded by a comforting darkness and music so loud the trunk vibrates with every beat and smoke so thick you'd swear it's fog. It all makes me feel so alive. Even if I do have to roll down the window to let in some fresh air.

"Well, if it isn't the famous English historian," Chuckie announces, leaning over the backseat and grinning like crazy as he slaps me on the shoulder repeatedly. "Those presentations are gonna kill your grade point average, Mar. No four-point-oh for you."

I shrug like I don't care about my grades even though I do. I care a lot actually. Chuckie teasing me about it is his way of reminding me the worst that could happen is I'll get a B in Advanced Lit. I can't sweat the small stuff in life and no matter how badly I want all A's, getting a B is *definitely* small stuff.

"You'll be all right, Mar," says Scuzz. "The way I figure it, if Ellington Prep is meant to be the school for us, it will be. If not, then so be it. School ain't life." He cranks the power steering–less wheel all the way to the left and peels out into the waiting night.

Scuzz and Chuckie are my best friends in the world. They're more like brothers, really. I'd take a bullet for either one without a second thought, and I can't remember ever not knowing them. We grew up in the same projects until my family moved to a one-bedroom apartment a few blocks away when I was ten and Chuckie's escaped to a duplex two years ago.

We've gone to the same schools and been in all the same classes practically our whole lives, so it's kind of crazy that Chuckie, Scuzz, and I all got chosen to be among the first group of financial-aid students to ever attend Ellington Preparatory High School.

Chuckie earned his scholarship by being a hard-core, straight-up, hands-down, indisputable genius.

Scuzz earned the first of eight athletic scholarships by dominating Morris Peak sports as the top athlete in school.

I earned mine the hard way. I studied my freaking ass off for it.

Now we're all going to this top private school and each doing pretty well for himself. For the first time in my life, I feel like all three of us might have a real future.

"So, Marley, what's up with Jen's party? You good?"

I shrug at Chuckie. "I'm ready to play."

"Yeah, that part'll be cool, but what I wanna know is, are you ready for *her*? You know she's gonna come on hard once she's got you there."

Scuzz slides me a slow grin. "She does want you bad, Mar."

I nod in reply. Jennifer pretty much feels the same way about me that I do about Lea Hall. Only difference is Jen is the type to get way up in your face about it. Constantly. It makes it hard to hang with her for more than an hour or two.

But not tonight.

Tonight I'm the DJ.

Tonight Jen could come at me all night long and I wouldn't care.

I figured we'd go straight to her place, but instead of heading south toward Jennifer's, Scuzz takes the freeway north.

"You making a run for the border?"

"Naw, man," he says, "gonna get some Mickey D's right quick. Could make a run for the border after the party, though, if you want."

I nod. "That'll work."

We get off at the next exit where the McDonald's drive-thru is.

Chuckie starts the loudest, most pitiful beat box in history, pressing his lips together in a massive fart sound and following that up with this overexaggerated sucking of air in and out, "*Puhuh, puhuh, puhuh.*"

Scuzz joins in with his own version of a beat box—a long, deep fart sound, followed by two higher, shorter fart sounds, the second of which seems to ask a question. This is the kind of shit they do when they're bored.

I don't pay them any mind. I focus on the scenery outside, and the other cars in line, and the fact that there won't be a single dish for me to serve tonight, or table for me to clear, or spill for me to wipe up, or dirty pot to scrub. Not one glass to fill or ass to kiss.

This is a typical scene among the three of us—Scuzz and Chuckie attempting to out-dork each other while I barely pay their goofiness any mind at all. This is my role in our crew, to be the chill one.

Chuckie is the crazy one. He's always into something shady and if you hang around him long enough, always getting you into something shady too. He's the only Chinese guy I know who stands almost six feet tall, with a sinister grin on his face and thick black hair down to his shoulders, and he's the only guy in our whole school with a goatee.

Girls dig him. He makes them laugh, and for some reason they decide if he's funny, he must be sweet too. Too bad he can only be sweet for like an hour before he starts saying all the wrong things. He's simply too goofy, too rude, and too incapable of taking anything seriously long enough to make it to the end of a date without ticking off the girl he's out with. The only thing he's ever taken seriously is his education. Chuckie's a straight genius, and the senior Have boys who stroll down the halls at school bragging to each other about their acceptance letters to Harvard and Yale have nothing on him.

Those boys have nothing on my boy Scuzz either. That's because their parents will fork out loads of dough for them to attend schools like Stanford and Princeton while Scuzz will go for free. Yup, over the next year and a half, every college he applies to will be offering him a full scholarship, and several more will try to chase him down in person.

While Chuckie is known as the comedian, Scuzz is known as the athlete. *The* athlete, with all the emphasis on the word *the*. Football, basketball, baseball, track, skiing, snowboarding, surfing, rugby, water polo, tennis, soccer, bowling, golf…land, water, air, it doesn't really matter. There is no sport he hasn't mastered or couldn't if he wanted to. Scuzz has it made and he's a pretty smart guy on top of his jock status, and good with the women too. Luck didn't miss him and neither did skill.

Like Chuckie, Scuzz sometimes comes off a bit shallow on the surface, but his soul runs deep. Both of them are the best friends a guy could have and that's where I'm the lucky one. I would never have gotten this far at Ellington without them. Hell, I would never have gotten this far in life if it weren't for Chuckie and Scuzz.

"Yeah, gimme a Big Mac Extra Value Meal with a Coke, two McDouble burgers, and an extra order of large fries," Scuzz hollers at the drive-thru speakerphone. "A sundae too. Fudge."

"Anything else?" the speakerphone muffles back.

Scuzz looks over at me and then back at Chuckie as if he's just remembered we're in the car with him. "Oh yeah, so you guys want something too or what?"

Chuckie leans over Scuzz and screams out the window, "Lemme have a large fry, a vanilla shake, and your digits, baby. You want anything, Mar?"

"Coke," I say, since McDonald's doesn't have root beer.

"Yeah, and a Coke for my boy. You got a friend in there for him too or what? I'll bet you do. What time're you off, mama?" Scuzz cranks the music back up and starts inching the car forward before Chuckie's done talking. "Aye!" Chuckie yells. "I'm trying to peep game here and you're pulling away."

"I want my food. I'm not trying to wait for you to spit game at some girl you haven't even seen."

Chuckie points to the line of cars in front of us that sit four deep. "Not like there's anywhere to go."

"Nowhere to go?" Scuzz asks, looking around confused. He continues to ease the Buick forward an inch at a time. "Nowhere to go?" he says again, jerking ahead. "You sure about that?"

Chuckie's eyes grow wide as Scuzz approaches the car ahead of us. "Scuzzy!"

Scuzz bumps the car hard, pushing it forward at least two feet. "Oops," he says, flashing each of us his best shit-eating grin.

"Will you look at that?" says Chuckie. "You could've done some real damage to that car!" But they're both laughing, having already moved over halfway up their usual prankster scale. The driver of the car in front of us has checked out

Scuzz in his rearview and apparently decided it would be wiser to stay in his car and keep quiet than to get out and get into it with the six-four, two-hundred-and-fifty-pound, slightly shady-looking black teenager with the shaved head. Scuzz "accidentally" bumps him twice more before we pick up our order.

"Speaking of chicks with big hooters," Chuckie says through a mouthful of food as we pull back out into the street even though nobody was talking about chicks, or tits, or anything else besides where's my fries, and hand me my drink, and did they put hot sauce in that bag? Scuzz and I follow Chuckie's gaze to the right and the two of them start spitting all kinds of foolishness to the three girls walking on the sidewalk beside us, trying to get them interested.

Not me. I'm lost in my own world thinking of Lea. I wonder if she's also on her way to a party somewhere. I wonder what friends she's with and how on earth that girl manages not to notice me gawking at her like an idiot during English even when I'm giving a freaking speech in front of the whole class. I wonder if she's really nicer than her Have girlfriends the way I keep hearing she is around school, the way I keep hoping she is. I am always wondering when it comes to that girl. I know I have to stop torturing myself thinking about her. But no matter how hard I try, I can't quite do it.

THE PARTY ENDS UP BEING PRETTY COOL, nothing too wild, just our main group of friends plus whoever they brought with them all going over to Jennifer Prior's place to chill.

"Ladies," Scuzz starts in the minute we walk through the door, "we have arrived!"

"The only three men you'll need to be forever satisfied," Chuckie finishes.

Everyone starts shouting out greetings, and Jennifer comes over to give us each a hug. She lingers when she gets to mine, then attaches herself to my arm and pretty much drags me around her apartment on a guided tour I don't really want.

Jennifer is one of only two white kids who're part of our junior Transplant crew at school. She's real tall for a girl, and stocky and muscular, yet still manages to be considered cute by the guys. Being a superstar athlete, and pretty, and white, she could've befriended the regular kids at Ellington easily, but she stuck with us Transplants and I've got mad love for her for that. I just don't have *love* love for her.

"How've you been, Mar?" she asks, as she shows me the kitchen/dining/living area, but what she's really asking me is, what are the chances of us hooking up tonight?

"I'm cool," I reply, which is supposed to translate as none. She walks me over to the bedroom she shares with her sisters and pauses in the doorway, watching me with a hopeful expression. "Jen..." I say, hoping the tone of my voice and the look on my face will be enough, but Jennifer never gives up that easily on anything.

"So you wanna go to the movies with me next Friday?"

I shift my weight from left foot to right and yank down on the brim of my lid, wishing I could stretch it out over my entire face and disappear. "I can't."

"Why not?"

"I have to work."

She flicks on the light, walks into the room, and plops down on her bed. "Maybe a night you don't work, then?"

"Jen..."

Jennifer frowns. "Yeah, I know. You don't like me like that, right?"

"You don't understand," I try to tell her.

"You're right, I don't," she says. "I used to think maybe you didn't like me because you don't date white girls. But now I hear you have a thing for Lea Hall, so I guess it's me that's the problem."

"Aw, come on."

"No, you come on," she tells me as she gets up, moves back into the doorway, and intertwines her arm with mine again. "I'll show you where I set you up to DJ."

I respond with a half smile stuck somewhere between relief and guilt as she leads me back down the hall to the main room. It's always this way with Jennifer. She comes on crazy hard and then lets up suddenly. I got off way easier than I thought I would, being at her house and all. She only hassled me for, like, five minutes. Five awkward minutes alone with Jennifer is definitely worth it when the trade-off is getting to DJ all night.

Playing for people is pretty much amazing. Even when it's only for your friends and sometimes *because* it's only for your friends. When I spin at home, I'm always picturing some imaginary club crowd dancing and smiling and really getting into the music. When I spin at parties, I get a chance to play for actual people and find out what they really think.

The parties are usually given by someone in our crew, but every once in a while I get a chance to spin at a Morris Peak party or a Roosevelt party and sometimes even ones thrown by kids from the old neighborhood, since Scuzz still lives there and is real good at talking me up.

The cool thing about getting to spin for a party like this one for only my friends is they're so psyched to have a DJ for parties at all they'd listen to anything and be happy. Hiring a DJ for a private party is the kind of thing the Ellington kids do, the kind of bullshit extravagance they can afford, so me being able to DJ at parties is a glamorous perk. It doesn't cost a dime, but it makes everybody feel like we've got it as good as they do for a change.

Plus, my friends inspire me creatively. Like, say for instance the song playing when I first got into Scuzz's ride sticks in my head and then something memorable happens tonight or on any night and suddenly that song always reminds me of that moment. Well, I might make that song the basis of my next mix.

The cool thing about getting to spin at a party for people *other* than my friends is I get to play for kids I don't know and see their true reactions. When I'm right about a track and play something that really turns people on, they smile wide, laugh hard, and dance like they mean it. When I'm wrong about a track, smiles fall off and heads shake, and if I'm *really* wrong, no one dances. That part sucks, but at least it helps me figure out what doesn't work.

The cool thing about getting to spin for *any* party, whether for my friends or for kids from another school, is it puts me in demand. So when I'm sweating like crazy, surrounded by hot water and steam and an endless pile of pots and pans at the end of a long Friday or Saturday night shift at work and my mind drifts to thoughts of some party I'm missing out on, I know whoever is there is missing me too. Radio play and mixtapes simply don't compare.

"Go!" Will shouts, signaling Scuzz, Chuckie, Denise, Juan, and Terrell to simultaneously flip open the tops on their Buds and drink as fast as they can. Of course, Scuzz wins easily. Beer chugging is practically a sporting event, which means he can't possibly lose.

About twenty-five of us are lounging in Jennifer's main room, shouting and laughing, and drinking and dancing. These are our friends, the junior Transplants from Ellington Prep, plus some of our friends from Morris Peak and Roosevelt, a mixture of black and Hispanic kids with a few white and Asian kids mixed in and a hundred percent of us living somewhere below the middle-class line with a guy/girl split of about fifty-five/forty-five.

"I got you a drink," Jennifer says, placing a large red plastic cup on the table where I'm spinning.

Not to say that what I'm doing is really spinning. Jennifer connected a stereo CD player to a set of speakers and then set up a second set of speakers for me to connect an MP3 player to. I plug my headphones into the CD player, skip to the song I want, then do a timed pull-out so the music plays through its speakers while I plug into my iPod.

I select the next track I'm going to play on my iPod, rewind the first few bars over and over until I get the beats to match up with the song I've already got playing through, and quickly switch out my phones with the speaker plug so the music can play through the second set of speakers while I use the volume as a fader to silence the CD player before the beats can slip out of sync.

Since there's no way to adjust the tempo of either the stereo or my iPod, I can't keep two songs playing at the same time for more than a few beats. Basically I have to spend time beforehand finding songs with matching BPMs that'll work well together and then switch back and forth between them quick-like. This is the kind of makeshift setup we'll usually come up with for a party, since we hardly ever have turntables. It's really hard to mix well this way, but I love the challenge of it. A drop mix—where I just switch from one track to the other—would be one thing, but beat mixing on a separate CD and MP3 player without any speed or pitch control? There aren't but so many people out there who can pull off something like that.

I stop long enough to thank Jennifer and take a drink from the cup she brought me. It's root beer. I never touch alcohol. Not with a boozed-up heroin addict for a mother. It's fine if my friends drink or smoke weed, but I'll stick with my root beers.

"Aye, Marley!" Chuckie calls out, making his way over with Will, Terrell, and Terrell's girl, Wanda. They all have these funny looks on their faces like they're about to pull a prank on Jennifer and me or crack jokes about us hooking up or something, which would suck. "Will has something to tell you," Chuckie says, his eyes lighting up in that way they do when he's about to pull a punk move.

I frown at Chuckie, already feeling wary. "Oh yeah?"

We all look to Will, who looks like he's about to explode. "The thing is, Mar," he says, "tomorrow night is your night."

"How so?" Jennifer asks.

"Because my neighbor broke his arm yesterday!"

"Okay," I say, "but what does that have to do with me?"

"Well, remember I told you about that neighbor who's a DJ?"

"Yeah?"

"And you know how I said he works at a club, right? Remember that?"

"Yeah, Will, I remember. What's up? I'm kind of busy here."

"Well, the thing is, the craziest thing happened. You won't believe it."

A long silence follows while we all hang on Will's next words, but they never come. He just keeps standing there cheesing hard.

"What! What!" Jennifer urges. "Come on, Will, spit it out!"

"I swear Marley'll want to hug me when I tell him."

"Tell me what exactly?"

"About my neighbor. You won't believe it."

"Look," Terrell cuts in, "I'm gonna get old waiting for him to tell you. His neighbor is a DJ who broke his arm and has to have surgery on it this weekend. He needs you to fill in for him tomorrow night."

"Yeah, I really hooked you up," Will says, beaming. "I told him not to worry, cuz my boy Marley could do it. You should've seen how smooth I was."

Another long silence follows, except now they've all switched from looking at Will to looking at me like they're waiting on me to do something. "What are you even talking about?"

"Will got you a DJ job for tomorrow night," says Wanda. "A real one."

I stare at them all in shocked silence. Then I laugh. "Whatever," I say, waving them off and moving to pull my next couple tracks. "I know you're fucking with me." Will looks at me with the same ear-to-ear grin he's been wearing since they first walked over. "Is this some kind of cruel prank or something, because it's not even cool."

"We're not that heartless," says Terrell.

Which is about the time I stop smiling. And start to realize what's really going on. *Holy shit!* "You guys are serious?"

Chuckie, Terrell, and Wanda all nod. Jennifer gives me a funny look like she's not sure she's buying it either.

"I ran into Collin yesterday," says Will. "When he told me about his broken arm and how he was in a bind I said that my friend is a DJ and could take his gig for a night, no problem. I told him you DJ at clubs all the time. Crazy coincidence me running into him like that with his arm in a cast and all, huh? Like it was meant to be or something."

I look over at Chuckie, needing him to reassure me this is for real. "It's true, Mar. He got you a gig. For one night you're gonna live your dream. You get to be a real DJ, in a real club. Paid and all that."

"Seriously?"

Everyone smiles and nods in reply and that's when I realize it's not just the five of them, the whole room is listening in. Probably something to do with the fact that I faded out the last track and haven't played music for several minutes. I look around at everyone now, suddenly desperate for an excuse out of this whole thing. It's just too crazy, too last minute.

"I have to work tomorrow night," I tell Will, who works as a part-time dishwasher at Spazio's. "No way will I find a sub on such short notice."

Will laughs a little too loudly in his excitement. "Nice try. I already called around, and Victor said he'd be happy to cover your shift tomorrow."

"But I don't have the gear to play out," I say. "All I have are my pop's turntables, which aren't reliable enough for a club, and it's not like I can show up with a stereo and an iPod."

"We were talking about this earlier," says Chuckie. "You're tight with that teacher of yours, Mr. Faulkner, right? He'd probably let you use one of the laptops from school for the night and borrow that DJ equipment he's got."

"No way," I tell him. "A school's not going to let me take its property off campus like that."

"A school like Morris Peak wouldn't," says Chuckie. "But this is Ellington Prep. And I'll bet you they will."

I shake my head. "I doubt it."

Then again, he could be right.

Mr. Faulkner is my music teacher. I signed up for his Beginning Jazz Band class as an elective, planning to learn keyboards, but when he went around the room asking what instrument each of us wanted to play, I blurted out "turntables" instead.

"Turntables?" he asked.

"DJ turntables."

Mr. Faulkner shook his head. "DJ turntables aren't a musical instrument."

"Sure they are," I said. He went quiet for a while, thinking it over, but eventually agreed we could look into it.

Chuckie is right—a fancy private school like Ellington, with first-rate teachers and plenty of cash flow, might let me borrow a laptop. After all, Mr. Faulkner not only let me develop my DJ skills in his class, he actually allocated school funds to purchase turntables and software. And at the beginning of this school year, he added a brand-new set of CD

34

turntables. No way would that ever happen at Morris Peak. Not even close.

"His number's listed in the school directory, if you wanna call and ask him," Terrell is saying. "And if Faulkner says no, we'll figure something else out. If we all ask around, at least one of us'll find some turntables or a laptop you can borrow."

"By tomorrow?" I ask skeptically.

"Anything's possible," says Chuckie. "Just say yes to the gig and we'll go from there."

"Say yes!" someone shouts.

"Yeah, Marley," someone else calls out, and then the whole room erupts in a volcano of encouragement.

"You were meant to do this, Mar," Scuzz says, moving in beside me and gripping my shoulder for a second.

"You really were," Jennifer agrees.

"Go for it, Marley!" Chuckie screams in a high-pitched girly voice. "Marley! Marley!" he chants, waving his arms in the air to get everyone to join in. And they do. A roomful of people chant my name, pushing me to get out there and take this chance. A roomful of friends. Now I have to do it.

"Okay, okay," I say, and everyone laughs and cheers. So I guess this is it. I guess I'm finally going to play out for real.

Everyone moves back into their own worlds, refocusing on whatever it was they were doing before, but for me the room is still spinning. I'm really about to do this.

"What kind of music do they want him to play?" Terrell asks Will.

"Collin said Saturday night is 'Be Kind, Rewind' night at DRC and that you gotta play all old-school R & B and hip-hop tracks. Real old-school, like Run DMC–style. Rick James and shit. And you gotta scratch a lot. I saw Collin spin a party in our building once, and I remember him scratching records almost constantly. But you can handle that, right, Mar?"

I nod.

"What time is he supposed to be there?"

"Eight," Will tells Scuzz.

"Get there at seven," Scuzz tells me. "Don't wanna take any chances."

"How many hours is this for?" Jennifer wants to know.

Will shrugs. "I forgot to ask that."

Chuckie turns to pat me on the arm like I'm a pet dog. Then he speaks to me very slowly and carefully as if I'm mentally challenged or something. "We'll. Find. Out. *Okaaay?*"

I nod again. I guess I am feeling a little mentally challenged right about now.

"How's he supposed to get in anyway?" Wanda asks. "Don't you have to be twenty-one? No one's gonna mistake Marley for twenty-one."

This is a really good question. I'm tall, but I'm lanky, with a face that looks very sixteen.

"I don't know, but I told Collin that Marley was sixteen, and he said no problem. Maybe it's because DRC is an eighteen-and-over club and not a twenty-one-and-over? I don't get how all that works, but he said you were fine to work at DRC at sixteen."

I don't know how it works either, but I know all the questions are making the spinning in my head worse. *How am I supposed to be ready for all this by tomorrow?*

That's my first thought.

My second thought is more of a realization. Because the truth is, it doesn't matter how soon it is.

I am ready for this. I've been ready.

People are asking ridiculous questions now, stuff that doesn't really matter, like what do the folks who run the club want me to wear, when Chuckie cuts everyone off. "Enough already," he says. "He's good. Now play some music for us, will ya, Mar, this is supposed to be a party. I mean, damn, what kind of DJ are you? Letting the music lapse like that..."

The group of friends standing around me all laugh and just like that I start to relax again.

"Yeah, okay," I say, refocusing on my makeshift setup, "I'm on it." Count on Chuckie to bring me back around. I get the music going again, purposely starting with a track I downloaded at school yesterday called "Dream It to Reality."

I look up and take in the scene around me. The shouting, the laughter, the smoking, the drinking, the making out, the friendships, the happiness. I watch it all, still swimming in a thick fog but starting to come around a little.

I'm going to play out tomorrow. Like, for real. Like, for the public. Me, Marley Johnnywas Diego-Dylan. Tonight I'm a nobody. But tomorrow night I'll be the DJ at DRC.

SCUZZ, CHUCKIE, AND I LEAVE JENNIFER'S around midnight. I need to get home. Out of nowhere tomorrow just became the most important day of my life. Of course Jennifer is right there to walk us to the door. "So thanks," I tell her. "It was cool."

"Thanks, Marley," she says, her eyes locking hard on mine. "Maybe you could come over again sometime when everyone else isn't here."

"Maybe," I say, but I know I won't.

"Good luck at the club," she calls after me as we head out the door.

Scuzz said he'd take me straight home but instead ends up skipping my exit and getting off the freeway three exits down, where the Taco Bell is. We hit the drive-thru for some quality late-night Mexican eatin'.

It's a good thing there aren't any cops around because they'd probably pull Scuzz over on suspicion of drunk driving, the way he's swerving back and forth and all. Scuzz never has more than a beer or two when he's in training, especially during football season, but he's so hyper right now he can barely focus on the road, both he and Chuckie having reached the full height of ridiculousness.

At the moment Chuckie is hanging across the front seat, and the two of them have the sides of their heads pressed together as they belt out a song that would make glass break and dogs howl out in pain.

"Make a ru-uuun for the bo-o-order..." they croon in a grossly out-of-tune chorus. *"I say a ru-uuun for the bo-o-order!"*

As for me, I'm in my own world and tonight that world is all about tomorrow. It's impossible to focus on anything else. Especially since, being that it's officially past midnight, today already is tomorrow. I'm nervous as hell, but at the same time I can't wait to get into that club.

"So look," Chuckie says once we've gotten our food and are back on the freeway, "about Jennifer. I'm thinking you go ahead and hit that. I mean, give the kid a break, will ya?"

"By having sex with her?" I turn and stare at Chuckie. "That's quite a break, don't you think?"

"But over a year now, Mar. Over a year that girl has liked you. That's, like, forever in crush time."

"I know it is. I'm just not into her like that. I don't know, she's not my type, I guess."

"Well, get into her. I'd get into her."

Scuzz laughs. "You'd get into anyone, Chuckie. Besides, you know he's been hung up on Lea Hall for, like, what's it been, Mar, like five months now? He's not trying to think about other girls."

"Oh, right. I forgot. Lea Hall. Like that's ever gonna happen."

"Shut up, Chuckie," I say.

"Yeah, at least Marley keeps the shit to himself and doesn't yap every thought he has about the girl out loud, like you did with Lauren. And with Yolanda."

"And Ashley," I add.

"Aw shit, he was the worst with Ashley. I wonder if Ashley ever thinks about me," Scuzz says, in his best over-exaggerated Chuckie voice.

"I wonder what Ashley is doing right now at this very exact moment within the grains of sand that make up time," I join in.

Then it's back to Scuzz. "I wonder what Ashley looks like when she's taking a dump."

"Hey, screw you guys," Chuckie says, glaring hard at each of us, but in that pissed but not really pissed way we do. Then he drops a comeback on me. "Hey, maybe Lea is on the shitter right now, Mar. You think she might be pinching a loaf?"

"Hmm." Scuzz overdoes a thoughtful expression. "Taking a shit...you know, that is a possibility."

"Hah!" says Chuckie, happy to have one of us back on his side. "Hey, Mar, you think it sounds anything like this when Lea Hall drops a big load?" He forces out a couple farts and then groans.

"Okay, okay, stop," I say, "you're ruining it for me."

"Well maybe you need us to ruin it for you," says Scuzz, but he's no longer joking. "I mean wake up, Mar. It's not like you can ever get with the girl. Sure she's cute, but she's a Have. Those're the only chicks in school who don't date outside their own crowd. It's like they've got their own religion or something."

"The I'm-Better-Than-Thou-Art religion," Chuckie adds.

"She'd never go for one of us. Even if she did, it wouldn't be like with other Ellington girls. Other Ellington girls are from a different world than us, no big deal. The Haves, though? They're from a different galaxy. You and Lea Hall? Never happen." Scuzz exits the freeway and makes a right onto South Grant Boulevard.

I know he's right. But I don't feel like admitting it. Instead I change the subject to something that's more important right now anyway. "So you guys gonna help me tomorrow or what? I have to find gear for starters."

"Hell yeah, we're gonna help you," says Chuckie.

"You know this," says Scuzz. "We got your back, Baby Bob. That and our fake IDs to get into the club so we can be there to hear you play. Tomorrow night, all that DJing we've watched you do over the years'll finally pay off. Me and Chuckie are real proud of ya."

I nod. I do know. Scuzz and Chuckie and I have been there for each other as long as any of us can remember. No way would they miss out on a night as big as the one I'm about to have.

"I'll make some calls," Chuckie says, "see if I can help you with the laptop situation."

"And I've only got two cars to work on at the shop tomorrow, so I should be done in plenty of time to run home, change, and swoop ya'll up by seven."

"Thanks," I tell them as we pull up to my building. "I don't know what I'd do without you guys."

"And you're never gonna know," says Chuckie.

"You either," I say, turning to grip hands with Chuckie and then Scuzz. "Later, ya'll."

"Peace *out*!" Chuckie replies, throwing up an exaggerated fist. I climb out of the car and slam the door shut behind me. "Peace, pla-yuh!" Chuckie calls out, climbing over the backseat and leaning out the open passenger-side window. "Peace, baby bruh-*thaaaaah*!"

Scuzz holds up two fingers in a V turned toward his chest and nods to me before pulling away from the curb.

TONIGHT, I HAVE THE MOST INCREDIBLE DREAM.

I'm not at Fever and I'm not DJ Lord.

I am a real DJ, getting paid to spin in a real club.

The club is a little spot downtown called DRC and I am myself all night.

I stand at the entrance, clutching the laptop and turntables I use when I'm at school. Chuckie was right about Mr. Faulkner. Not only did he not have a problem with me using them for the weekend, he actually met me at school on his day off to get them, telling me all the while how proud and excited he was to see how far I'd come. I stare at the closed metal door, holding my borrowed equipment and feeling nervous as hell.

"You the DJ?" the doorman asks.

I'm about to shake my head no when I have this crazy thought. I *am* the DJ!

"Yeah," I hear myself say.

The word is still pounding in my head as he opens the door and lets me in.

Scuzz and Chuckie get in on their fakes without any problem, and Scuzz picks up a woman without any problem. Chuckie picks up a few different women but has all kinds of problems getting any of them to stick around for more than five minutes, leading him to chug beers at the bar alone the majority of the night and end up pretty heated.

I play through it all, caught on an incredible, unreal plane somewhere outside of my life for one beautiful night. It's nothing like I'd imagined it would be, with me starting out all nervous and messing up at first and getting booed by the crowd but then getting it together and winning them back in the end and watching them cheer. I guess that stuff only happens in movies.

The crowd doesn't boo. They don't cheer either. I don't think they even notice I'm here. The DJ works from a little room with a window that overlooks the dance floor where you don't see him unless you're looking up. Besides, everyone is too busy being into themselves and each other to notice any of the workings of the club.

But I am here, standing in the DJ booth playing radio rap and R & B circa 1970 to 1990, like they asked me to.

Tonight, I have the most incredible, amazing, unbelievable dream. But I'm not asleep when I have it. I am wide awake. I am so very awake.

IT'S FOURTH-PERIOD LUNCH ON MONDAY, AND Scuzz and Chuckie have been talking nonstop about Saturday night at DRC.

"Marley was amazing," says Chuckie, "cooler than cool...." He pops a cigarette in his mouth, lights it, takes one puff, and stubs it out again before the lunch monitors can catch on. "Cooler than cool," he says again, shoving the cigarette back behind his ear.

"Marley," Scuzz says, taking a long pause after my name for effect, "was so creative"—another pause—"and so smoooooooth" — another pause — "he had that crowd, man, in the palm of his hand." He looks around the lunch table with wide, serious eyes as he shakes his hand, palm open, like he wants to be absolutely sure he has every person's undivided attention.

"In the palms of his two talent-filled, record-spinning hands," Chuckie adds.

"He played these Isley Brothers tunes and then blended them into Notorious B.I.G. and Ice Cube," Scuzz explains before shoveling a forkful of spaghetti into his mouth. He chews, swallows, and twirls another spoonful onto his fork. "The transitions came out real cool cuz Biggie and Cube used Isley Brothers tunes for melodies."

"It was genius, Marley, mixing them all up like that."

"It was sick, ya'll. Like you're hearing this Isley Brothers tune you've never heard before but could swear is so familiar and then all of a sudden it turns into something you know and you're just like, damn, is that where that melody came from?"

Chuckie nods and pounds the table. "You were on, Marley! You were *on*!"

He pulls his cigarette from behind his ear and reaches for his lighter again, but Scuzz snatches the lighter from Chuckie's hand before he can touch it to the end of his cig. "No smoking at the table while the rest of us are trying to eat."

"I know, I know," Chuckie says, holding up his hands in apology. "I just need it sometimes."

Scuzz glares at Chuckie a moment longer before turning his attention back to the rest of the table. "Marley was going for this classic old-school hip-hop vibe with a dash of R & B sexy sprinkled on top, right, Mar?"

I continue to work on my burger, crouching over my food like I don't hear him. I'm not much for being put on the spot.

"He was so great," Chuckie says, gazing at the ceiling to make it all seem more dramatic, "in his little booth with the brim of his hat pulled down low...."

"Like always," Jennifer says, smiling at me.

"The crowd loved him," Chuckie is telling everyone.

"Okay, the crowd did not love me," I finally say, because all the hype is starting to get to me. "They didn't cheer or clap or anything."

"But they didn't hiss or boo either," Scuzz points out. "DRC is a black club. If they didn't like you, they would've let you know. You know how our people get, Mar."

"They would have let you know, Marley," Chuckie agrees, nodding vigorously. "I was nervous for you. I was sure you were gonna fuck up, but you didn't."

"That's great, son," K.C. says.

"I'm so proud of you, Marley," says Denise.

"When do we get to see you?" Jennifer asks. "I'd like to come to the club sometime." She watches me with questioning, hopeful eyes.

"It was just a one-time deal," I tell her, as if she didn't already know.

She leans across the table and throws a dreamy smile my way. "Well, maybe somewhere else, then. I'd really like to see you in action."

"I'll bet you would," Chuckie says, gyrating in his chair and making moaning noises.

"I meant his music," Jennifer snaps, but everyone is already shouting teasing comments and laughing.

I get up from the table. "I have to get to music class."

"Lunch ain't over for another twenty minutes," says Will.

I answer with a shrug as I grab my pack and pick up my tray. "I'll see you guys later," I say, and rush off. This, of course, is all a reaction to Jennifer, who hasn't eased up one bit. That and the teasing from our friends.

But once I leave the cafeteria, my mind really is on music. I'm hoping Mr. Faulkner is in the band room setting up or something. I want to tell him about DRC and thank him again for letting me borrow the laptop and decks.

I've been really pumped since Saturday. I barely slept these last two nights, and all morning I've been dying to get to Beginning Jazz so I can work on some new ideas.

I crank the volume in my headphones as I cross the main courtyard. The trees sway, the wind blows, the students' bodies move to the beat of a Damian Marley song called "Confrontation" that's dramatic and raw and powerful and that I'd love to put in a mix. There's nothing like reggae to make you feel alive and connected.

And then, I see her. The angel in girl's clothing. My curse in life. Lea Hall.

She strolls the walk that sits parallel to the one I'm on with her friends Brittany and Melanie. Three super rich senior Haves trail along behind them. It's kind of nice to watch Have boys squirm a little. Especially these particular ones who happen to be unusually big jackasses. The tall, wimpy-looking blond one grabs Lea's hand, but she pulls away. That's Todd Bitherman. Total rich boy. Total creep.

He moves in again, dropping a limp arm across her shoulder, but Lea ducks away and begins to walk faster. Is she mad at him? No, Todd looks too confident. He continues to stroll and grin in his usual cocky way as if nothing is wrong at all. She must be teasing him, playing a game.

I move to a nearby tree and lean against it, waiting for the group to pass. I'm a little torn between wanting to stay out of sight and wanting to watch her walk by.

Lea has an amazing body. Her girlfriends look more like two sticks piercing the pavement with their bony bodies. You can tell they work hard to stay thin so the boys will like them more. Probably take a second look at their food in the bathroom after every meal.

Lea Hall is not thin. She isn't overweight either. She's athletic-looking, but in this soft, sexy sort of way, and I'd knock over both her skinny, stuck-up friends to get to her. I watch her hair blow in the wind as she pushes Todd away a third time.

The group is passing me now and Lea suddenly glances my way. I drop my gaze and continue on toward the band room, walking twice as fast on the path I'm on as they do on theirs. I don't look back. I'm dying to. But what's the point?

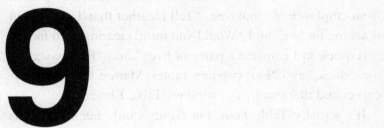

9

THE RESTAURANT WHERE I WORK, SPAZIO'S, CAN
be a pretty crazy place. Sure, if you're dining there it seems
calm, and organized, and warm, even a little romantic. You
sit, you order, and delectable dishes are served to your
table. You eat a fabulous meal, you drink a bottle of the best
wine, and you pay the hefty check. Simple as that.

But beyond the kitchen doors nothing's simple. Food spills,
glasses break, dirty dishes pile up faster than they can be
washed, and everyone is shouting.

Then you push through the kitchen doors and are greeted by peace, candlelight, the graceful sounds of music played on a baby grand.

The same craziness from behind the kitchen doors still exists, but now it's conducted in hoarse whispers, passed from employee to employee. "Tell Heather that Table Seven is asking for her," and "Would you mind clearing Two for me real quick so I can seat a party of five?" and "Eighty-six the roast duck," and "I sat two new tables, Marley. One in the far corner and that one by the window, Table Eleven."

It's actually Table Four, but Sandy's only been a hostess here a week and it takes a while to get the table layout memorized, since there's no numerical logic to it. I nod to her so she knows I've got it.

It's 7:10, the middle of the evening rush, and I'm running through everything I have to do in my mind to the beat of a medley of underground hip-hop songs I'd like to mix with. Right now I'm putting my own spin on a Cannibal Ox song called "Pigeon" I've got rolling through me. *I'm just a pigeon, with one mile left, finish clearing Two and Sixteen, check on coffees for Twelve, deliver water and bread to Tables Four and Nine, and serve desserts for Dennis cuz he just got slammed....*

I bus tables, refill glasses, deliver bread, and basically kiss rich people's privileged butts here six nights a week. That amounts to somewhere between thirty-six and forty-eight hours a week of water pitchers, bread baskets, coffeepots, and dirty tables, and that's before the second part of my shift as a dishwasher has even started.

It's a great job, though. The work is fast-paced and the hours feel long, but the waitstaff is tipped well on the expensive dishes they serve and tip the busboys out pretty decently in turn. Besides, I'm the youngest busboy here by, like, seven years. A lot of adults would kill for this job, and I almost didn't get it, so I'm lucky. Very lucky.

The diners at Table Six are rising and reaching for their coats, which means someone from the host stand will be on me or Julio to get it cleared, cleaned, and reset fast for one of the next set of reservations who're already starting to show.

Julio managed to slither out for a smoke break right in the middle of the rush, leaving me to cover his section, and my two new tables will get impatient for their warm bread, olive oil, and water quick if I'm not on top of that too. I clear and clean Table Two and drop fresh place settings before picking up Dennis's desserts from the kitchen. Tim's coffee drinks aren't ready yet, which leaves me just enough time to fill two baskets with warm bread.

I deliver the first to Table Four with a small dish, which I carefully fill with olive oil, a dash of vinegar, and a sprinkle of freshly chopped garlic. I grab the second basket of bread, for Table Nine, and nearly drop it on the floor when I see who the diners are. Justin Hall, a senior and a defensive lineman on Ellington's football team, spots me right away and smiles. Justin is very rich. He's also one of the nicest guys I know and the only Have who's really well liked by both the regular kids at Ellington and us Transplants.

Sitting across the table from him is a tall, heavyset, dark-haired man, with a mustache and stern eyes. This must be his father. A pretty, older woman, who wears a ton of makeup and jewelry and has to be Mrs. Hall, sits beside his father.

I'm totally staring. But it's not Justin or his parents I'm

staring at. It's his sister. Lea Hall, *the* Lea Hall, is seated in my section at Spazio's, studying a menu.

I slowly make my way across the room, which now feels more like a speeding treadmill I can't quite keep up with, and approach the table with an air pocket caught in my lungs. It takes everything I have to keep my cool as I place the bread-basket on their table. I am completely horrified.

"Diego-Dylan!" Justin exclaims. "Wow, what's up, man?"

"Hey," I manage, staring straight down at the cream-colored tablecloth. I put down the glass dish and pour the olive oil with a slightly shaky hand. My eyes feel hot and red. If I were to lift them and shift them slightly to the left, I'd be looking right at Lea. I keep them focused on that tablecloth like my life depends on it. As it is, this is the closest I've ever been to her.

"You know this young man?" Justin's father asks.

"He goes to Ellington," Justin says. "This is Marley Diego-Dylan. Marley, these are my parents. And I'm sure you've seen my sister around school. In fact, you guys have some classes together, don't you? Don't you, Lea?"

Lea doesn't respond. At least not verbally. If she gives her brother some sort of secret reply with her eyes or something, I don't see it. Justin rolls his eyes at me and shrugs when she doesn't say anything, but I don't say anything either. I can't bear to even glance in her direction. I'm too nervous. I can't believe she's right here, right now, sitting at a table at Spazio's, connected to me in this moment.

Mrs. Hall breaks the silence. "So you go to Ellington Pre-paratory and you work at Spazio's," she says, clasping her hands together. "Oh, how wonderful! And what a clever way for your family to teach you responsibility, with a part-time job. I love it!"

I decide not to tell her that I work full-time to support that "family." Somehow I don't think Mrs. Hall would understand. "Thank you," I say instead, but I doubt she hears me, since I've folded over into my shyness and my voice is practically nonexistent. "I'll be back with some water for you. Would you prefer sparkling or still?"

"Still water will be fine," Mr. Hall says.

"Oh yes!" Mrs. Hall agrees excitedly. "You're doing an excellent job, Marley." I nod in reply, then move away from the table as fast as I can, resisting the temptation to break into a full sprint.

"You okay, Mar?" Latreece asks as we pass each other between Tables Two and Six. "You look funny," she says frowning. "Did something happen?"

"Table Nine," I say.

Latreece looks past me. "They need something?"

I shake my head. "*They* are Lea Hall and her family."

"You're kidding!" Latreece's eyes grow wide. "Lea Hall? As in the love of your life? She's here?"

Love of my life? I wish. Most perfect thing to ever exist? Hands down.

Latreece takes off in that direction before I can ask her not to be all obvious when she checks out the family at Table Nine. I cringe on instinct as I watch her stop to talk to them, but really I have nothing to worry about. No way would she ever sell me out like that.

Latreece James is my favorite server at Spazio's. We've been tight like family since day one. In fact, if it weren't for her, I would never have gotten this job. I was just past my fifteenth birthday when I applied to work here, not old enough to take the dishwasher position they had available. At least not without written consent from a parent or guardian. But I needed a job real bad.

We went on a strict budget after Pop died, but it still got really hard to make ends meet, what with Ma being too broken to work more than two or three shifts a week at her waitressing job and no other income coming in.

When our Section 8 finally came through, things started looking up. We got to move into a little two-bedroom apartment at half the price of our one-bedroom place. With our rent dropping so dramatically, we did all right for about a year.

Then the drugs took over. Ma started disappearing on binges for days at a time. She lost the few shifts she had left at the diner. We were in trouble.

That's why I forged her signature on the form. Which seemed all right, not like the people who ran Spazio's would know the difference. Until I got there, that is, and found out they wanted a parent or guardian to actually be with me when I turned in the form. *No problem,* I told them, smiling. But the smile was as fake as can be. Because really I was screwed.

I passed a waitress on my way to the door. My true feelings were all over my face when we made eye contact and she saw my disappointment right away and gave me an understanding smile. I smiled back for real that time, as much as I could manage to, and then left.

"What happened?" someone called out as I was starting down the street. "Allen didn't turn you away, did he?" It was that same waitress coming out after me. When I explained that he'd offered me the position, but I couldn't bring a guardian in to talk to him, she got it right away.

"I can't believe you're going to lose out on this job over some ridiculous law," she said, shaking her head in disgust.

"I was really counting on the money," I admitted, because even though I didn't know her, she was surprisingly easy to admit things to. "Thanks for your kind words, um…"

"Latreece. And I have to get back to my tables, but I want you to stay a few moments longer. Can you do that? Can you wait here a couple minutes?"

I shrugged. "Sure." It seemed like the least I could do, since she was being so nice to me.

Latreece went back inside and I waited for her in front of the art store two doors down from the restaurant, wondering what I was going to do. This was the only job I'd been offered in almost four months of looking, and now I couldn't complete the paperwork to accept it. Meanwhile we had ten days to come up with a payment plan for the nine hundred dollars we owed in back rent or Mrs. Schermer, our landlady, would have no choice but to start the eviction process.

Latreece never returned. But a couple minutes after she went inside, Allen, the general manager, came out, his hand already extended to shake mine as he apologized and explained that he didn't realize I was Latreece's cousin and it was fine for her to vouch for me being sixteen. A month after getting hired for the night dishwasher position, a better job as a part-time busboy that included tips opened up. I took that job and still kept my dishwashing one and that's how I first went full-time and became the "breadwinner" holding the family together.

As for Latreece, we've been tight ever since meeting that first night. At thirty-five, she is big and brown-skinned and warm-hearted, more like a mother serving home-cooked meals to her family than a high-end waitress serving four-course dinners to some of the wealthiest people I've ever seen. She also happens to be the most popular member of our waitstaff, with customers constantly requesting her section when they first make their reservations. Nobody serves up more care and comfort to a table than Latreece.

But the best thing about Latreece is that I can talk to her. I mean really talk to her, really tell her stuff. I've never had that with anyone before. Sure, I was close with my pop when he was alive, but I was so much younger then. And yeah, I tell Scuzz and Chuckie most stuff, but I still hold back sometimes. I hold back with everybody. Except Latreece. I don't know why, but she's that one person I can say anything at all to.

She's the only one I told about Lea. My boys figured it out pretty easily on their own after catching me staring at her a half dozen times at school, and then word sort of got around after that. But Latreece knew first and she's always known the most and I'd like to think some of the stuff she's told me she'd never tell anyone else either.

"So have you been to her table yet?" she asks when we cross paths again in the kitchen.

"Yup."

"And? What happened? Did you speak to her?"

"Nope. I don't think she even knows who I am."

"Are you going to speak to her when you go back? I think you should."

"The only thing I'm going to do is this," I say, gesturing to the six waters I've poured and set on a tray. "I can't talk to her, Latreece."

"Well, I switched tables with Rob so I can check her out and make sure she's good enough to date my Marley."

I sigh. "Believe me, there is no risk of us dating."

And with that sad truth admitted, I pick up my tray and head off to deliver the waters.

Moving through the kitchen doors and back into the calm elegance of the dining room, I try to focus on our pianist Sharon's fingers flowing back and forth over the piano keys and the calm beauty of her playing. My heart feels like it's exploding in my head. *Stay calm.*

I drop waters at Table Four and eye the Halls' table. My nerves feel like they're eating away at my insides. *Stay calm....* I can barely hold my tray steady as I approach. *Staaaaay calm.* I pick up a glass of ice water and place it in front of Mrs. Hall.

"Oh, thank you," she says, smiling.

I pick up the next glass and place it on the table in front of Justin.

"Appreciate that, bro," he says with a nod.

I set down Mr. Hall's glass. He's busy telling a story but still pauses to give me a quick, "Thank you, son."

They are one of the nicest families I've served at Spazio's. Hardly anyone bothers to say "thank you" to a busboy, and certainly not everyone at the table.

Lea Hall. She is sitting on the opposite side of the table. She is stunning. She is waterless. I move to her chair, my eyes glued to the tablecloth again. I reach for the last glass on the tray with a trembling hand. *Please don't spill this water. Please don't spill half the glass into Lea's lap.*

When I lean in toward the table, her light, flowery perfume fills the space around me, sending my stomach into a marathon of flutters. I place the water glass in front of her without spilling a drop and take a step back. Lea stares at the water for a moment but doesn't say anything.

I have to return to Table Nine three more times before the Halls finish their meal and head out into the night. Each time I clear a dish or refill a water glass, Mr. Hall, Mrs. Hall, or Justin take a moment to be kind and appreciative, but not Lea. She never even looks in my direction. As far as she's concerned, I might as well not exist. I hate that my friends were right about her, but I guess they were. She's a Have and I'm a Transplant. Who we could be together in another world doesn't matter because we're living in this one and, in this one, I'm just another busboy.

10

TONIGHT, I HAVE THIS INCREDIBLE DREAM. I DREAM my family is together and happy. My father is still alive, still sitting in his lounger smoking weed and sipping on Hennessey. He works hard at the shop fixing people's cars and spends as much time as he can at home. Ma still works her old waitressing job at Jake's Diner. She smokes weed and drinks sometimes, but that's it.

When Ma isn't working she's home. But she doesn't lie on the couch letting the pillows suck away at her soul. She spends her time with Pop. When he cooks, she hangs out in the kitchen; when he watches TV, she keeps him company. She's healthy and she's happy.

Later in the dream, I walk down a narrow, brick-layered path and come across a massive home, a two-story white mansion with deep green trim and an actual picket fence surrounding it. I climb the front steps and, as I do, the door swings open and there is Mrs. Hall with her hair done, her diamonds intact, and her makeup set. She opens her arms wide and gives me a warm, gentle, motherly squeeze.

"Welcome, Marley," she says as she holds me tight. "Lea is waiting for you inside. We're all so pleased that she's dating you." She places a delicate arm around me and leads me into the house.

On Friday night, I dream these things.

But when I wake up Saturday morning, my mother is still sedated, lounging in our front room with the new loser boyfriend who replaced Frederick. The fridge is once again empty except for the half a stick of butter and the jar of applesauce that has now begun to mold over. And my father is still dead.

"What's with you guys and the food lately?" I call into the front room as I toss out the applesauce, but no one seems to hear. I know the harshness in my voice comes from the fact that some cokehead named Don is sitting in Pop's lounger instead of Pop, but at the same time, I really would like to know what's happening lately to all the groceries I buy.

"You know, it's okay to make a trip to the store to buy more food when it runs out. Can you do that please?" I walk into the front room and glare at Ma's new boyfriend for a moment before turning to Ma, who's posted expressionless in front of the TV, slowly transforming into just another couch cushion.

Sometimes, when I look at her, I think about taking off, running away to see what she'll do. My hope is that she'll suck it up and get her act together and get a job. But then I walk outside our building and see what will become of her if she doesn't. One long look at the homeless addicts that line the streets in our neighborhood and I change my mind every time.

Some of the women even make the trip down to Fourth Street to do tricks for drugs or for money to buy drugs with. That could have been Ma if it weren't for me. That could still be Ma if I'm ever unable to hold things down. She's that far gone and only wasting away in an apartment instead of on the cold, hard concrete because she has a "responsible" son to take care of her.

Well, I don't want to be responsible. What I want is to go off on my own, not fight to succeed in school and come up with money for us to live off of. I want to go out and party and be sixteen while I still can. I want to accept the truth — that she's a lost cause, a full-fledged dope fiend who can barely function anymore.

But I can't leave her. I'm all she has now. Sure, there's the revolving door of boyfriends, but they're only good for keeping her company and helping her get high. I'm the only one doing her any good and I'm big-time burned-out on coddling her. I know she's been through a whole lot since my father was killed in that hit-and-run accident, but then I've been through a whole lot too. Pop dying didn't just happen to her; it happened to both of us.

I stand there for a minute, waiting for my mother to answer me about making a trip to the store and buying food next time, but she keeps watching her show like I'm not even in the room and suddenly I have to get away from her. I go to my room and double-lock the door behind me.

My bedroom is like this little eight-by-ten square of freedom in the middle of our apartment. I've got a twin bed, a dresser, a bookshelf, and a tall metal desk I keep my turntables set up on. The mere sight of my decks is enough to make me breathe easier.

My turntables are the only thing I really have left of my pop. He loved these tables. Back in the day, when he used to throw parties in our studio apartment in the Eaver Projects, he'd pull out his turntables and spin. There were always people over. Our place was constantly bubbling with energy and all kinds of action, yet the only action I wanted any part of when I was a little boy were my father's decks. I'm positive those turntables are what saved me from ever even getting curious about shooting up when Ma started using.

Why put a needle in my arm when I can put a needle on a record?

I remember when I was little I would stare at Pop in wide-eyed fascination as he pulled record after record, carefully placing them like fragile china plates onto the left or right deck. He'd listen in his headphones to things the rest of us couldn't hear, then suddenly switch songs without ever missing a beat. Each time he changed up a track, something exciting and new would take over the room, something so great I couldn't even remember what the song playing before it was.

My memories of him spinning are just as fond as the rest of my memories of my father. Unlike Ma, who never really took to the idea of parenting, Pop worked hard at being a good dad. Maybe because he lost his own parents at such a young age, I don't know. But to me he was like a superhero who did things I was convinced no other human being could possibly do.

"Little Mar," he'd say, "choose a record for me." I would rush over to his crate of records and choose one with a cool-looking cover, since I couldn't read well enough to pick one with a cool-sounding name. I was five years old and already had my whole life figured out. When I grew up, I would be a DJ just like my pop. It was one of many ways I wanted to be like him.

Then it was my sixth birthday and my parents were inviting all their friends over to celebrate. "Little Mar, choose a record," my father said. I eagerly picked out an album with a cool-sounding name from his crate. Even though I wasn't in school yet, Pop had been teaching me how to read and I loved to practice on the weird band names sketched across his album covers. I selected the next track he would play, walked my chosen record over, and tried to hand it to him, but he shook his head no.

"It's your turn now, Little Mar. Pull the record out of the sleeve. Go on. . . ."

I carefully placed the record onto the left turntable like I'd watched him do so many times before.

Pop stood behind me and gently guided my arm with his big, dark hands as I picked up the needle and swung it over to the record.

When the needle touched down and I stepped back and my father pulled off his headphones and pressed them to my ears so I could hear the song I'd picked playing, I felt like I was on top of the world.

Pop smiled at me and winked as he re-cued the track and slid the control lever over from the other deck in one swift movement so Digital Underground's "Doowutchyalike" flowed from the speakers for everyone in the room to hear, and I laughed and turned to hug him tight.

"Check out my son, y'all!" he'd shouted. "My boy is gonna be a star one day. DJ Marley Johnnywas!" Everyone had cheered and I'd beamed with pride at my six-year-old accomplishment.

I gaze down at those same turntables now. They're super old-school, belt driven, with homemade slipmats, and a dying motor, but they're still full of moments spent with my father.

I've been saving for several months now to buy a laptop. Once a month I put fifty bucks aside for emergencies and fifteen or twenty aside for myself. I used to spend the money I put aside for myself on music, but now I'm investing it in my future—in my laptop. Sure, college is my main goal for the future, but as long as my grades stay where they are, graduating from Ellington will pretty much guarantee me full scholarships to several good schools.

What it won't guarantee me is a future as a DJ. How will I ever get gigs if I don't even have the tools of the trade? It's not like I can borrow a laptop and decks from my high school when I'm twenty-one, and I can't drag my pop's rickety old decks from gig to gig. I only need forty more dollars for the laptop I'm planning to buy, and then I'll be ready to save for some sturdy secondhand Technics 1200s.

I'm saving for a cheap laptop and used decks so I can get them soon, but for my mixer I'm willing to put away money for years if that's how long it takes to purchase something top-of-the-line. I've got my eye on that Rane/Serato Scratch Live combo. That way I'll be able to download and mix with any song I want as if it's vinyl, but I can still play all the records I've collected over the years and inherited from Pop. Then I'll really be ready to get out there. It'll be a major investment but worth the wait.

I run my hand across my metal desk in front of Pop's old Technics. By the time I've saved enough money to purchase my own gear, there might be something available that's so ingenious it hasn't even been invented yet. But no matter what I buy in the next couple of years, I'll never, ever get rid of these.

I scan my records, which fill five crates at my feet, slowly trailing my fingers over thin, worn jackets that cover amazing sounds of joy, love, anger, sadness, courage.... For the next few hours, my life belongs to me.

I am at peace in the silence right before I play when my headphones are quiet and my mind is free. I pull a record from its sleeve and hold the large, flat, circular black disc by its edges, and smile to myself for a moment before placing it onto the left turntable and pulling on my headphones. I start the left deck spinning, and align the needle to the second track, "Enter My Domain."

Music starts, and I breathe in the beat like oxygen, absorb the melody like a sponge, feel the singer's voice in the tips of my fingers and the soles of my feet. I begin to come alive, and my blood starts to really flow as my imagination stretches out in every direction like rays of bright light.

This is when I feel closest to my father. When I'm playing music, I'm bringing Pop back to life, almost as if he's in the room with me. I can talk to him through music. It's always been our connection, and the connection is still here, even though he isn't. I know he's watching over me, making sure everything is cool. Even when things are bad, I know they could always be worse, and I know it's Pop who's up there somewhere keeping the worst away.

I grab my next record and place it on the right deck, dropping the needle in a premarked spot two-thirds of the way between the first and second song and then patiently tracking it in my phones and fine-tuning the beats of "Darker than the Light" until everything fits. I swim in the feeling of control over the vinyl beneath my fingertips as I pull the record backward, then forward, then back again over the beat I want to start on, like I'm giving it a massage.

I love this part, when I have all the control of when I drop that new track and no one else has any clue what I'm about to hit them with, or when, or how. I slide the crossfader over halfway with my left hand as I drop the new record into the mix with my right.

Usually I spend about half my time spinning spontaneously, letting the way each track makes me feel inspire the next one I play. Then I practice a couple of what I like to call my preset mixes, blending the same records and the same premade beats at the same time every time, sort of like a piano player playing scales. After that, *it's on*!

At school I've started to work on my own tunes—totally original stuff, thanks to the amazing support and encouragement I get from Mr. Faulkner, who's also been teaching me to play the keyboards and helping me create my own beats on a computer. My work on originals is still in the beginning phases, though. Most of my time is focused on trying to hone my current skills, not create new ones.

I'm starting to get really good and I know it. It's rare for me to train wreck these days even when I'm improvising with unfamiliar tracks and my musical tastes continue to grow. I am lucky enough to love all kinds of music, so I work with a little of everything: hip-hop, house, reggae, R & B, drum and bass.... I'm proud to have schooled myself in so many different genres. But now I want to find ways to pull other music into my mixes too: jazz, Latin, blues....

I want to find ways to add samples of tracks DJs usually wouldn't even touch, like country or death metal. And one of these days I've got to find a way to mix with elevator. Elevator music doesn't get nearly enough credit in this world. I happen to love the stuff. Sure, it's made up of cheesy renditions of famous songs never meant to be played on a stringed instrument, but that's what's so great about it.

One time I heard an elevator music rendition of Jimi Hendrix's "All Along the Watchtower" with flutes and violins each taking a stab at the melody and every other instrument that has no business playing that song performing in the background. It was just plain wrong. I died laughing. The entertainment value of Muzak is priceless and I'm determined to find a place for it in my sets.

That's the thing. I don't want to be the DJ who simply gets people dancing. I want to be the one who makes people think and surprises them and shows them something new and takes them on a journey and gets them moving on the dance floor to tunes they used to hate but that I've made beautiful by pulling sounds, switching beats, adding samples.

I spin for most of the day, caught in a trance, floating on air and living in an alternate state of consciousness. Then it starts to get late and I have to return to reality and leave my safe haven to clean the apartment and cook for Ma. I stop playing suddenly, and the return to the real is like a massive jolt to my system, but that's the way it has to be. Otherwise, I'd go on mixing forever.

I drag two bags' worth of dirty clothes down to the laundry room in the basement of our building and start three loads. I scrub down the bathroom and kitchen, and clean the main room as best I can, considering I have to work around my mother, her scrawny, grungy, mega-loser new boyfriend, Don, and a couple of their friends who've all been sitting comatose in the living room the whole day, taking on a vegetative state. I prepare a huge dinner for Ma that I'm hoping will be enough food to last her all weekend.

I'm giving the kitchen floor a quick once-over with the mop before leaving for work when my cell rings. I pull it out of my pocket and see a number I don't recognize.

"Hello?"

"Hello there," a man's voice says. "I'm looking for Marley."

"I'm Marley," I tell him, picking up the mop again.

"I saw you last weekend. I was watching you."

"'Scuse you?" I answer a little harshly, hoping what he said came out wrong.

"I said I was watching you. I watched you and then I asked about you and got your phone number."

I don't respond. What do you say to something like that? The guy sounds like a straight perv, and I'm about ready to hang up on him.

"Marley? Are you still there?"

"Yeah, for about ten more seconds. Where is it exactly that I'd know you from?"

"From DRC."

He says more, but I don't catch it. I'm too busy thinking back to a week ago at that club DRC. For the most part no one paid me any mind, but there was one exception. A funny-looking guy who showed up during my second hour. He sat on a bar stool and stared up at the little DJ room.

He was much older than the rest of the crowd, and white, with dark, thinning hair and Coke-bottle glasses, and the only time he wasn't keeping an eye on me was when the club manager came over to shake his hand and chat with him. This has to be that same guy.

"Sorry?"

I cradle the phone between my ear and shoulder and begin to mop the floor again. I missed pretty much everything he said.

"Look, Marley, my name is Lonnie Kert. I have a twin brother named Donnie Kert."

I'm not following him at all. "I think you have me mixed up with someone else," I say, thinking I need to get off the phone if I'm going to finish cleaning before leaving for work. "I don't know who you're looking for, but I've really got to—"

"We own a club, my brother and I."

"Oh yeah?" I say, because now he's got my attention. What if he's not a stalker at all, but a guy who likes my music? And if he's calling for the reason it's occurring to me he could be calling...

"I went to DRC to see Collin Stan, a DJ I've been hearing

good things about. I wanted to talk to him about possibly working at my club one night a week as a warm-up DJ, but, wouldn't you know it, the guy broke his arm and wasn't there. But you were there that night. I saw you play and thought you were quite talented. The manager over there, Freddy, says you spin house music too. Is that right?"

"Yup," I reply, and then sigh because the phone call suddenly makes sense. I know exactly what's going on. "So which one of them put you up to this?"

"Excuse me?"

"It's okay, you can tell me. Was it Chuckie or was it Will?"

A long silence follows. And then, "I don't know a Chuckie or a Will. I'm calling because I'm interested in hiring you to DJ as a regular at Cream."

I don't remember letting go of the mop, but I do hear it hit the floor with a loud wooden clatter. "Hiring me?"

"Of course, you'd still need to audition for my brother, so I'd like to have you come to Cream and spin next Wednesday night. Assuming you're available."

"Cream?"

"Cream is a club."

Like hell it's a club. Cream is one of the best-known clubs around. Oh man, everybody's heard of Cream.

"Here's the thing, though, Marley. I noticed you use a laptop."

"Yeah?"

"And I think the things you can do as a DJ with the software out today are incredible."

"Yeah."

"But I need someone who works with vinyl. I wasn't even

going to call because I knew it'd be a long shot that you'd know how to work with both software and vinyl, but—"

"I do!" I blurt out. "I work with both. I use vinyl. It's all I've got at home."

"You sure?" he asks. "Because I find more often than not these days it's one or the other with DJs, and I know laptops are really the future."

"I'm sure," I tell him. "I'm just as good with vinyl."

"All right then," he says, "you've got the audition."

"Do I need to bring turntables?"

"Of course not. Just your records. If the audition goes well, I'll give you the eight-to-ten spot on Wednesday nights."

"You mean like every week?"

"Yes, every Wednesday night from eight o'clock to ten o'clock. The pay would be seventy-five a night. I know that's not as good as some clubs, but it's better than others, and we pay in cash. Besides, our club is pretty well known. We've been featured on late-night TV on club-life shows like *The Nightshift* and *VIP Room*. And if you do well, we'll bump you to a hundred a night after a few months."

"A hundred," I repeat, in a monotone voice like some kind of idiot robot.

"Well, seventy-five to start, but yeah. If everything works out. So are you interested?"

"Uh-huh."

"You'll come in and audition on Wednesday?"

"Uh-huh."

"Great, then be at Cream at seven thirty this Wednesday night and ask for Donnie. Normally we'd have you bring a demo in first, but since I've already seen you in action, that won't be necessary. You can bring a history of your experience for us to review during your audition, though. Oh, and bring your ID. I hate to even ask, but you look so young, and our spot is strictly twenty-one and up. You are over twenty-one, aren't you?"

"Uh-huh."

"Perfect. Wednesday night then. Who knows, maybe Collin Stan's broken arm will end up working in both our favors. Good-bye, Marley."

There's an abrupt click and his end of the line goes dead.

I hit the End button on my phone and put it back in my pocket.

I feel like I should do something.

Pass out maybe.

Just pass out right here on my freshly mopped kitchen floor.

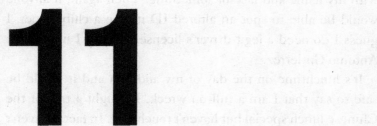

11

"ANTONIO GUTIERREZ?"

I stare at the picture, then look across the table at Scuzz and frown.

"What?" he says defensively. *"What?"* He tilts back a full can of Coke, finishing the whole thing in one long swig.

"The guy already knows my name is Marley. How am I supposed to explain my driver's license saying I'm Antonio Gutierrez?"

K.C. smirks. "What'd you think, son, Scuzz would find you

an ID of a guy that not only looks like you, but also happens to have the same name as you?"

"I don't know what I thought." I guess maybe I figured Scuzz would take a picture of me and make an ID out of it with my name and face or something. Then again, if anyone would be able to spot an altered ID it'd be a club owner. I guess I do need a legit driver's license. Even if I have to be Antonio Gutierrez.

It's lunchtime on the day of my audition and it would be safe to say that I am a full-on wreck. I bought a tray of the Chinese lunch special but haven't touched it. In fact, I haven't eaten since lunch yesterday, and on top of that my chest is starting to feel all tight.

I look over the ID some more. I've never had a fake before. Antonio Gutierrez's height and weight are close enough to mine, but the face is all kinds of wrong. "Scuzzy," I say, "this guy looks straight Latino."

"So?"

"So I'm Puerto Rican and black."

Scuzz sighs and looks over at Chuckie who shakes his head and rolls his eyes like I'm a lost cause. "Once again," Scuzz tells me carefully, "what the hell were the odds? Look, I know the guy doesn't look mixed, but at least his skin tone is pretty close, right? Keep your lid on and pull it down low like you usually do and you'll be fine."

"You need to calm down, man," Chuckie says as he pulls out his lighter and fires up a cig. "You're all spazzed out." Two quick puffs and he stubs it out again. "Where's the coolest guy I know? The mellow, kickback one?"

What is he, kidding? A crowd of people are going to be

dancing to my music. Every week from now on if tonight goes well. This is my dream I'm about to audition for. They couldn't possibly understand how stressful it is to know that one night could change your whole life or doom it. It's a lot of pressure on a guy. "This is five years earlier than expected," I say. "Five whole years!"

Chuckie doesn't look too impressed. Neither do Scuzz or K.C. They're right. I'm losing it.

*   *   *

I am the epitome of total, complete, and utter wreckage. I am the aftermath, the miserable remains. Dinner is out of the question — cooking it, that is. Ma will have to fend for herself tonight. As far as eating goes, I'm freaking starving all of a sudden. I pull down a can of tuna from the cupboard and mix in a couple spoonfuls of the mayo I bought yesterday.

It could never compare to the four-star tuna fish sandwich our line cook, Billy, fixes for me to eat after my shift at Spazio's, but tonight it tastes like heaven. I eat it right out of the can and then start in on some cornflakes, devouring three bowls' worth, since nobody drank all the milk for a change.

Ma is calling from the front room. Probably whining something about the fact that she can't smell dinner cooking from her permanent spot posted in front of the television set. I don't respond. For once, I'm the one who's not listening. It's not intentional, it's just that everything she says has become muffled and everything around me is a blur.

The only thing all evening that holds any clarity is the subway ride to Cream. The sound of the train wheels rumbling over the tracks is crisp and edgy. The rhythm soothes my nerves. *Badoomp, badoomp, badoomp, badoomp* . . . I clutch the handle of my suitcase tighter and shut my eyes. All those nights outside Fever . . .

The train pulls into the station and screeches to a stop. I stand. I wheel my suitcase to the doors, waiting for them to open up and let me out.

But I feel the opposite.

Like I'm waiting for the doors to open up and let me in.

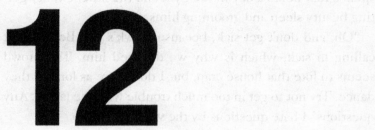

12

"COUCHES, BAR, DRINKS ON THE HOUSE WHILE
you're working, yada yada yada, statue that sprays cream
instead of water, which is really powdered milk, whatever
whatever, belongings here, Hogan, office, dance floor, and so
on and so on, eight to ten, seventy-five cash payout…"

I've been following Lonnie's twin brother, Donnie, around
Cream, listening to him ramble on nonstop. It's hard to keep
up with what he's saying when I'm so busy worrying about
the actual audition, plus the fact that I had to get a sub for
work again.

It's also hard to believe this guy and the guy at DRC could even be brothers, let alone twins. The guy at DRC had long, messy hair, thick glasses, adult acne, and frumpy, wrinkled clothing covering a beer gut. This guy Donnie looks like he spends four hours a day in the gym and the other twenty getting beauty sleep and grooming himself.

"Oh, and don't get sick, because Hawk's guy Benny kept calling in sick, which is why we dropped him. The crowd seems to like that house crap, but I don't care as long as they dance. Try not to get in too much trouble with the ladies. Any questions? I hate questions by the way."

"No questions," I tell him, even though I didn't understand hardly anything he said.

"Great. You'll do great, guy. I gotta go and you've got everything. There's nothing to it. Go make something of yourself out there." Donnie flashes a set of super white teeth before turning and slipping away toward the back of the club.

Go make something of yourself. It's the only thing he said that sticks. I close my eyes and take a deep breath. *Make something of yourself, Marley. You can do this.*

Wednesday nights at Cream represent my first big chance, maybe my only chance to be a real DJ, and whether I land the job or not is up to me. I have to be braver and more determined than I've ever been if I want anything to come out of tonight. *Make something of yourself.*

There is music playing overhead. Soon it will be my music playing throughout the bar. Anything I choose for the next two hours.

It's half past seven now, and my nerves are actually causing me physical pain. I find the bathroom and expel every morsel of food I ate: all the tuna, the cereal, the bag of M&M's inhaled on my way to the club....

I wash my hands at the sink and remove my lid to wash my face, looking into the bathroom mirror at my barely-sixteen-looking features and feeling grateful for my height. I got away with the ID. I couldn't believe it. I had a speech all ready about how my real name was Antonio but everyone calls me by my nickname, Marley, but Donnie barely glanced at the driver's license before handing it back. I get the feeling he doesn't really care. I also get the feeling he doesn't have much interest in running this place. He simply wants to look like he runs it.

Yanking a couple paper towels free from the dispenser, I dry off my face, then stare hard at myself straight in the eyes. I'm starting to feel a little panic-stricken, but my eyes look steady enough. If only this were like DRC. For all the talk I've heard of DJs getting caught up in nerves and train wrecking their mixes their first time playing out, it felt surprisingly easy. My instincts took over and I played on autopilot the entire time.

But that was a single night in my life at a little spot hardly anyone's even heard of yet. This is different. I've fallen into an opportunity to become a regular at Cream based solely on luck. Some DJs spend years working to get an audition for a regular gig. I'm about to do it in a club that's been featured on national cable shows. At sixteen! Talk about being in the right place at the right time.

The thought of it makes my hands tremble. Not the best scenario for someone about to spin records for two hours, but I can deal. As long as my brain is functioning, everything'll be okay. As long as the creative juices are still flowing—and they are. I can do this. That's what I tell myself as I walk determinedly out of the bathroom, pulling my suitcase along behind me as I cross the room to the bar.

For as famous as Cream is, it's actually really small. In fact the only thing in the place that's big at all is the black marble fountain that sits right in the center of the room. The bar is situated to the left of the fountain. Wooden and shiny, it wraps around toward the back of the club where the office and bathrooms are.

The dance floor is a tiny little square of space on one side of the fountain. As for the DJ booth, there isn't one. Instead the decks are set up right on the counter behind the bar, and the DJ spins back there, with the bar staff passing back and forth behind him. It's a cheap-ass setup, yet still glamorous somehow.

"Get you a drink?"

I look up in surprise. Probably a little too much surprise for someone used to hanging out in bars. I have to remember I'm supposed to be twenty-one. "Got any root beer?" I ask, because faking I'm legal is one thing, but pretending I drink is something I'm not willing to do for anyone.

The bartender nods and places a glass of ice on the counter. "Don't worry about all that crap Donnie was rambling on about," he tells me as he fills the glass from a deck gun. "The guy is a little eccentric, know what I mean? Anyway, I can help you settle in."

"Thanks."

"What's your name?"

"Marley. Uh, Antonio."

He offers me his hand across the bar. "Welcome to Cream, Marley Antonio. I'm Hogan."

Hogan looks like his name—a tall, heavyset, friendly, twenty-something dude in a long-sleeved shirt rolled up to the elbows with jeans and a black Kangol. I like him right away. "So you ready for this?"

"Yup."

"Well, come on back then and I'll show you the setup. We've got twelve-hundreds—you familiar with those?"

"Definitely." I move behind the bar and crouch down to unzip my suitcase.

"Got any questions?" Hogan asks.

"Well, one," I say, debating whether it's cool to ask it and finally deciding I need to be bold and ask regardless. "I was wondering if you knew how many DJs have already been in. Or maybe how many others are expected to come in after me. You know, so I'll know what kind of competition I'm up against?"

"I'd say there've been a couple DJs a night asking for management. I swear it's like they knew we had an open spot before Benny knew he'd lost it."

I nod. Not exactly what I wanted to hear, but it still helps to know.

"Now, as far as actually being invited in to audition, I think you're the sixth guy. Yeah, there's been one in every Wednesday night since he got fired."

"Any idea when they'll decide?"

Hogan shrugs. "Wish I knew, but you never can tell with Lonnie. He's the one you wanna impress, you know. You do need Donnie's approval, but Lonnie is the one who really runs this place. Who knows with him? He could be waiting for 'the one' to walk in. Personally I think he just wants to see twenty DJs or something ridiculous like that as a comparison to be sure he's picking the right one.

"Hell, in the end he might choose the first guy who played. Excuse me, Marley." Hogan moves down the bar to serve a group of clean-cut, yuppie-looking guys. He's got incredible expertise and skill, his hands moving at the speed of light as he pours, blends, serves, collects. I wonder if he had to compete to get *his* job. I imagine he would've smoked all the other bartenders if he did.

I try to clear my head as I pull my first few records and put a dozen more near the front of my suitcase that I'm thinking I might want. It's 7:50—only a few minutes left to get it together. My first track of the night will be a song called "In Flight." I discovered it one day at school while searching Internet sites during my computer lab and fell in love with it instantly. It's got this crazy melody that's hypnotizing and a chorus that'll get fixed in your head for days if you're not careful. Even though its tempo is a little slow for a house crowd, I knew it was the song I wanted to start with the moment I saw an article online describing Cream's music as "generally techno."

My hands are still trembling slightly as I pull the record free from its sleeve. I drop it onto the left deck and stare at it as it spins, needing to focus on something besides the growing crowd. The place seems pretty busy for a Wednesday night and it's getting harder and harder to appear calm as my pounding heart takes over, *badoomp, badoomp, badoomp...*

like the subway train wheels chugging over the tracks, hard and fast.

At 7:58, the overhead music cuts out. Crowd voices take over the room as I pull my second record, which is made up of nothing but break beats, and drop it onto the right deck. I pick track six, which is perfect for "In Flight" with a tempo paced for a dance crowd, and even though I'm going to start with "In Flight" and then drop the beat at the end of the intro when the tune really starts, I cue up the beat track first.

It's 7:59. Sixty seconds. *Stay focused, Marley. You've done this a thousand times before.*

"In Flight" needs some serious pitch adjustments to bring it up to speed with my beat track, and that takes me a lot longer than usual. But eventually I get there. I re-cue the beginning of the cut, holding the record gently in that between-song silence, while the platter beneath continues to spin. It's 8:03. It's now or never.

I take a deep breath, slide the upfader to the top, and *let go*... of the record, of the air held in my lungs, of my fears of failure. I let it all go the moment the intro to "In Flight" begins to pour out of the speakers around the room. It envelops the crowd like a suspended net falling, trapping their interest. In my headphones the beat completes the track, but I keep it to myself for now, only pumping in my right ear. I eventually pull it back and hold on to it just before that first kick.

The intro to "In Flight" is long, with steely violin notes that ring out in chorus, then circle into a single saxophone that sings alone. It gives no warning of what's coming, which I really dig, but at the same time grabs everyone's attention like a magnet hidden within those first few notes, which I dig even more.

And then that crucial moment arrives when I drop the volume on my low knob to pull out the bass line and ease the right upfader in nice and slow. I let the beat grow gradually before dropping the bass hard on the first beat of the chorus, pumping the song full of energy and letting it expand like a filling balloon. It builds and builds until it's stretched to its limits, exploding into a double-time beat made to draw people to the floor. My audition has begun.

Heads nod and a few people continue to look on in interest, but no one approaches the dance floor. I go for my next record before I have a chance to focus too hard on the dance floor's emptiness, then fade out "In Flight," leaving the beat alone as I replace it with "Bring It," in my headphones, a track I'm hoping will do just that. It slides easily into the beat with minor pitch adjustments and my fingers lazily trailing the platter to slow it a little. My fingers flowing over the ridges of the platter is a motion that's always made me feel really good. Tonight, it does nothing for me.

"Bring It" is edgy and decisive, with its own solid beat, allowing me to bring it in slow, pull beat track six out fast, and slip on my next record. I try not to look, but out of the corner of my eye I see it anyway—the dance floor. Still empty. Even though I force my focus back onto the decks, I can feel that small vacant square of space watching me, taunting me, its heat melting away the confidence I worked so hard to build only moments ago. I mix a track called "What, When, Why" into "Bring It" and let them blend, intertwining easily in a smooth introduction and eventual fade.

Thirty minutes into my set the dance floor is still empty. The crowd bursts with energy all around but shows no desire to dance. My eyes flicker from spot to spot involuntarily, searching for Donnie or Lonnie. Donnie isn't anywhere that I can see, and I don't even know if Lonnie is in the club. It doesn't really matter, though. One or both of them are out there somewhere watching that vacant dance floor. "The crowd likes house, but I don't care as long as they dance." *Shit!*

I've fallen into an autopilot state now like I did at DRC, but this time not in a good way. The music sounds hot and my mix feels on, but then I guess it isn't, going by the reaction of Cream's customers. Or should I say lack of reaction. This is my worst nightmare and all I want to do is wake up from it, find myself lying in bed never to return to this place ever again. Suddenly I wish the reality *was* only a dream.

Almost an hour into my set, the dance floor still sits lonely beneath three enormous spotlights. It's torture. I want to break down. But I fight my emotions with a fierce mind. No, I'm here and I'm going to finish what I started even if it kills me. I know I can't go on like this for sixty-seven more minutes. But I'm going to anyway. *Come on, Marley. Keep your head up. Pull your next record, you know the one.*

Yes, I do know. A song called "Drip," with a clubby, contagious, house sound I'm going to trance out and shade in deep, dark life. I follow that up with a track called "Broken Soul" and one of my favorites, "Fall into the Beat of Energy." By the time I drop "H2O," I'm finally in the zone.

"Aye!" someone shouts.

I look up in surprise with tired, frustrated eyes that now

sting when I move them. A Filipino-looking dude in a sweater and jeans with gelled, jet-black hair is standing in front of me. "You're good," he shouts over the music, "I'm digging your sound. It's sort of all over, keeps us guessing, you know?"

"That's the goal," I say, "but I don't think it's working for anyone but you."

He frowns in confusion. "What are you talking about?"

I gesture to the empty dance floor to prove my point and my heart drops out from under me.

Where only moments ago there was no one, there are now seven people. Seven! Which actually looks like quite a few on that tiny floor. Hell, it's almost half full! "Thanks for the compliment," I say right quick, because now I have no time to socialize. I've got people to please. *Finally.* I grab my next record, determined to keep them from walking away, then stop short and put it back, turning to study the crowd and try to get a sense of what they'll want to hear.

I reach for a new record but stop again and finger a third. The fourth is the one. I know it the moment the track I want starts to flow into my ear, and when I do drop it, three more people hit the floor. Music bleeds together like colors of a rainbow, radiating through a dream that leads into a dream that feeds off a dream and drifts amid a dream.

My insides pulse with excitement and nervousness as I watch the dance floor. *Don't get too excited. Keep your focus on what you're doing. Don't pat yourself on the back yet; you have work to do.*

A few beautiful notes pinpointed and accented here, a sad tune played over and over there, an increasing intensity that makes the whole room quake beneath my fingers, spreading hallucinating sound into all four corners. I float a high note in a multiple echo above a magnetic melody and feel the energy around me swell.

I remember every moment of my set, every second, every breath, every perfect record chosen, every wrong record mixed away as fast as I can switch it out. People dance, people drink, people speak to me in flashes I sort of hear, sort of don't.

"Who's that song you're playing by?"

"You the new regular guy or just filling in?"

"I can't remember what it's called, but can you play it for me? You know the one."

"Hand over the money and no one gets hurt."

What? I lean forward, knowing I must've heard the last guy wrong. "What was that you said?"

The guy does a quick shot of some kind of clear liquor, slams his glass down on the bar in front of me, and looks around him like he thinks someone might see him doing something illegal and bust him for it. "I said," he repeats, "step away from the tables, young buck. Your day in the sunshine has clouded."

"'Scuse you?" I say, because the guy isn't making any sense.

That's when he leans across the bar and flashes a first-rate, nasty-ass smirk. "Step off," he shouts angrily. He is much shorter than me but looks at least forty. Blond hair hangs past his shoulders in thick "white guy" dreads. His face is closed in and dark, engraved with a deep scar that runs the length of one cheek. "You hearing me?"

"I hear you fine," I tell him, starting to feel a little heated myself by his tone, "but I don't know what you're getting at, so why don't you go ahead and get to it in plain English?"

And that's when he uses the kind of slow, careful pronunciation people use when they're trying to get someone to understand a language they don't speak. "Get…OFF… my…tables! It's ten o'clock."

His tables? Ten o'clock? Oh! "No problem," I say, wondering why the dude had to get all complicated and spout off stupid metaphors instead of simply saying, *Hey, I'm the other DJ.* I move aside and start repacking my records. He doesn't seem like the friendly type, so I move out from behind the bar quick, only waiting long enough for him to start his set and hand me my last two records before moving down the length of the bar and taking a seat at the other end of it.

What an asshole.

Hogan walks up and refills my root beer. "You did good," he says. "Real good."

I shake my head. "For like half my set there was nobody on the dance floor. If I'd gotten people dancing earlier, I think I might have had a shot."

Hogan shrugs. "It's always that way early on. You know how it is when you're the warm-up DJ. Who wants to dance at eight? No one at Cream, that's for sure. People are still settling in." He moves on down the bar to make some sort of fruity drink for a brunette lady seated a few stools away.

That makes sense, I guess. I hope it's true. Either way, it's not like there's anything I can do about it now. I take a sip of root beer and look around at the people who make up the crowd at Cream. It's not huge and glitzy like Fever, but it's way more sophisticated than DRC: sort of like sitting in the middle of a mini movie set.

The women wear sexy bodies and pretty faces and carry

around flirty drinks in wide glasses with umbrellas and fruit hanging off the sides for decoration. The men loiter in different sections of the club according to type: yuppies by the fountain; club regulars in the far corner; awkward types near the front entrance; sleazy, on-the-prowl types spread out all over the club claiming territory and harassing any woman unfortunate enough to pass their way.

I spot Donnie at a table in back with some of the club regulars and wonder if he was there all along. I watch him check his phone before standing and heading my way. As he crosses to the bar I take a deep breath and stand too. This is it, the moment of truth.

But then he passes right on by in a flash like a strong gust of wind, somehow managing to slip three twenties, a ten, and a five into my hand before moving on down the bar and disappearing into the dim lighting at the back of the club without a word.

I stare down at the money in shock. Seventy-five, as promised.

But he didn't say anything. So do I wait for him to come back or what? Is he planning to critique me later when he has more time? Or maybe handing me the money like that was his way of saying thanks, but no thanks? Maybe I can call him tomorrow to ask what he thought of my set?

I want to wait and call tomorrow. But what if he comes back to speak to me and I'm not here?

My mind is rattling like crazy in confusion. I can't leave, not without knowing. I have to try to stick around to see if he comes back. I decide to stay for twenty more minutes.

I sit back down on my bar stool as my eyes flit across the

bar, taking in images but not really processing them. My stomach gurgles anxiously. What am I even doing here? Any second now someone's going to notice how young I look and kick me out.

I close my eyes and try to focus in on the one thing that always calms me—the music. I take in the beat, devour the melody, lose track of why I was stressing in the first place in the way the tunes seep into each other like liquid. The way the tracks blend is so natural and so crazy clever at the same time, like spurts of thought that make you forget where you were trying to go, but end up taking you somewhere better than anywhere you could've ever hoped to be.

My eyes fly open again. I turn my attention to the other end of the bar and just stare at him. Because, asshole or not, that DJ is incredible.

He spins with years' worth of confidence and dances around behind the bar with spastic energy, never missing a beat and never, ever playing anything the crowd doesn't seem totally into. I watch in awe for the next three and a half hours.

It takes me off guard when the bartenders announce last call and his set ends ten minutes later. The club starts shutting down a few minutes after that and customers are bustled out the door.

I get up to go. "Thanks for your help," I tell Hogan, dropping a generous tip on the bar.

"Anytime," he says, offering me his hand. I shake it and head for the door.

I reach it and stop.

Even with the bar closing down for the night, it still feels wrong to leave. It's like somehow I know if I walk out this door, I'll always regret it, and I've gone through too much already to end up regretting this.

I have to talk to Donnie. I have to at least know I tried. It's pretty clear the dude isn't planning to hire me. But maybe if I approach him with a thick skin, I can take whatever feedback he gives me as constructive criticism. Even if it's bad, I can learn from it. After all, I have five more years to get it right before my next audition.

Which is why, with the little courage I have left, I turn my back on the easy way out and cross the bar to the office.

I take a deep breath, and knock on the door.

"Sir?"

"Come in," Donnie calls back.

I open the door and peek inside. Except that it isn't Donnie at all, but his brother, Lonnie, who's seated at a desk looking up from a massive pile of paperwork. So he *was* here.

Lonnie eyes me expectantly. "Can I help you with something?"

I go blank for a moment. I was expecting his brother. "Uh, sorry to bug you, but I was looking for the other guy, um, what I mean is, Donnie?"

"He's left for the night," Lonnie says before returning to his work punching numbers into a calculator and copying figures onto an oversized chart, making it clear he has nothing more to say to me. I shift my weight from one foot to the other. I'm dying to turn and run, but I know I won't be able to forgive myself if I don't talk to Donnie. It's like even though I know I failed, I need the closure of hearing the guy say it out loud. Lonnie glances up again when he realizes I'm still here. "Was there something else?"

"Well, yeah. I don't know if you remember, but you saw me at DRC and then called me up for an audition? Anyway, I played earlier tonight and was hoping to speak with Donnie about that right quick. You know, before I left and everything. Did he leave a message for me or anything by chance, sir?"

Lonnie stops writing and eyes me again over thick, Coke-bottle lenses. "I'm sorry," he says, shaking his head. "He didn't leave any message." He turns his focus back to his work and begins to write again. "You can probably catch him next week before your shift, Marley. He should be around."

Next week? My shift? Shock washes over me so fast it nearly knocks me over. "So I got the gig?" I ask, the shock now replaced by a huge wave of excitement.

"You mean he didn't tell you?"

"No, sir."

Lonnie shakes his head. "That's my brother for ya. Well, congratulations, then. Your shift starts at eight o'clock next Wednesday night. Do not be late."

"Not a chance," I say. "Thank you so much. You won't regret this." I leave the office, shutting the door behind me and practically collapsing against it.

I did it.

I actually did it.

I can't believe it. I got the job.

I am the newest DJ at Cream.

Me!

A real DJ! Paid and everything.

No way can this be for real.

Except that it is.

13

"HOW 'BOUT DJ BOB?" CHUCKIE SUGGESTS. "YOU know, for Bob Marley?"

"No one'll get the connection," says Scuzz.

"DJ Reggae?"

"Weak!" Scuzz snaps.

"How 'bout DJ Youngin' or DJ Kid?"

"Uh, hello? The last thing he needs to do is draw attention to the fact that he's young? Too young to be in that club?"

"DJ DJ?"

Scuzz stops and stares. "Was it my imagination, Chuckie, or did you say DJ DJ?"

Chuckie throws up his hands in surrender. "What do you want from me? I'm getting tired."

Scuzz shakes his head and walks on ahead of us. "I'll say," he calls over his shoulder.

Tonight will be my third Wednesday-night shift at Cream, and Chuckie and Scuzz have been trying to come up with a DJ alias for me all morning. Personally, I think I'd be better off calling myself Marley. Or I could always be DJ Antonio Gutierrez.

I feel like I'm living someone else's life all of a sudden. Someone older and super talented and free and alive and confident. Somebody who's really got things good. I keep wanting to pinch myself to see if I'm dreaming, but never do. Just in case I am.

At school, word has spread fast about the junior with the secret nightlife working as a DJ at the famous club Cream. Every Transplant at Ellington knows about it now. I told Chuckie and Scuzz not to tell anyone, but that's kind of like telling the sun not to shine.

My Advanced Lit class just ended and Scuzz is walking me and Chuckie to the gym. "Something really weird happened in English today," I tell them.

"Oh yeah," says Scuzz. "What?"

"The Haves were nice."

Chuckie laughs like I'm joking. "What do you mean, nice?"

"I don't know. It's, like, they weren't jerk-offs for once. Richie even said hello. Why would they switch up like that?"

Scuzz eyes me and Chuckie with a guilty half smile. "I may have told the football team about you working at Cream, and that may have included a few of the Haves. They thought it was a trip, you being a junior whose after-school job is DJing at a twenty-one-and-over nightclub."

"Scuzz!" I exclaim, stopping and staring at him. "The whole football team?"

Scuzz shrugs. "Terrell was telling them too."

"If the whole football team knows," Chuckie points out, "that means every kid in school knows by now."

"Maybe that's a good thing," says Scuzz. "Maybe the reason they're being nice is they think if they buddy up to you, you'll sneak them into the club and hook them up with drinks."

Maybe. But I doubt it.

* * *

The hot lunch in the cafeteria consists of hamburgers, grilled cheese sandwiches, and today's special—a shady-looking rendition of chicken potpie. Me, Scuzz, Chuckie, Will, Jennifer, K.C., Tanika, Cara, Juan, Terrell, and Denise all lounge at our usual table. Chuckie and Scuzz are still refusing to let the whole DJ name thing go, and the bickering is starting to get on my nerves.

"How about something real confident-sounding, like DJ King!"

Scuzz shakes his head. "That's weak too."

"How about I just go with DJ Marley," I finally say. "It's not like I've ever bothered with a DJ name before."

"Um, duh, of course you haven't," says Chuckie. "You were

playing for *us* before. And maybe a party here and there, but a *high school* party. Shit, Marley, you're getting paid now. Not only that, you're a regular DJ at one of the hottest clubs in existence. You're not just you anymore — you're the dream version of you. This whole thing is mad crazy."

"That's the first thing Chuckie's been right about all day," Scuzz says. "Seriously, Mar, think about what's happening. They believed you were twenty-one. Twenty-one! Even with that baby face of yours, they still bought it. That's how good you were. This is *huge*. Way too big for you to be using the same name you use when you're being your plain old sixteen-year-old self, that's for damn sure. You're gonna be a star and you need a star's name."

Chuckie looks up in surprise and grins like he's particularly pleased with himself. "I've got it!" he says, "and it's definitely a star name, nothing weak about it at all."

"Whachu got, son?" K.C. asks.

"DJ *God*!"

"Now, that's simply going too far," says Scuzz.

"Well, shit, Scuzzy, I'm the one doing all the work here. Why don't you think of something instead of putting down everything I come up with?"

"Fine," Scuzz answers, leaning back in his seat. "I will."

But five minutes pass without Scuzz making a single suggestion.

Chuckie leans across the table. "Not so easy, is it?"

Scuzz brushes him off, as if Chuckie is merely disturbing his brilliant thought process. "How 'bout…" he says, but then pauses, unable to come up with anything. "DJ…" He tries again. "Um…DJ…mmmm…A.M."

Chuckie stares at him, dumbfounded. "DJ A.M.? Did you say DJ A.M.? And you think *my* stuff is bad? At least I didn't come up with anything that was already *taken*! You better let that man rest in peace, Scuzz. Trying to steal DJ A.M.'s name…"

"How about something to do with being cool?" Jennifer offers. "Marley is known for being reserved and mellow. What about DJ Chill or DJ Ice or something like that?"

"How about DJ Ice?" Chuckie announces excitedly, like it was his idea and not Jennifer's.

Cara nods. "I like DJ Ice."

"Yeah, that'll work, Mar," says Scuzz.

I was sure I just wanted to be Marley, but I think I might like it too. I don't know if "Ice" will go over well at the club or not, but there's something about the fact that it's my friends who came up with it that feels really good. Almost like if I let them name me, I can take a piece of them into the club with me every time I go. DJ Ice…

"Well, look who's here," says Chuckie.

I look over my shoulder to see Justin Hall approaching our table. "Hey, guys!" he calls out.

Justin Hall really is a decent dude. There's no doubt he's super rich, is a member of the popular, stuck-up Have crowd, and has a lot of influence at this school, but for some reason he doesn't care about any of it and doesn't seem to want anything to do with their status bullshit. Justin is like this peace guy who likes and is liked by everybody at Ellington while some-how still managing to remain one of the untouchable elite.

At least most of us like him. I watch Will scrunch up his nose like he smells something bad.

Scuzz grips Justin's hand and shoots Will a warning glance at the same time. "'Sup, man?"

"Hey, Scuzz." Justin crosses to the other side of our table, turns a chair backward, places it right next to Will, and straddles it, proving in that single motion that he couldn't care less about any social clique bullshit the rest of the Haves live by. "So, Marley," he says, "good running into you at Spazio's. I hope my family didn't make you too crazy that night."

"No, they were nice," I say as I tug my lid lower, not wanting to be the center of attention, not needing to have everybody stare.

"There's a rumor going around that you scored a major DJ gig at Cream," Justin says. "That true?"

"Hell yeah, it's true," says Chuckie.

Justin smiles at Chuckie and nods. "So yeah, you must be real good to be spinning at Cream."

I shrug. I'm not the bragging type. But Chuckie is and so is Scuzz, and the two of them start a tag-team session that could win them a world wrestling match.

"Marley DJs with this other guy," Chuckie explains. "Marley's kind of the opening act, and the other guy is supposed to be like the headliner, see, but Mar is so much better than him it's embarrassing. I think he would get more time if he didn't threaten the other dude so much. Huh, Scuzz."

And there's the tag. "I think the other guy is really good," Scuzz says thoughtfully. "DJ White Night or Midnight or something like that. I like him. But Marley..." He pauses to look around the table all dramatic-like. "Marley's on a whole other level. This is what he was meant to do with his life, know what I'm sayin'?"

"Hell yeah, it is," Chuckie agrees.

Justin looks back and forth between them like some poor schmuck caught up in a tennis match that never ends. When they finally do stop talking, he looks to me like he's hoping I'll let him in on what is and isn't true.

What is true is this—Chuckie and Scuzz haven't been to Cream. We thought it best that I not be seen with other teenagers, so even though they've got fake IDs, they're staying away. Because of this, they've never heard the other guy spin, so they can't compare us. Also, the other DJ's name is Hawk, not White Midnight or whatever crap Scuzz pulled out of his ass.

I decide not to bother explaining any of this to Justin. Instead I look at him sideways from under the brim of my Etnies and shrug again. It's typical of me to not say more than twenty words in one sitting anyway, and I'm easily over halfway to my quota for this lunch hour, so letting others speak on my behalf until I have something to add is almost expected. Mostly I want to escape at this point.

"So look," says Justin, "I like to have these little get-togethers whenever my folks go out of town. Nothing major, just a few friends hanging out at my place. You know, super casual. My parents are taking off for a couple of days a week from Sunday, so that's when the next one'll be. I'm planning to hire a DJ to spin."

"You pay a DJ to spin for a 'little get-together' that's 'super casual'?" Will says smugly. He rolls his eyes at the rest of us for emphasis.

"Yeah, I like to invite over a handful of close friends to my house to chill every once in a while," Justin says, totally missing Will's put-down. "So what do you say, Marley? You interested in the DJ job?"

K.C. spits out a spray of the milk he's drinking and coughs like crazy.

"Me?" I say.

It seems like a dumb question, being that he just asked, but not if you go to our school. A Transplant at a Have's party? It's never happened. I doubt any non-Have has ever been to one of their parties.

Chuckie points a warning finger at Justin. "How much you planning to pay him?"

"I hadn't thought about it yet."

"Well, think about it."

"It'd be like a three-hour job…" Justin says, silently calculating my worth. "Three hundred dollars sound okay?"

Jennifer sucks in her breath and stares at Justin, then at me. Will laughs in a loud, forced way.

The rest of our table remains silent, waiting to see what'll happen next. Some of the kids at the tables around us watch too. It's pretty rare to see Haves socializing with Transplants on their lunch hour. It's pretty rare to see Haves socializing with anybody.

Chuckie gives me a questioning look as if to ask if I'm going to accept or decline Justin's offer. It feels like every other student within earshot is waiting for my answer too.

The answer is, I have to do it. It's three hundred dollars, for crap's sake. I give Chuckie a nod.

"Three hundred will be fine," Chuckie replies smoothly, grinning like a salesman who's just ripped someone off.

"Awesome," says Justin. "What kind of music do you play?"

I shrug for the third time. "What kind you want?"

Justin frowns. "I don't know. Can you play any hip-hop maybe, or house or something?"

"I can play pretty much anything," I tell him, because I can.

"All right," he says, nodding and smiling as he stands. "I'll give the music some thought and get back to you." He glances around at everyone else. "See you all later." Scuzz grips his hand once more. "See you at practice, Scuzz."

"Fo sho," Scuzz replies.

"Thanks, Marley."

"Aye!" Chuckie screams, causing half the cafeteria to turn and stare. "That's DJ Ice to you!"

"DJ Ice, huh?"

I nod. "Looks like it."

Justin nods back. "Good name."

MY FOURTH WEEK DJING AT CREAM I GET ASKED to fill in for the opening DJ on Friday night.

Friday night…

A month ago I would've stressed hard at the mere idea of playing for Cream's weekend crowd, gotten all nervous and worried I wasn't good enough to pull off a weekend slot.

But I never worry anymore. I'm too at home behind the decks at Cream to get nervous now, no matter what the circumstances. This is my place in the world.

My skills on the tables are improving at a mad pace and I

feel confident and in control when I'm standing behind the bar. Even the way I wear my lids has changed. I no longer switch colors. Sure, the dark gray one will always be my favorite, but these days I find myself reaching for the red one before going to Cream. Why, I don't know. Maybe because it was the one I was wearing the night of my audition. Or maybe it's because red is such a bold, loud color, and I'm usually not anywhere close to being bold or loud but feel that way when I'm DJing. All I know is I wouldn't think of wearing any of the others. Not while I'm working.

But then maybe it isn't the way I wear it as much as the way it feels on my head now. My constant hat-wearing, the rim pulled down low over my eyes, has always been a sort of security blanket for me. Not in a weird way or even in a way I was ever aware of before. I've just always been more comfortable with them on than off.

I still wear all of them at school, the way I always have, but when I reach the club and grip hands with the bouncer Rick outside before pushing through the cream-colored doors, my red lid becomes something different, the same way everything becomes different. It's like it somehow frees me to do anything I want with my music in a way that's almost as amazing as Cream itself.

I no longer feel like a teen struggling to get by. I feel like a DJ known for his T-shirts, and his oversized jeans, and that mysterious red hat hiding his face. When I step behind the decks, I simply take over this place that is becoming a part of me now and that I am becoming a part of. Cream cures me of that lost feeling, that incompleteness that used to follow me, hovering over my every move and waiting to swallow me whole.

Wednesday nights get busier earlier now and some of the regulars even greet me when I walk in. I am making a name for myself. I am DJ Ice. And then I walk back through those cream-colored doors and I'm Marley again, except now with that wholeness, that fulfilled dream always in my midst.

Even home doesn't seem as bad as it did before. Sure, Ma and her druggie boyfriends still get to me. Their drug use is still sickening and unbearable. After all, my mother isn't the one who's changed. It all sucks a little less, though.

The change in me goes unnoticed at home and school, being that it doesn't really exist outside of Cream, and the six days I'm at Spazio's still feel familiar and necessary in a "taking care of my shit the way I've always had to do" sort of way.

As for this moment right here, right now, performing for the Friday-night crowd at Cream, I can't help smiling at the room around me, at the projectors that spray movie clips onto all four walls, at that random-ass marble fountain in the middle of the club that sprays "cream," and, of course, at the people who really pack it in tonight, doubling my Wednesday-night crowd.

And amid all the alcohol and the people and the swelling, pulsing life is my music, flowing through the room like a contagious laughter that makes each and every person feel a little more alive. Like a wildfire that spreads through people's bodies, moving their feet, lifting their heads, turning their torsos, and filling their minds with incredible fantasy.

I pull my pounding beat back a bit, shrinking the track down into a single hollow note that drips with loneliness and soul-filled agony: a new sound with no color at all, just a cool, light, easy feeling, a background to the clinking glasses, the laughter, the shouts of release.

I plan to move into a more melodic, transient-like sound but feel the crowd vibe with the moment and change my mind, instead giving them more of that same lonely melody, echoing atop a lonely melody, echoing above a great agony, whispering of an old pleasure that has been torn away but is always remembered, always played out in the depths of the soul to feed a burning pain.

* * *

When my shift ends, Donnie asks to see me in the office. I didn't think he even used the office. I figured only Lonnie did any real work in there.

Donnie and Lonnie might have been born on the same day to the same parents, but those have got to be the only things on earth those two have in common.

Donnie wears wrinkle-free designer suits with expensive ties and gelled-back hair. He has a corner of the club he likes to hang out in with his friends and any girls he thinks have the potential of going home with him for a night.

His job in the bar seems to be to look and be "the shit." He's the type of guy you expect to see standing outside a spot like Fever overseeing the line and deciding who is and isn't good enough to get in.

Lonnie is the polar opposite of his brother in every way. He lives, thinks, and breathes nothing but Cream. All day long it's Cream, Cream, Cream. Phone calls, e-mails, meetings with distributors, interviews with promoters, private-party arrangements with customers. He unlocks the doors for business at six p.m. sharp and locks up at the end of the night after the employees head home. Then, when he's done with all the paperwork in the office, he retreats to his apartment directly above the bar to plan the next business day.

So it's weird that Donnie is the one who wants to see me. Shouldn't it be Lonnie? Shouldn't Donnie be busy getting drunk with his buddies and women who wear too much makeup and too little clothing?

Apparently not, because here he is sitting at the worn-out oak desk, eyeing me curiously as I hover near the door and wonder if I'm about to get the ax. He waves me to the extra chair and takes on a pondering pose, leaning back with his fingers interlaced in his lap, fronting a serious look. He has a pose for every occasion, and this one appears to be his *boss* pose. I take a seat and wait.

"How's everything?" he asks.

"Fine."

"Money, environment, people?"

"Sure."

"Tonight was good?"

"Tonight was great."

"Yes, it was. Friday, then." He watches me like he's expecting a reaction. I have none. I have no idea what he's talking about and finally have to ask.

"Friday, then? Did something happen or—"

"Exactly." He rises from his chair. He checks his reflection in the little mirror that hangs on the wall above the desk, smoothing a hand over his dark, slicked-back hair and straightening his already perfectly straight designer tie. "Exactly."

Music fills the room as Donnie opens the door and strolls back out into the club, then muffles again as it shuts behind him. I sit there alone for a few moments before walking out of the office myself and heading over to the bar where I claim a stool and continue to wonder what the hell just happened. "Hey, Hogan?"

Hogan places a glass of ice on the counter in front of me and fills it with root beer. "How's it going, man?"

"I'm not sure. I had a talk with Donnie."

"Yeah, I saw you go in the office." He leans over to wash glasses behind the bar, dunking them in soapy water, then disinfectant water, then clean water before setting them on a rack to dry.

"Donnie said, 'Friday, then,' but I have no idea what he was talking about. Was he trying to remind me it's Friday or something? Ask me to sub again next week? I don't know. I tried to ask and he said 'exactly' a couple times and walked out. I feel like I never know what that guy's talking about."

"Nobody does," says Hogan. "But he said Friday?"

"Yeah."

"You sure?"

"Yeah. I'm sure."

"Wow!" Hogan nods to some customers and opens three bottles of beer. "I'm impressed."

"So you know what he meant?"

Hogan grins. "I do," he answers, before moving down the

bar to serve some sort of clear liquor drink and a draft beer to a couple businessmen types.

"What does it mean?" I call after him.

"It means you're coming over to my place after work," he calls back as he moves farther down to where the high-end liquor is shelved. "We gotta celebrate. You, my friend, just landed the opening Friday-night shift permanently."

I stare after Hogan in disbelief. "You're kidding."

"Nope."

"You mean..."

"Yup. Mackie is moving to LA. Dorian's getting his Saturday-night shift, but nobody knew who'd get Friday night. Guess you're the lucky winner. Weekend spots are prime. They'll pay you more on Friday nights too. You're the real deal now, Ice."

Thoughts spin around my head like some awesome mix, blending together, absorbing each other, sliding easily into grooves of imagination. I'm DJing on Friday nights! I can't believe it. And apparently I'll even get paid more to do it. I'm already making seventy-five on Wednesdays, which means I'll be making more than a hundred and fifty dollars a week to do something I'd do for free. Shit, forget free, I'd pay Lonnie and Donnie to be here!

I already switched my night off at Spazio's from Tuesdays to Wednesdays, so if I drop Fridays and keep my other five shifts, I should be able to work seven nights a week and still make ends meet easily. I should even have more extra cash to put away each month. And with Justin's party coming up this Sunday, I'll have way more than enough money to buy my laptop by the end of the weekend.

This is the real deal, like Hogan said. I'm a professional DJ now. What could be better than that?

*   *   *

Hogan lives in a two-bedroom, one-bath apartment within walking distance of Cream. I figured everyone went home after the club closed, but, it turns out, aside from me and Lonnie, the Cream crew all go over to Hogan's every night after work.

When I walk in, everybody's already there. Hogan standing in the kitchen mixing drinks. Donnie buried in a corner, cuddled up to a girl who frequents the bar. Dana, who bartends at Cream on weekends, seated on the couch smoking a cigarette and looking pissed-off. Standing five foot eight, with short, spiky black hair, a sheet-white complexion, and these pouty lips she covers in bright red lipstick, she's not a bad-looking girl. But she's not very pleasant and always has an expression on her face like she just sucked on a lemon, which wipes the cuteness right off her.

Rick, the bouncer at Cream, is busy rolling a joint on the counter that connects the living room to the kitchen as he chats animatedly with Hogan. Like Hogan, Rick is an all-around good guy. He looks like your typical bouncer, six-four and muscle-bound. He's all business when he's working the door, but all heart when work is over.

Greg, the bar back, takes swigs from a bottle of Heineken and dances in circles around the living room to some music a Cream regular named Dave's got playing on the stereo. Greg's a little guy who wears thick black eye makeup and pretty much works his ass off between handling Dana's demanding requests and rushing to help Hogan out. He's a tiny dude, only about five feet tall and super skinny and gay and hilarious. He's also brilliant: a second-year law student who somehow manages to party all night and still do well in school.

Everybody who works at the club has some sort of dream.

Greg's is to be a trial attorney.

Donnie's is to own a bigger, more glamorous, Fever-caliber club.

Dana is an Administration of Justice major in junior college, training to be a cop, which I can totally picture.

Rick, who wants to be an actor, auditions during the day and has traveled to both Hollywood and New York City to read for parts. So far he hasn't had much luck, but I imagine when he does, he'll end up typecast in roles like "bodyguard" and "tough guy" and, well, "club bouncer."

Hogan is the only one who isn't trying to become something else. He's been a bartender for eight years and loves it. And, of course, then there's me, living out my dream right here, right now.

Several Cream regulars also get invited to the after parties at Hogan's. From what I can tell, Tony, Cynthia, Leon, Dave, and Asia all dream of one thing and one thing only—partying.

In addition to the Cream crew and the regulars, a girl I've never seen before is wandering around shouting, and laughing, and kissing everyone she sees. Her hair is black with purple streaks, and her makeup is heavy and sort of rainbow-colored all over her face, but you can still see how smooth her medium-brown skin is beneath the makeup and how well built she is beneath her lacy black dress. Basically, she's beautiful. I watch her crouch down to kiss Donnie and then kiss the girl he's cuddled up to. Donnie frowns and wipes off his cheek. Weird.

The girl dances across the room to where Dave is and grabs his face in her hands and kisses him on his forehead, his nose, his mouth, and that's the moment I first see them. And damn are they beauties. I can hardly believe my eyes.

I walk toward them, moving in slow like they might disappear or something if I approach too fast. But as I get closer, they only become more beautiful. No, it's not my imagination at all. On a wide wooden table in the corner are the sweetest turntables I have ever laid eyes on.

I figured Dave was playing tunes off his iPod and didn't pay him any mind, but what he's actually been doing is playing a record on an M5G deck! Not only that, he's got three of them. How could I have missed them?

I move around next to Dave and eye them hard. Oh man! This is the first time I've even seen a third deck in person. I only know of a handful of DJs who can play on three at once, and they're international stars.

What would Hogan be doing with all this? Does he DJ on the side or as a hobby or something? He's never mentioned it. But this is some equipment he's got. Not exactly hobby quality.

"Like 'em?" Hogan calls out from across the room when he sees me staring.

Like 'em? What, is he kidding? "They yours?"

"Naw," he says, but he doesn't bother telling me what he's doing with such high-end equipment, plus a bookcase packed tight with vinyl, if he doesn't spin. "Go on, Ice. Play for us. Dave, move aside and let a pro have at it."

"Gladly," Dave replies, stepping away.

I scan the albums lining the width of the bookshelves rising five high to the right of the decks and pull down a few titles I recognize and a few I don't. The moment I start thinking about the music I want to play and the type of mix I want to create, everything else in the room fades away.

The first record is special, a track I've been keeping an eye out for at Gecko and John Z. Records for, like, forever. I haven't even been able to find it anywhere online, which is really kind of crazy. Yet here it is, right here on Hogan's shelf. The guy has a collection going any DJ would approve of and most would envy.

Fur-covered headphones slip around my neck and my head tilts to the left, cradling them against my shoulder. The needle drops *riiiiiight* there, and my soul begins to fill with music. Soon that music is seeping from the speakers and trickling through the room like the smell of freshly baked chocolate-chip cookies floating out of an oven into the open air. I sift in a second track with a hard, confident beat to counter the melody—and look up long enough to see Hogan dancing through the kitchen as he pours a new batch of drinks one by one into waiting glasses.

Donnie and his girl are busy making out in his little corner of the room to my left. Lips and tongues move together, hands travel over curves, skin touches skin. It's kind of gross, really.

Hogan must think so too because he hollers, "Get a room, Donnie! And I don't mean mine!"

That makes me smile, but only for a second, and then I'm absorbed in music again, switching a record, altering a beat. When the sound I'm creating is exactly where I want it to be, I let my eyes close and relax and take in the energy of everyone in the room, letting it pulse in my hands, throb in my palms, then slip off my fingertips, and flow out in every direction.

When I open my eyes and look around again, I see Dana and Greg sitting side by side on the couch, simultaneously dropping pills of some kind and washing them down with quick shots. E and tequila, I think. In the same breath Dana leans over a painting and does a line on the glass through a tightly rolled bill. She sits up and shakes her head back, sniffing the air.

Watching them, I wish there was a way I could show them all the things I've seen drugs do to Ma and her friends. The withdrawals. The depression. The desperation that makes them lie, and cheat, and steal, and screw up every relationship in their lives.

But I can't show them. And I sure can't tell them. Nobody listens to speeches like that until they're ready to quit using.

I should know.

I turn my attention away from their drugs quick and try to focus on the rest of the room so I don't have to think about what Dana and Greg are doing to themselves. It's a very real part of the nightlife, but I don't want to see it. At least not right now. I know I'll have to find a way to deal with the drug use going on around me if I want to be here, and I will find a way to deal somehow. Because I do want to be here. More than anything I want to be here and come back here again and again and somehow become a part of this.

Everything I set eyes on pumps me with new ideas. Rick

and his girlfriend moving to the center of the room to dance. Dana stepping onto the coffee table, not even bothering to move the painting or any of the glasses out of the way first. She raises her arms and moves them in slow waves above her head as she swings her hips back and forth, her eyes shut and her mouth curled into a rare smile. Greg moves all of the glasses to one of the end tables and the painting onto the couch before climbing up onto the coffee table beside Dana. A Cream regular named Leon dances in circles around the room.

All of it becomes a part of the mix I'm creating, which is about the party scene itself from the very beginning of the night until the very end: gritty, beautiful, fake, real, colorful, dark, full, empty, lost, found, with surging emotion everywhere that encompasses anything and everything.

It's nice to see Rick be the one who gets to dance, free to relax and party and enjoy himself for a change, as if he's hanging out inside the club instead of working the door.

And I love watching Dana's peaceful face. Is it the drugs that melt her fiery anger, or is it a natural high from the music that's making her feel so good? I hope it's the music.

In the kitchen Hogan looks up from a blender full of some sort of thick orange drink and gives me a nod of approval and a smile. I smile back, and just like that I realize I already do belong. Almost as if there was a gap somewhere in this group that I'm here to fill. I feel a connection to these people. Even to the ones I don't know. We're connected in energy, me and these adults who don't act like adults at all. The whole room swells with it, and it consumes me, and I'm dizzy with music and happiness and people and life. I don't ever want this night to end.

15

I DON'T REMEMBER CRASHING AT HOGAN'S, BUT I must've knocked out at some point because the next thing I know I'm waking up on his couch and it's almost one o'clock in the afternoon and everyone is gone and the place is totally quiet. I look around the room thinking it's weird for me to still be here and that I need to find my shoes, my pack, my jacket, and be on my way.

But then my eyes catch sight of those turntables set up on the other side of the room and I know I'm not going anywhere.

I run my fingers over some of the soft cardboard covers of hundreds of records displayed on the adjacent shelves. Oh, wow! I pull down one, then another and another, studying several for a long time before picking the ones I want. My body grows jittery with excitement as headphones slide around my neck, records drop, needles work.

Deep, flowing sounds move through Hogan's empty living room like a cool breeze I can almost see. Bright blue wind dances on furniture and bounces off walls, filling the room with a warmth and light every room deserves on a sunny Saturday afternoon as I suck in music like it's oxygen I couldn't possibly live without.

This time here alone at Hogan's place is a chance to work on all the things I can't do at home. I may never get my hands on equipment this pimp again. I have so many ideas in my head that involve adding depth to my sound with delay and echo combinations, flanging, phasing. . . .

"What in the hell is all that racket?" a voice growls. "Making my ears bleed. *Fuck!*"

I look up suddenly, startled by Hawk's tired, irritated face. I didn't think anyone was still here. In fact, I didn't even know he'd come over last night. "It's nothing," I say, quickly turning down the volume.

"It's something, all right. I didn't know which would explode first. My head or my brand-new speakers."

Hawk's speakers. His tables. His unbelievable record collection. Of course. He and Hogan must be roommates. I should have known none of this was Hogan's. What kind of sense would that make?

Hawk goes into the kitchen and pours himself a cup of coffee. He doesn't bother to offer me any, not that I'd expect him to. "Who taught you to spin anyway?"

"Nobody."

He chuckles, returning to the living room and taking a seat on the couch as he slurps from an oversized mug. "Nobody? What, you just walked into Cream one day and started droppin' beats?"

I don't respond. I could tell him my father taught me the basic mechanics of drop mixing when I was a kid, and then I taught myself to beat match. But I know if I say anything, I'll only be opening myself up to more low-blow potshots from asshole number one, and I'm not interested in sinking to his level.

"You sound like it," he continues. "You spin like you walked up to the tables for the very first time that night and started screwing around."

I pull his headphones from around my neck, set them back on their hook, and say nothing. Hawk watches me for a moment, waiting for me to react to his insult. "I'll tell you something else. The guy you replaced was better than you. Seasoned, you know?" He lights a cigarette and eyes me with a cold gaze. "You, on the other hand, are nothing but a goofball amateur. It's clear you don't know shit about music."

I'm starting to figure Hawk out. The guy's got two moods — his bad mood, which is crabby and rude, and his bad mood, which is harsh and cruel. This morning, he's in a bad mood.

I choose to ignore his abuse and not play into his game as I slide all the vinyl I pulled back into the exact spots where I found them on the bookcase and start grabbing my stuff. The guy keeps laying into me, though, and won't shut up about it.

"You think that crap you play is music? Hah! You don't deserve to spin on my tables. You haven't earned that right!"

"I wasn't really spinning," I say, as if it matters what he thinks. It doesn't. But the guy is seriously starting to piss me off, so the words keep coming. "I was experimenting with sounds is all, hoping to trigger new ideas for an original mix I've been trying to compose. It's not like I was serious."

"Original mix?" he scoffs. "You don't even know what the word *original* means, Ice. And what's up with that anyway? *DJ Ice!* Seems like an awful big name for a guy who doesn't know shit."

What a dick. I'm about ten seconds away from going off on the guy the way I should have that first night.

"Original?" he says again. "Original? Shit, I'll show you original." He moves to the desk in the opposite corner of the room, next to Donnie's make-out spot, and switches on the computer. "Original," he grumbles as he drags down a menu and opens a file. "Listen to this, *DJ Ice*. Now this, this is original." I move a little closer without actually getting close and listen to the music playing through the computer speakers.

And what I hear is amazing. Beyond amazing. Techno blended into a powerful African rumba broken up by strong salsa beats with flowing, echoed keyboard chords interlaced throughout the melody. "Wow, that's nice. Where's it from?"

"It's not from anywhere except right the fuck here!" he says. "It's mine."

"You put that mix together?"

"I didn't put anything together, *Ice*. I wrote it. Every beat, every note." He leans back and grins with satisfaction at the computer screen. "Now that's original. And I've got tons of 'em." I notice how the scar on his face moves when he smiles, and realize I've never seen him do it before.

"The music's really good," I say. This is an understatement. The music is unreal. What I would give to create something like that out of thin air. I mix with records that aren't half as good as this. In fact, so does he. "Who's playing the keyboards? They're good."

"I am, of course."

I consider telling him I've been learning to play for a couple months now but change my mind. "How long you been a DJ anyway?"

"Long enough," Hawk answers, anger returning to his voice almost as fast as it fell away.

"The stuff you play at Cream is really good, but this…this is on another level. Why don't you ever play any of it at the club?"

Hawk cuts off the music. He swivels around in his chair to face me and points an accusing finger. "When you're on your own time, you play what you want. When you're on their time, on the clock, you play what they want, what the crowd wants to hear." He stares at me in disbelief and disgust. "Didn't anyone teach you anything?"

I shake my head. "Most of what I know I taught myself on my father's tables."

"You don't know much," he says. "In fact, I'm surprised you know how to work with vinyl at all. Why aren't you into the DJ software scene like everybody else?"

"I am. They told me no laptops allowed at Cream."

"You're damn right," says Hawk. "And there never will be, not as long as I'm working there. DJ software is banned. It's in my contract."

"In your contract?"

"That's right. There's a no-laptop clause in my contract."

I wait for him to explain, but he doesn't and I have to ask. "So it says somewhere in your contract that you won't use a laptop in Cream?"

"Wrong. My contract says *no one* can use a laptop in Cream. Ever. Wax only!"

"Oh," I say. "Wow."

"That's the kind of power I've got there, *Ice*. You think other clubs have rules like that?"

"No, I don't," I say. "But why do you have a rule like that? What does it matter?"

"Because I want to play in a club with artists, that's why. Spinning records is an art form, and the only true form of the art is vinyl. Staring at a computer screen is not art. If you could create a picture on a computer but didn't know how to draw, would you be an artist? No, I don't think so. We're musicians. Turntablists. If you can't use vinyl, you can't call yourself a turntablist."

I shrug. "All right."

Hawk smirks. "You *saaaay* all right, but only because you don't have a choice. If you did, you'd be using a laptop instead of vinyl."

"To be honest, I don't know which way I would've gone if I'd had a choice. I guess if I was asked to play a type of music I don't own a lot of, I'd hope I could use a laptop. I have a lot of records that suit the Cream crowd, but not hundreds like you. Working with software is so much cheaper. It's what makes it possible for guys like me, who can't afford many records, to become DJs. And software like Serato and Virtual

DJ and Traktor open up so many options. Like you can take a track and double it instantly, and with vinyl I'd have to buy two records to do that, and who's to say I could even find two if they're rare tracks let alone afford them, and artistically DJ software opens up all kinds of new avenues, plus you don't have to lug your records around because—"

"Hey hey hey," Hawk cuts in, "that's enough of that. There's nobody here who cares. What are you, a salesman for Serato? You sound like a fucking ad."

"I don't mean to," I say. "I just wanted to point out that software also has its place in the DJ world."

"Well give it a rest. And hone your craft if you wanna keep working at Cream. You've got a whole lot to learn."

I shouldn't ask. It's stupid, and useless, and pride-breaking. But between what I've witnessed in the club and this, I have to. It's like I need to be able to walk away from here knowing I at least tried.

"All right," I say, looking him in the eye deadpan-style. "You think I've still got a lot to learn? Fine. I feel where you're coming from and I'll even agree with you. I have a lot to learn. And I want to learn. So why don't you teach me?"

Hawk's expression turns to shock. Then anger. He stands abruptly.

He glares at me silently for a few seconds, before picking up his coffee and walking out of the room. A door slams somewhere down the hall so hard it makes the windowpanes rattle.

No surprise there.

I grab my stuff and bail.

So much for a mentor.

JUSTIN DECIDES ON ROCK, POP, AND RADIO RAP for his party. Works for me. Then again, for three hundred I'd sing karaoke tunes for three hours straight if he wanted me to.

A hundred bucks an hour...I still can't get the amount to settle in my head. I never thought I'd make anywhere near that kind of money, even as an adult.

Very few people on this earth will ever make a hundred dollars an hour. My first paid private party. Cooler than cool. And on top of the coolness factor, three hundred bucks will actually put me over what I need for my laptop and start me well on my way toward purchasing my Rane mixer.

I arrive at the Hall residence at noon to check out the brand-new Pioneer CDJs Justin rented for the day. I brought a few compilation CDs with me, plus a thumbdrive of songs by artists Justin said he wants to hear during the party. The Hall residence is unreal. I call it a *residence* because calling it a house would be a gross understatement. The sucker is four stories tall, with two tons of lawn space out front. My whole apartment could fit on that lawn, like, six times over.

The inside is even more unbelievable. I try not to look as surprised as I feel, but I don't think I do a very good job of it, since Justin keeps telling me to take it easy. "It's only a house," he keeps saying.

Only a house? Maybe to him. To me it looks more like a museum I should be careful not to touch anything in. Every room has these fancy-looking hardwood panels that've been oiled to a glistening shine. The floors are covered in marble, the walls are covered in expensive-looking art, and there are too many rooms to count. Most of them stand two stories tall and make my mouth gape open.

Justin's friends start showing up around one o'clock. The senior Haves.

It's funny, though. Now that I'm here up close and personal, they don't seem that different from anyone else. In fact, with the exception of Todd Bitherman, who's a jerk-off in any crowd, they actually seem pretty nice. I watch in amazement as each of them greets me before moving on into the living room.

Watching the five guys and four girls settle in and begin to drink an obscene amount of alcohol makes it pretty obvious this won't be anywhere close to my scene, but I don't even mind, because the music sounds amazing and feels even better. My juices are really flowing today.

I take tracks from artists like Lady Gaga, Eminem, Rihanna, and Lil Wayne that're kind of played out but also total crowd pleasers and remix them with fresh sounds and classic beats that leave them fully recognizable while at the same time reinventing them as something that feels more my style. Some of Justin's friends get up to dance, and I can't help noticing the songs they dig the most are the same ones my own friends are really into.

It's like music is such a universal connector it can break right through all the bullshit barriers that divide people into opposite groups. I may not understand most of the stuff the Haves do, but I know what they want to hear, what'll make them feel good. Watching the senior Have girls pick themselves up off oversized leather couches and dance together, I feel like a king on a throne, totally in control without ever saying a word. I feel like Pop, like the man of the hour he always was when he DJed his parties. He could command any crowd, make anyone feel more alive with his music.

I can feel him here with me now, listening and beaming with pride. We laugh together as I drop little lyrical snippets into my mix that express what I'm thinking as I watch Justin and his friends. Things like "money can't buy you happiness" and "we're all the same."

"Hey, Marley, sounding good," Justin comments, strolling up and smiling.

"Thanks," I say, but my attention is focused on Todd

Bitherman, who's stepped up beside him. Standing six foot five and skinnier than I am, Todd is just about the biggest ass I've ever met.

I eye him warily as he places a hand on Justin's shoulder and leers at me. "I thought you said his name was DJ Ice. What a completely idiotic name."

I pull away my headphones and lean forward. "Well, I was thinking of going with the name DJ Todd, but I didn't want anyone to mix us up and think *I'm* the one who's the total asshole."

"Ice," says Justin, missing our exchange, "right! How could I forget?"

Todd hones in on me with stony eyes. "Say, Justin, I like this new idea of getting a DJ to play while we hang out, but why hire a low-life nobody from school to do it?"

Justin's smile fades. He is no longer oblivious to the heated exchange going on between me and Todd. "I hired him because I heard he was talented, and he is. You got a problem with me deciding who'll play music in my own house, Todd?"

Todd puts his hands up in surrender. He'll give me shit all day, but he knows better than to mess with Justin. "I don't understand why you'd get *this* guy when you could've hired one of the DJs who play our real parties, that's all I'm trying to say."

"Dude, that's uncalled for," Justin says, eyeing Todd carefully.

"Dude, *he's* uncalled for," Todd replies.

Justin turns back to me. "You mind taking a little break? There's plenty of alcohol on the table in the backyard if you want a drink. Down the hall to the end and through the glass doors. Make yourself at home."

"Thanks," I say. "I'd take a root beer or something like that if you have it."

"There should be something out there for ya," Justin says, which seems to translate as "disappear for a few so I can bust Todd's chops," which is exactly why I like Justin Hall and why he actually deserved to be homecoming king this year.

I make my way to the backyard where a picnic table covered in bottles of liquor has been set up a few feet away from a massive swimming pool. I'm hoping for root beer or a Coke or juice, but it's like there aren't any mixers on the table at all. I'm searching the pile for tonic, or regular water, or something, anything nonalcoholic, when I notice the girls. There are six of them lying side by side on long lawn chairs on the opposite side of the pool. One of the six is Lea Hall. She is the only one of the six who isn't glaring at me.

"What are you doing here?" Melanie, who looks anorexic in a black bikini, calls out. The contrast of the black against her sheet-white skin isn't too flattering either.

"Looking for something nonalcoholic to drink."

"No, I mean what are you doing *here*? At Lea's house."

"Melanie, stop," says Lea.

Melanie eyes me hard from across the pool, burning me to a crisp with her eyes. "Oh, sorry," she says, but she's still giving me that death stare. Brittany smirks at me from the lawn chair beside her.

"Ignore Melanie," Lea tells me. "You're totally welcome here. And there's nonalcoholic stuff in the fridge in the kitchen. Take the hall on your left when you walk into the house."

"Thanks," I mumble in reply before walking back across the yard and through the stained-glass doors as fast as I can and still call it walking.

I never do get that drink. I'm too flustered from seeing Lea Hall wearing nothing but a bikini. Instead I return to my rightful place behind the decks. My mood has turned, though. Not because of the way her friends were acting. I could care less what they think. It was the fact that Lea didn't act that way. The Melanie Jergenses and the Brittany Daneses and the Todd Bithermans of the world can look down their stuck-up noses at me all they want. Lea told me I was welcome in her home. She welcomed me here.

I'm not stupid. I know she doesn't like me, doesn't even think of me, in fact, except when I'm standing in her backyard on a break from working for her brother or fetching her water and bread and clearing her dishes away while she dines with her family. But she seemed, I don't know, decent.

If only I'd said something back. Something clever. If only I'd had the balls to say something to her right there in front of all those bitchy girls. But I didn't. And right now that's okay because it isn't what I'm here for anyway. In under an hour I'll have made three hundred dollars doing something I love. In under an hour I'll finally have the money to buy my computer.

I weave one last random pulled lyrical phrase into my mix, but this one isn't meant to be a silent message to the Haves. This one's for Lea and Lea alone. What I would give to be able to talk to her for real.

"If I knew what, if I knew how..."

If I could tell her the things I'm feeling, what's inside me. I'd find a way to give her the whole world if she gave me a chance to.

"If I knew where,
"If I knew when,
"If I knew you ..."

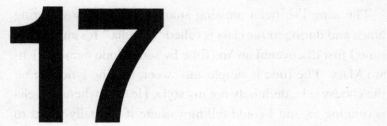

THREE DAYS AFTER JUSTIN'S PARTY I FIND myself behind another set of turntables, standing in my place in the world, the one where I, and only I, belong between eight and ten every Wednesday and Friday night.

It's really pretty unbelievable how good things have gotten. With my music turning into a mini career, I've started spending more and more lunches in the band room at school experimenting with new tunes and continuing to school myself on Scratch Live. I've been working on more original stuff too, stuff I now know is total crap, thanks to Hawk, but I can't get better unless I keep at it and, being that I don't have a teacher or a mentor to guide me in the art of making music that isn't total crap, I'll have to keep trying to get better on my own. Besides, Hawk might think my DJ skills suck ass, but people are paying to hear me, so I can't be all that bad.

The song I've been messing around with the most during lunch and during music class is called "Angelia." It's an eighties tune I first discovered on YouTube by some dude named Richard Marx. The tune is simple and sweet, but the lyrics are on the cheesy side, definitely not my style. He asks where Angelia is running to, and I could tell him where if he really wants to know. As far away from him and his sappy crooning as possible.

I'm in the midst of deconstructing the whole song. The only lyrics I'm even keeping are the few in the chorus where he asks where Angelia is going, because I think that's the weakest part of the song and will therefore be the greatest challenge and the most rewarding triumph once I transform it into something incredible.

I'm keeping that plus a tiny cut from the instrumental break. A little keyboard here, some echoed samples there, a bumpin' beat throughout, and it's on its way. I mask it enough that the little of the song that still exists does so only in flashes. When I'm done with it, it'll be so good that Angelia herself will turn around and run right back to Richard Marx.

This is one of my favorite things about DJing, something I love almost as much as I love the way it feels when you discover a brand-new tune the mainstream knows nothing of and daydream about how you're going to go about sharing it with the world and that head-swelling, heart-constricting moment when you actually do.

132

Mixing with "Angelia" is almost as good, except in the opposite way. It's more about covering something up than sharing your soul. Like instead of taking a tune that you know is brilliant but that no one has heard before and introducing it to the club world, you're taking an old song that you know nobody would dance to and morphing it into something that makes them move and cheer and ask, "What is that? It's awesome!"

That's how it will be with this song. When I'm through with it, my "Angelia" remix will pull people onto the dance floor like an invisible arm, and that perfect beat I'll find to intertwine it with and the melodic sounds I'll mix it into will keep them there, mesmerized, forever moving, unable to stop even when they tire from their overpumped hearts and aching feet. I will turn "Angelia" into a masterpiece of true beauty for the real-life angel they call Lea. Not that she'll ever hear it.

I hunch over the tables in the back of the band room, lost in that vast space that exists between my headphones, in a trance I only feel when I'm working, mixing, creating.

Life has seriously been looking up lately. I can't remember ever feeling this happy. In fact, the only thing that feels hard at all anymore is being so crazy busy all the time trying to juggle school, and homework, and working seven nights a week. The minute school is over, I have to bail out to study and get ready for work, so I hardly ever get to spend time with my friends anymore outside of lunch three days a week and maybe a minute or two in between classes. And even though I've been studying every chance I get, half my grades have slipped from As to Bs.

Today I fell asleep in the middle of lunch. I was so out of it from working at Cream on Wednesday night and hanging at Hogan's after, and then having to stay up half of last night cramming like crazy for a big exam, I knocked out as soon as I got to our table. I slept right there in the cafeteria sitting between K.C. and Will, my right arm sprawled across the table barely missing a bowl of mac and cheese.

It's all worth it, though. Even when I think about getting Bs in school, and barely seeing my friends, and not being able to keep an eye on Ma the way I should, I know it'll all be worth it in the long run. All my sacrifices are temporary and they'll all pay off when I become an international star. They all pay off now, every single time I stand behind this bar spinning my records and watching the goings-on of the club around me.

Not just because it feels so good to be doing the thing I love most either—they're paying off literally. And this is only the beginning. One day I might make a living doing nothing but DJing in clubs every night. It's a crazy thought, but it's not nearly as crazy as it used to be. The wax beneath my fingers and the crowd before me vibing with the beat are totally real.

I feel like a scientist watching the reaction of one chemical to the next every time I look around the room. I add more of one potion or another, experimenting with unchartered sounds, testing out new tracks, doing whatever it takes to get that compound *just* right.

And when I'm done, I add in a few extra drops of that chemical they call excitement. Every musical compound needs excitement to exist. It is the base; and all good chemists know their base just like all good DJs know their bass.

I know my bass. It sings out deeply and makes the floor-boards vibrate. I know its certainty, its depth, its repetitive addiction. When I'm spinning, I am caught in that whirlwind of pleasure that every addict seeks. Music is my drug and when I'm done mixing my chemicals, everyone on the dance floor will be addicted. Every person in Cream will be high on life.

18

"HEY, ICE," GREG CALLS OUT, "YOU GONNA PLAY
for us or what?"

It's a few hours later and everybody's over at Hogan and
Hawk's celebrating the end of a super-exhausting Friday-
night shift. I eye Hawk's tables thinking of how badly he
trashed my skills the last time I was on them.

"Hey, Ice!" Greg calls out again.

"Naw," I tell him, "I'm done for the night."

I scan Hawk's records, pulling down ones that look interesting and checking out their song lists. There are several

crates in the living room that weren't here before, and they're all full of records too. I check out every single title. I'm dying to play. But no way will I do it. He may not be in the room with us, but he's definitely here.

It wasn't until my third time over that I found out where Hawk goes while everyone else is here partying it up after work. He doesn't go anywhere. Hawk is here too: in his bedroom sleeping with earplugs shoved in his ears and an early-morning shift at his day job on his mind.

I don't know if he's in there sleeping right now or not, but I know I can feel him whenever I look at his decks. If I use them or anything else of his, he automatically wins the silent battle going on between us, and I refuse to give him the satisfaction.

"Ice." Hogan motions to me. "Come over here a minute, will ya?"

I cross the room and take a seat on one of the bar stools. Hogan lines up seven glasses and pours whatever concoction he's created into six of them.

"So look," he says as he pours Pepsi into the last glass and places it on the counter in front of me, "I've got something here I'm supposed to give you. Real good news."

I eye the envelope in his hand. "What is it?"

"Look inside and see," Hogan says, handing it to me and standing back. "Go ahead," he urges. "Open it."

It's got *DJ Ice* typed across the front. I look up at Hogan questioningly and he nods to me, still grinning. He did say good news. I rip the envelope open, pull out the letter inside, and start to read. And as I begin to understand what it is I'm reading, my mouth goes dry and my stomach gets queasy.

Dear **DJ Ice** ,

You have been cordially invited to participate in Fever's 1st Annual DJ Battle. Six DJs from around the city will take part in this exciting event. There is no monetary prize. There is no second or third place, only a winner. The winner's reward will be the title of top DJ in the city, plus a coveted spot on Fever's regular DJ rotation.

The competition will take place on January 21 in front of our Saturday-night crowd with the crowd reaction counting as one vote. Four guest DJ judges brought in especially for this competition will account for the other four votes.

Each contestant will be allowed a forty-five-minute set. You have been randomly assigned a competition time of **10:00 pm.** You are to arrive at Fever to check in twenty minutes prior to the assigned time listed above.

You must RSVP your acceptance of this invitation to the number listed below by December 7 in order to compete. Best of luck to you!

Sincerely,

Jorge Sanchez   Timothy Campbell   Adrian Lo

Jorge Sanchez, Timothy Campbell, and Adrian Lo
Fever Club Owners

OH. MY. GOD.

I read the letter two more times before looking up and real-izing everyone in the room is watching me, waiting, grinning the same grin as Hogan, the same grin my friends wore at Jennifer's party when they first told me about the sub gig at that little spot DRC.

I've come so far since filling in that night for the regular DJ, becoming a regular myself at a major club, honing my skills, building my confidence, experimenting with my creativity on the ones and twos. And now this. Oh man. I'm waiting for someone to say "psyche," but nobody does. I don't know what to feel. Except confused.

I look around the room at friends, co-workers, club regu-lars, strangers. They're all looking back at me, and all I can think to ask is, "How?"

No one answers. They all keep giving me these expectant looks, waiting for me to say more, but I can't think of any-thing else to say.

I try to picture myself standing in the DJ booth inside Fever, looking out at some sophisticated crowd full of club veterans who expect me to master the turntables and impress them with something new, some innovative sounds unlike anything they've heard before.

Oh my God. Oh my God. Oh my God. Those three words are turning, churning, the only words that'll stick in my head. Until they're finally replaced by four others, four horrible words that will disappoint everyone in this room: I can't do it.

There's no way. I'm not good enough yet, not to spin in a club like Fever. Besides, I wouldn't have the first clue how to compete against other DJs.

"I'm not ready," I say. I know I'm disappointing everyone, but it's the truth. No way am I ready. Not for something like this. Not even close. I'd make a total fool of myself and screw up any chance for a big-time DJ career later on.

"We'll get you ready," says Greg.

I look at him skeptically and frown. Did I somehow miss the fact that Greg was a professional DJ who could coach me to perform in front of a massive crowd in a competition? "You spin?"

"Actually," Greg says, beaming, but then his smile drops off, "no. I don't."

Exactly. He can't do anything to help. None of them can. And I'm simply not ready for this. Not now and not a couple months from now. I've got to be the luckiest guy in the world to be holding this letter in my hand, but I can't do it. I won't half-ass it either. No way. Not at my dream club.

But a moment later, Greg's face is lighting up again. "I know someone who can help you," he says. "Hawk! Hawk could coach you!"

Hawk. I picture him glowering at me, despising me. I picture him despising my music. He ignored me earlier tonight. I'd finished my set and was moving aside to let him take over. "'Sup?" I said. He looked at me and growled—literally growled.

"Just one problem," I say. "Hawk hates me."

Hogan's grin doesn't break for a second when he hears my revelation about his roommate. "Hawk doesn't hate you," he says in a tone close to laughter.

"He does. Believe me, you don't even know how much he does."

"Not so," Hogan insists, still smiling.

"If he were here," I say, "he would tell you himself. He loathes having to share the turntables at Cream with me. He thinks this friend of his that used to have my spot is way more talented and experienced and should still be there because he's so much better than I am."

"What, you mean Benny?" Hogan and Rick look at each other and crack up. "Ice, you're a way better DJ than Benny, believe me. He had years of experience, sure, but he was never as good as you are."

I shake my head solemnly. "Hawk doesn't think so."

Rick takes a seat on the other stool. "Look, Ice," he says, "take some time and think it over before you decide. Meanwhile let me share a little something with you that might help make up your mind. One of the owners of Fever is a good buddy of mine. Tim ran this whole contest thing by me to see what I thought of the idea and I told him I thought it was great except for one thing. DJs can't just enter. They have to be invited to compete and, to me, that kind of sucks. How is a nobody supposed to get discovered if he can't even get in without knowing a *somebody*? That's not fair."

He's got a point. If the goal is to find undiscovered talent, but it's not an open contest...

"That's how they chose to do it, though. He said they didn't have time to weed through a ton of people with auditions and they weren't about to risk having someone who sucks play for their prime weekend crowd. So six of the top DJs in the city were each given the opportunity to put the spotlight on the most talented up-and-coming DJ they know.

Invites were extended to those six DJs, and those six only, so getting invited is a real honor."

I sit there trying to take in everything he's saying. I can't get my thoughts straight. The opportunity of a lifetime is sitting in my lap. I can feel it between my fingers, words typed out on a sheet of plain, white paper.

But why would I be one of the chosen ones?

Then it dawns on me.

Holy shit! I know why.

It seems impossible, but no one else could have done it. My eyes grow wide with shock. "Hawk did this?"

Hogan nods. "Guess he must not think you suck so bad after all, huh? Considering his reputation is on the line based on how you do."

"I guess…"

Hawk? Choosing me? He would never. This is way too much at once. Hawk chose me. Of all the people he knows, mine was the name he submitted. And if his rep is really on the line, he must be planning to work with me, at least a little.

I feel shocked and baffled and dizzy all at once. "I don't know what to say."

"Say you'll do it."

"Hawk's planning to help me?"

"Yup."

"You're sure?"

"I'm positive, man."

"Then yeah, I'll do it. At Fever? Hell yeah!"

Everyone breaks into cheers and applause. "This calls for a drink!" Hogan announces. Rick slaps me on the shoulder and laughs. I laugh back. It's unbelievable. I am holding a letter in my hands from the owners of Fever. The owners!

And Hawk of all people is the one who made it happen. Hawk, who has never had a single positive thing to say when it comes to me, who's told me time and time again how much he hates my music, how I don't have one ounce of talent.

It definitely goes to show. You never know what life will toss your way. And even when you do think you know, when you're sure you have it all figured out, life'll totally surprise you. Just to remind you that you don't know shit.

19

THE NIGHT AFTER GETTING THE NEWS, I WORK
a shift at Spazio's. It is the longest shift I can ever remember
working. By the time the restaurant closes for the night and
Julio and I finish clearing and cleaning the last few tables and
I start my dishwashing shift, the oversized clock in the
kitchen has stopped moving altogether.

I stare at it over the water spray and steam and steel con-
veyer belt, trying to will time to move faster, but every time I
think I'm done for the night, a new pile of dirty pots and pans
appears. I feel like I'll never get to Fever.

I've been thinking about the end of my shift at Spazio's all day, wondering what it'll be like to make the trip over to the club tonight, knowing I'll be playing there. Will sitting across the street feel different now? Of course it will. It has to. Life is different now.

I end up having to stay late and it's one o'clock by the time I get out of work. I almost forget to grab the tuna sandwich Billy left for me in the employee fridge, I'm so eager to get there.

When I do finally come around the corner and see Fever up ahead, bathed in colored lights, buzzing with people, and surrounded by excitement, I wish I could kiss the ground in front of it and wrap my arms all the way around it and hug the building itself. That's how hit up with emotion I am. I feel edgy as I drop into my usual spot on the other side of the street, popping open the top of my root beer can and pulling the wax paper away from my sandwich.

Across the street the line is getting long. I sip on foamy, sweet root beer and watch a girl exit the club through one of the side doors. From far away she looks like Lea. Then again, a lot of girls remind me of Lea from a distance. I suppose that's what I get for thinking about her so much. She looked fine as hell today. I stared at her all through English and, as usual, she didn't notice.

I take a bite of the most perfect tuna fish sandwich in the world and wash it down with a couple swallows of root beer as I watch the girl move around to the front of the club and start down the block. Suddenly she looks across the street and stops short. "Marley?" she calls out, squinting her eyes like she isn't sure what she's seeing. "Marley, is that you?"

My heart flutters erratically as I put down my sandwich and stand. It flutters because I don't have to squint. I know exactly what I'm seeing. It's her! Not only is it her, she's looking at me. Talking to me, even.

"Hey, Lea," I call back, as if it's no big deal to see her here. We watch each other in surprise from opposite sides of the street, from opposite worlds, but neither of us says anything more. She looks as beautiful as ever in sleek black pants and a white tube top, her blond hair twisted into a bun at the back of her head except for some loose strands that frame her face. I watch her step into the street.

Shit! Is she coming over here? I can't imagine why she would after all the time she's spent ignoring me. But she's halfway across already, only a few feet away, waiting for a car to pass. Then all I can think of is, what's she going to say once she gets here? Once she's on my side of the street? She's never spoken to me before. I'm pretty sure she's never even looked at me before.

Hell, forget what she's going to say—what am *I* going to say? I'm way too shy for this. I watch in shock as Lea Hall steps onto the sidewalk on my side and we come face-to-face for the first time. She doesn't look past me or at the ground either; she looks directly into my eyes. And she smiles. Actually smiles. I haven't moved but somehow feel totally out of breath.

Now that we're standing together, I'm noticing all kinds of things I hadn't before. Like how delicate her fingers look when she does that thing where she curls loose strands of hair behind one ear. And how big her brown eyes really are when she looks at me. And she's smaller than I thought, even, five-four at the most. I literally tower over her.

I pull at my mind for words to say but come up empty. This leaves us with an amazingly long and awkward silence during which Lea just watches me curiously, waiting for me to speak. I watch her back with my heart, which radiates through me as I shift my weight from one foot to the other.

I almost don't want us to talk. I want to stay in this place we're in forever; a place where she pays attention to me and I get to look at her all I want for the first time — probably the only time.

"What are you doing here?" she finally asks, but not in a harsh way like her girlfriends do when they want to point out that you're not one of them and don't belong. Her words carry a gentle tone, as if she's simply curious. "Were you here for Todd's party?"

I chuckle and say, "Yeah, right," realizing too late that I'm being rude. "Oh, hey, I'm sorry," I tell her. "I didn't mean —"

"No, don't be sorry," she says. "That was just about the stupidest question I've ever asked anybody."

I let a grin slip out. "Probably," I agree under my breath, but loud enough for her to hear.

Lea smiles, and I swear it's the most beautiful smile I've ever seen, because it's not just a smile. It's a smile directed at me.

"I was at Todd Bitherman's birthday party," she explains, gazing back across the street at the club. "We're supposed to be leaving soon, but I was sort of over it already, so I snuck out early to get some fresh air."

He had his birthday party here? At *Fever*? "But you guys aren't even old enough to get in."

"Todd rented a private room with a separate entrance.

They rent it for parties and you don't have to be twenty-one; you just can't drink openly there or access the rest of the club." She frowns. "My brother talked me into going." I nod like I understand, even though I don't. "So what are you doing here then?"

She eyes the can of root beer and the half-eaten sandwich sitting on a paper bag at my feet.

"Dreaming," I tell her. And I don't want to be as distracted as I am, but it has occurred to me that Lea Hall isn't just paying attention to me; we're actually having a conversation. She's standing within the boundaries of my dream space, my most personal spot in the world. I'm not even nervous about it. It's like I'm too excited to finally be talking to her to even worry about feeling nervous.

"What is it you dream about?" she asks. "Partying at Fever?"

"DJing at Fever."

Lea's eyes light up. "No way!"

I shrug. "You've heard me spin before. At your house?"

"Well, sure," she says, "at my brother's party. You were good."

"You think so?"

"Yeah."

"But you're surprised that I'd want to be a DJ here at Fever?"

"Well, sort of. It's just that... I don't know."

"What?" I urge.

"Well, it's just that there were only a handful of people at my house for Justin's party. Honestly, Marley, when I imagine you in front of a whole crowd of people, I sort of picture you spilling flash cards all over the floor."

148

"Ouch!" I exclaim, "that's cold, Lea." But Lea just laughs again, and her laugh makes my stomach flip, which makes it impossible to pretend my feelings are hurt for more than a second.

I don't even know what to say next. If I could say anything I wanted, I'd ask her why she's always ignored me before and now suddenly doesn't seem to mind talking to me at all. But no way can I say a thing like that. I can't chance ruining this. "So what about you, Lea?" I ask instead. "What do you dream about?"

"Me?" she asks, shooting me a sideways glance. "Well, that's a secret."

"A secret?"

"Yup. But maybe I'll tell you someday."

I stare at her in surprise as she rubs her arms. "Okay, then. Someday...maybe...I'm going to hold you to that."

"You do that," she says, rubbing her arms a second time.

"Are you cold?"

Lea nods. "I forgot my coat in the club."

I look down at the gray hoodie I'm wearing. In my dreams I'm a guy who's suave enough and brave enough to take it off and drape it over her shoulders. But I'm not that guy in real life. Which is why I'm more surprised than she is when I unzip it and take it off and hold it out to her.

Lea hesitates.

Then she reaches out as if she's going to take it but pauses at the last second.

"It's okay," I tell her, "really. Take it. Please, I don't need it."

And then she does. She takes my hoodie from me and she actually puts it on. Even zips it up. It's massive on her, and

I'm probably grinning like some kind of idiot at the sight of her swimming in it, but I can't help it. She looks freaking amazing wearing my clothes.

"*Lea!*" a guy's voice calls out. "What're you doing over there? Come on, we're leaving."

I'm watching Lea when that jackass Todd Bitherman shouts to her from across the street and, if I didn't know better, I'd swear I see disappointment cross her face for a moment. Not like she's crazy about me and can't live without me or anything as major as that, but maybe like she'd rather be here than go with those fools. Almost as if she wouldn't mind abandoning that sheltered world of hers for a while.

But then I shake those thoughts loose. Because I do know better. Girls like Lea Hall don't think like that. They're lucky to have been born in their world and they know it.

"Lea! Let's go!"

"I'm coming!" she shouts back, quickly unzipping my hoodie and taking it off.

"You can keep it if you want," I say. "At least hold on to it until you get your coat back."

"It's okay," she says, glancing across the street at the group of Haves now mulling in front of the club, then looking back at me again. "Thank you, though."

"Sure." I take my hoodie back.

I want to grab her so bad it hurts. Nothing out of line or anything, just her hand, long enough to find out what those delicate fingers of hers feel like. I wish I could reach for her and tell her not to go.

But I can't say something like that, not really. And like she said, it's okay. Hell, I'm grateful to even get to talk to her.

She's not what I expected at all. After Justin's party I figured she was kinder than her friends. That alone was a nice surprise coming from a girl who's avoided eye contact with me all this time like I've got some deadly disease she might catch if her eyes ever met mine. But I never would've pictured her being funny or clever.

"Well, it was nice talking to you, Marley."

"Yeah," I say. "It was real nice talking to you, Lea."

"I'll see you around," she says in a casual tone, like it's normal that we both happened to be at Fever at the same time and ran into each other and talked like this.

She's halfway across the street before I can even get out the word "good-bye." I watch her walk to the end of the block and duck into a waiting car. The car pulls away from the curb and makes its way down the street and around the corner and then she's gone. Just like that.

I put my hoodie back on, sit back down on the sidewalk, and pick up my sandwich again. But I can't finish it now. My mind is too full to take another bite.

Running into me was no big deal for Lea. She's probably forgotten all about it already. Out of sight, out of mind.

But for me? Running into her means a lot. Lea Hall just wore my hoodie. I sniff it to see if it smells all flowery like she smelled that night at Spazio's, but it doesn't smell like anything, and for a second I wonder if it was even real, if she was really here.

I try to run the conversation we just had back through my mind and can only remember little pieces of it. But the little pieces I remember are all real cool. She was witty and bold. And somehow, in some way I would never have predicted in a million years and still can't quite believe, so was I! Once we started talking, all the shyness I usually feel with girls just sort of fell away.

Yeah, she was definitely here, smiling at me and talking to me and somehow managing to make my old gray zip-up sweatshirt look hot.

I try to study the action across the street, try to think about something else, but even as I watch the goings-on outside Fever I catch myself absently humming the chorus of that tune I've been working on at school, "Angelia." Suddenly I can't get it out of my head.

20

THE FIRST THING I HEAR IS MUSIC. THE FIRST thing I've always heard is music. Dark and melancholy, the melody has this crazy edge to it that blends surprisingly well with a funky, exotic Latin beat.

The second thing I hear is Hawk's voice. Deep and angry, it travels across the room with a hint of that strained sound that lets you know he's totally annoyed with you. It's a sound I've now learned is a part of his voice even when he's not annoyed. Of course since he's working with me, he probably is.

I'm spending all my free time at Hawk and Hogan's place now and it feels really good—like escaping to some kind of safe house or something, a place totally separate from my real life. I can't deal with home or my mother or her interchangeable druggie boyfriends anymore, especially not now that all these good things are starting to happen. I want to surround myself with positive stuff as much as I can. I want to be here. I want to work my ass off for that competition at Fever.

"You have forty-five minutes to show off every bit of talent you've got," Hawk is saying. "That's all you're gonna get, so you better make it count. The key is to give them a little of everything so they can see how well rounded and versatile you are. That's your biggest strength and will be your advantage over the competition. But at the same time you gotta focus on the music your audience wants to hear.

"You've got to get that entire crowd on their feet. Not one person should be sitting or leaning against a wall, because this isn't about you—it's about them. The whole point of this is to figure out which DJ is most entertaining and most popular with their patrons, so the crowd vote is worth more than the vote of every judge combined. The whole time you're on, I want you asking yourself, is this something that would draw me to the dance floor? Trust me, you win the crowd over and the judges will follow."

Hawk's been working on a playlist with me and so far it's about twenty minutes long. The rules don't prohibit guest performers, so Latreece is going to sing during one part of my set, and now I'm apparently having a conga player and sax player join in at one point too. "So you've played with these guys before, right?" I ask Hawk when he first brings up the idea.

"I used to play with them all the time when I was over at The BASSment back in the day," he says.

"Will I have a chance to practice with them?"

"No. But unlike you, these guys are professionals. They can improvise over anything you do, so shut up about it already."

Jewel eavesdrops from the kitchen, where she's preparing a huge pot of spaghetti for dinner. She's the wild girl with the purple-streaked hair who was running around the apartment kissing everyone, only now her hair is parted into two neat afro puffs with black roots and green tips that match her eye shadow.

"No! No! No!" Hawk screams at me three days later. "What are you doing?"

"Don't listen to him, Ice," Jewel says. "His nickname in high school was Oscar the Grouch." I glance over at her curled up on the couch skimming a copy of *Rolling Stone* magazine. She looks back at me and winks. Jewel is way hot, with medium-brown skin and a gorgeous smile and more piercings and tattoos than any girl I've ever seen. She is also Hawk's girlfriend and never more than a few feet away from him.

It's kind of sweet, really, that Jewel and Hawk never leave each other's side. If you see either of them, the other isn't far behind. They even work together at Trader Joe's during the day. Jewel usually hangs out at the club Wednesday through Sunday nights when Hawk spins and in the living room while Hawk works with me. She's also almost always in the living room partying with everybody after the club closes down. I don't think that girl ever sleeps.

Two days later and Hawk is still yelling. "No man, *jeeeeeeez!*"

He sighs, exasperated. "I'll be damned if I let you go into that stupid, miserable club and embarrass me."

Stupid?

Miserable?

I look over at Jewel and we catch eyes. Then hers roll into the back of her head in response to Hawk's drama. Today, my seventh straight day rehearsing, she twirls in wild circles when music plays and makes goofy faces whenever Hawk stops me to complain about something I've done that he doesn't like.

"Are you hearing yourself? It's all wrong, all wrong!"

But then there are those other times. My favorite times. When Hawk helps me with my own music I've been attempting to compose and we both fall into a kind of zone where there are no insults, no frustration, only the exchange of ideas and the excitement and pride when things fit.

I spend as much time as I can playing his records, and creating sounds on his computer, and making up tunes on the music room keyboards at school, and when I play whatever I've come up with for Hawk, he never fails to find a way to make it better. There are moments when I stop and look at him and feel awe at the way his mind works and all that he has to teach. With Hawk's skills and creativity, it seems impossible that he isn't a big-time star at Fever, like DJ Lord. At the very least.

"Okay, don't play that, that sucks," he tells me now.

"Ignore him," says Jewel. "You're gonna do great, Ice."

"You better, *Ice*," Hawk snaps, putting emphasis on my DJ name like he wants to remind me that even though he thinks I've got a little talent, I'm still not worthy of it. "I'll kill you if you fuck up when you spin at that piece-of-shit club."

Hawk's got me playing every moment I have away from school, and Spazio's, and Cream. I'm almost always over at his place and crash here two to three times a week. I hate going home now.

In the past I hardly ever crashed at friends' houses. The need to check up on Ma always brought me home. If I didn't keep an eye on her, who would? Nobody, that's who.

But now that I'm spending all this time at Hawk and Hogan's place, it's like I let myself put my hand in the cookie jar for the first time and am suddenly addicted to sugar. I dread going home, and taking care of Ma feels more like a painful chore than ever.

Hawk and Hogan's apartment is warm and colorful and full of life, with people walking in and out at all hours of the day and night. My place is cold and dark and depressing. On Thanksgiving last year, I just cooked a regular meal for Ma and then went over to Scuzz's place and hung out watching football until it was time to go to work at the restaurant. Ma and I didn't even wish each other a happy Thanksgiving.

But on Thanksgiving this year, Jewel invited me to spend the day at their place. She told me everybody who didn't have family close by would be there, and sure enough there were fourteen of us. Everyone brought food and drinks, and we had a proper sit-down Thanksgiving dinner, all seated on folding chairs around a bunch of desks and tables shoved together.

It's like no one is related, but everyone at Cream still treats each other like family—an amazing, happy, loving family whose members choose to spend time together because they want to and who always support one another.

Today, two days after Thanksgiving, I work on my music with Hawk until it's time to head on to Spazio's. We pick up where we left off later on when Hawk gets back from the club and end up working half the night.

I wake the next morning curled up on the floor with a blanket thrown over me. I grab my jacket and my music notebook and start putting on my shoes.

Rick eyes me from the couch where he and his girlfriend are cuddled up sleeping after a long night of partying. "You headed out?"

"Yeah," I reply as I walk over to Hawk's tables. The mere sight of them widens my smile. Even with all his bitching and complaining, I can hardly wait to get back here.

It's a five-block walk to the train, and as I look around me at the sidewalk scene, everything seems extra stunning: the way the trees sway in the brisk morning wind, the way the birds chirp with excitement. The way the train wheels feel rumbling across the tracks below, that soothing, rhythmic sound like the pounding of my heart before I play. I could never get tired of that sound. *Badoomp, badoomp, badoomp, badoomp, badoomp.* I wish I had a way to record it to use in a mix.

A woman sitting across from me is busy knitting. A group of elementary school boys hang out at the other end of the car shouting and laughing together. Several men and women sit alone, reading or checking their phones. I wonder where all these people are going. All of them headed in different directions, to live different lives. The only thing we will probably ever have in common is this moment together on this train.

A couple down the aisle fawn all over an infant dressed in pink, with a pink bow in her barely-there hair. I watch her carefully, wondering what it would be like to be cared for that way, loved that way, kissed and hugged that way.

I reach my stop and walk the seven blocks to my building with my mind full of thoughts of music. That and the laptop I'm going to buy today.

I've been eyeing the laptop I want in this discount computer store near the restaurant and I can't wait to finally get it. This'll be the first time I've splurged on something for myself other than music since I bought my iPod two years ago.

I enter the apartment and head straight for my room, ignoring my mother, who sits in her usual spot on the couch, ignoring her latest loser boyfriend, Don, who hit the six-week mark, making him two weeks past due to disappear, and ignoring the mess the apartment has turned into after only one night of me not being home.

"Where've you been?" Ma asks as I pass by her without a word.

"Yeah," says Don, "you need to buy some more food." *Loser.* I reach into my pack for the key to my room, then stop dead in my tracks when I see my bedroom door.

What in the hell?

There's a huge, jagged hole to the right of the doorknob like someone chopped through it with an ax or something. I try the knob and my door falls open. It's unlocked!

Panic sets in as I rush inside.

"Fuck!" I yell as I look around me.

My room is in shambles. Half my drawers are open with clothes spilling out. My bookshelf has been turned over, and everything that was on it is now strewn across the floor. The mattress on my twin bed is flipped over too. And my desk!

The desk itself is fine and sits upright like always, but it's bare. Pop's tables are gone! "No!" I holler as I rush over to it. "No!" I yell even louder. I knock the desk over myself and let out a scream of crazy anger. "No! No! Not this! *Not! This!*"

I wave of devastation hits me dead-on like a two-ton truck. I want to destroy everything left. I want to destroy whoever did this.

I don't even have to look to know the money is gone. It's what they really came for. The turntables were just a bonus. But the money? I kept my entire savings rolled up in a rubber band in the back of my sock and underwear drawer. I wanted a bank account, but Ma wouldn't co-sign for me to open one unless she had access to it, and there was no way I was agreeing to that.

I always assumed my room would be safe, that the two locks on my door would be enough to discourage anyone from going in my room. I thought the money would be okay here. I was stupid! I underestimated the power of a desperate drug addict. They don't think about where you might have hidden your valuables; they just rifle through everything and take whatever they find.

I pull the half-open drawer out the rest of the way and immediately hang my head.

Gone!

All of it.

Like it never existed.

A second wave of devastation pelts me in the face. But the second wave is one of outrage and fury, and this is the one I hold on to. I get why they'd take my money. But Pop's Technics? How could they take those? That's just cruel. My hands begin to tremble as I push the drawer back in and slowly walk out of my ransacked room.

"Where is it?" I demand, in a massive wave of fear, and spit, and intensity.

My mother looks up from her couch with a questioning stare. I barely see her. My view and my interpretation have gone crazy. The whole room appears in jarring angles. Everything feels red and fiery hot. "My stuff, Ma! What did you do with it? Where's my money? Where are Pop's tables?"

Of course, I already know the answer to where the money is. It was used to buy drugs or booze or both.

"I don't know what you mean," my mother says in a voice thick and slurry with emptiness. She's almost too high to communicate, but the look on her face is sincere. She doesn't know what happened.

Her boyfriend, Don, leans back in my pop's lounger and takes a long swig from the stupid liquor flask he's always carrying around. I stare at his pale, skinny arms, his baggy pants, his long, messy, brown hair, and his little ratlike face. I look into his beady, bloodshot eyes and feel his heightened high. He looks away and my heart drops out from under me.

"Don?"

He looks up again but only to see what's happening on the TV show he's watching. He won't meet my eyes again.

"Don!"

But there is no point now. The money is gone. All of it. He found it and spent it, wasted it. I can't believe it. I don't even know why I can't believe it. Most of the money they buy their drugs with is stolen. But still. I've let this dude stay in our home and this is how he repays me?

"How could you?" I say. My voice has lost its anger, though. It's turned to dismay. It is the voice of a boy whose mother has betrayed him by bringing selfish, idiot, drug addicts into their home and letting one of them steal the extra money it took him months to save. Extra money that was mostly there for *her* in case something really bad happened.

All that time scraping and sacrificing to end up with nothing. It's all gone, just like that. All the tables I've bused, the dishes I've washed, the parties I've missed out on, the blocks I've walked. "I hope you're happy, Ma," I say, my teeth clenched, my mind still swimming in shock. "And I hope you guys got a quality high with my money. You sure deserve it."

"Don't you talk to us like that, you little fucker!" Don snaps, finally shooting his glazed-over eyes at me and pointing a threatening finger. "Tell him, Roselia."

"Did you call me a little fucker?" I ask, my anger returning as fast as it fell away. "I'm a foot taller than you, you asshole!"

"Don't you...don't you do that! Rosie, say something. Because he...make him stop yelling. I want respect!"

"Stop yelling at Don," my mother says in a sleepy, sunken voice. "I'm your mother and he's my man and you have to respect him."

"Respect him?" I repeat. "*Respect* him?" I drop onto the couch next to her. "What exactly is it I should respect, Ma? That he keeps you company when you take off on binges? That he robs people to pay for your drugs? That he takes the time to shoot that shit into your veins for you?"

"Yeah," Don slurs, "don't you, cuz that's right, and so I'm gonna..."

162

I try to ignore them when they're like this, because they're more useless than normal and there's no point in wasting time trying to have a conversation, but I can't ignore Ma. Not anymore.

"I have to respect him because you're my mother?" I say again. "You think having sex with Pop with no protection makes you a mother? It makes you irresponsible, but that's about it. And where in the hell are Pop's turntables?" I am shaking. My entire body trembles. "Those belonged to my *father*, Don! I want them back. It's not like you can get much for them on the street anyway; they're too beat up."

Don takes a long swig from his flask. "I got twenty dollars for 'em."

"You sold my pop's decks for *twenty dollars*?" I stare at him and then at Ma in utter shock and disgust. "How could you let him do that?"

"I'll do what I want," she says. "It's not your business."

"And this is really what you want? Because if it is, I'll leave right now. I'll go for good. I'll mind my own business and let you be another homeless junkie on the corner."

My mother's eyes go wide. I've never spoken to her like this before and my words have totally stunned her. It's the first time I've ever told her off for real and it feels like therapy. I should have gone off on her a long time ago. Maybe a dose of reality would have done her some good.

"Get out!" Don suddenly hollers. He is barely slurring now. His anger has finally sobered him. "Get out of here! This is your mother's house!"

"My mother's house?" I say in disbelief.

"*My* house!" she says.

"I will not get out, Ma. I pay the rent. I pay for the water you drink, the heat you enjoy, the electricity that keeps your TV going twenty-four/seven. I cook to make sure you get enough to eat and then I can't even have a bowl of cereal because your boyfriends eat all our food and I am *tired*!"

"I hate you!" she suddenly screams.

And then I go quiet.

She hates me. She really said it. My own mother hates me. It's like venom, her words. Venom seeping through my veins and sinking right into my heart. Suddenly I am the most hurt and the most angry I have ever been in my life. "Yeah, I'll bet you do hate me," I say as I get up from the couch and move away from her. "Because you're too high to feel anything else."

That's when my mother starts yelling obscenities at me. I stand there silently, steaming and glowering, watching her and that useless, miserable, sorry-ass, thief boyfriend of hers sitting there, both too high to move but sober enough to drill their hate into my soul.

Then a thought occurs.

Don may have spent all my money, but he couldn't have used up all the drugs already without a whole lot of help from his friends, and the only people here are him and Ma. He may have found my hiding place, but I know where theirs is too.

I move through the swinging door into the kitchen, pulling the Mystery Machine lunch box down from the back of the cupboard and emptying the bags of heroin and weed inside of it out onto the counter. For a moment I just stop and stare. I've never seen so much heroin in my life. It looks more like evidence from a major drug bust on *COPS* than a party supply for two. Don really outdid himself.

I sweep it all off the counter, back into the lunch box, and carry it through the front room with me. The sight of me holding the big blue lunch box perks up my mother, who starts to yell again.

Don becomes hysterical and struggles to lift himself up out of Pop's lounger to let me have it. He makes it to his feet and takes two steps in my direction before tripping and falling into the glass coffee table, which gives under his weight, smashing to pieces on the carpet. Ma begins to wail as she rushes to him and tries to help him up. They call out together in an eerie harmony.

I stand there and watch them for a moment before moving on out of the room.

"*Nooooo*," Don hollers after me desperately. "*Noooooo. Nooooo. Nooooooo.*"

I reach the bathroom and open the baggies one after another after another, pouring half the drugs down the toilet and flushing. Then the other half.

My mother rushes up behind me and almost knocks me over trying to get to the toilet. She sticks her hand into the bowl as our savings and my last connection to my father circle down the drain.

I leave her there screaming and crying like a baby, kneeling on her knees on the tile floor with her forehead resting against the toilet seat. I go back to my wrecked room, grab my pack, and make my way to the front door.

Don is still lying in the pool of glass that was once our coffee table. He's bleeding through little cuts in his hands and arms, but I'm positive he can't feel them and wouldn't care if he could.

"I'll kill you," he says, fumbling to get a hand into his back pocket. He pulls out a switchblade and flips it open.

"I'll bet you would kill me," I reply in a calm voice, because I flushed my pain down the toilet with the drugs and now refuse to care.

"That there was my high," he says. "Mine!"

"*No!*" I say, pointing at him accusingly. "Those were my turntables. That there was my high."

"Get out!" Don shouts. "And don't ever come back, you hear me? Not ever!"

He jabs the knife in my direction again. Watching him lying there on the floor waving a knife at me isn't exactly threatening. Just hurtful.

"Get out!" he hollers again. "Get out!"

"Don't worry," I tell him. "I'm going."

I open the door and walk out of my apartment, leaving the door sitting wide open behind me.

Then it's down the stairs two at a time, three flights' worth in a matter of seconds. I rush out the front door and gasp desperately at the outside air.

I crumple in front of the entrance to our building as my mind blurs into an endless sea of nothing.

TONIGHT, I HAVE THE MOST INCREDIBLE DREAM. I walk into my apartment and take a seat in Pop's lounger. The apartment around me is clean, but I know I haven't cleaned it.

When I walk into my room, it looks exactly like it did before Don wrecked it except for one change. The laptop I wanted is set up on my desk along with Pop's turntables.

But the best part of the dream isn't the laptop, and it isn't seeing Pop's decks back where they belong. The best part is my mother. I turn to see her standing in my bedroom door-way looking alert. She's slightly overweight, but it's healthy weight. The color has returned to her face and she's smiling. I know without asking that she doesn't have a boyfriend, Don or otherwise.

She tells me dinner is ready, and when I follow her into the kitchen there is food everywhere. On the table, on top of the fridge, all along the counter, in boxes on the floor, and it's all cooked food, enough for an army.

At the end of the dream, my pop walks in and sees all the food. He looks at it and laughs. We all laugh together. I feel incredibly full even though I haven't eaten a bite.

Of course, it's only a dream.

In the real world, I sit on a train feeling lost as I gaze out the window at the world passing me by. Eventually I get off and just start walking.

I don't even know where I'm going. I have no plan. I know I could go to Chuckie's or Scuzz's or even Will's, but I'm not ready to tell them what happened, at least not yet. And I'm definitely not ready to hear the words *I told you so*, which I know would be coming, and rightfully so. As I walk from one block to the next, the houses grow bigger and bigger, and that's when I realize I'm heading into the wealthy Fountain District.

Soon I'm gazing up at the massive estates, at the identical trees that line each side of the street, at the enormous, unnatural-looking squares of grass that sit perfectly manicured in front of each home. I'm only a few blocks away from the home where Lea lives, where I was once allowed to work for a day.

I've been thinking about her nonstop ever since seeing her at Fever. Thinking about us standing together talking and

168

laughing makes me wonder what it'd be like to see her again. Would she be like that? Or would she go back to the way she was before, not even noticing I'm there?

The sun starts to set and the air around me begins to grow cold. Cold like the deep waters that chill the ocean floor. Cold like a mother's heart while she looks you dead in the eye and tells you she hates you.

I turn around and start to walk back in the direction of the train station, still thinking of these things.

And then I think of my father. Wishing I could just walk around the corner and find Pop waiting for me there. Wishing I could let go once and for all.

THE FIRST THING I HEAR IS MUSIC. THE FIRST thing I've always heard is music since the day I was born amid all those peaceful reggae sounds.

The second thing I hear is laughter and voices as a red BMW pulls around the corner.

I watch it drive by.

Then I watch in surprise and confusion as it brakes to a sudden stop and backs up.

It pulls parallel with me and stops, but I keep on walking.

The window rolls down and I pick up the pace.

"Who is he?" I hear the driver ask. "You sure you know him?"

The next voice is a girl's. "I'm sure," she calls out over the music. The sound of her voice stops me dead in my tracks.

"All right," the driver replies reluctantly.

I turn back toward the car and my breath catches as the back door opens and Lea steps out. "Marley?"

"Lea! Hey."

"Marley, what are you doing here?"

"Oh, well, I..." But I can't think of anything to say. I'm three blocks from her house with no reason to be here. I eye the red Bimmer stopped in the road behind her. At first I figured the car was full of junior Haves, but I don't recognize the driver, and when the guy in the passenger seat peers out at me, I realize I've never seen him before either.

Lea follows my gaze. "Friends from my church group," she explains.

"Lea, what's going on?" a girl asks, leaning out the open back door. "Are we driving you home or what?" But Lea doesn't take her eyes off me.

"No," she says, her brown eyes studying me hard. "I'm gonna walk home from here with Marley. I'll see you guys next week, okay?"

"Okay, then. Later, Lea." The back door shuts.

"Bye, Lea!" the driver calls out. He nods to me as he pulls away.

"So," Lea says as the BMW reaches the end of the block and disappears around the corner.

"So," I say back, shoving my hands in my pockets.

"This is twice now," she says.

"Yeah," I say.

"I always run into you on sidewalks," she says.

I look around me and then back at her. "Yeah," I say again. "But this isn't what it looks like."

"Oh?" Lea tilts her head to one side and watches me curiously. "What is it, then? No wait! First tell me what it looks like. Then tell me what it is."

I smile. "You're clever," I say.

"Don't change the subject," she says back.

I nod. Busted. "I was going to say that I know it must look like I'm a stalker or something, me being so near your house and all."

"I don't think you're a stalker," Lea says. She starts down the street only turning around long enough to motion for me to join her.

I fall into step beside her and survey the scene—Lea looking crazy beautiful in a white pullover sweater with jeans. Me looking impossibly opposite of her in all black. The sunset, which is in full display now that it's past four o'clock. The enormous homes rising up on either side of us.

"What are you thinking about?" Lea asks, watching me curiously.

"You," I admit. "What are you thinking about?"

"I'm thinking that I pictured you being shyer than this," she says.

"Honestly?" I tell her. "I am. I'm usually really shy."

"But…"

I shrug. "I don't know."

"Maybe it's me," she suggests. "Maybe I bring out your bold side or something."

"Maybe," I say.

It's definitely her. But I'm not sure I'm ready to say that much yet. I steal glances at her profile as we walk in silence for a while. It's an easy silence, a good silence. Like I feel nervous to be walking with her, but also really comfortable and excited and unexpectedly happy.

It's crazy that I'm here walking through the streets of the wealthy Fountain District with Lea Hall against a backdrop of stunningly colored sky. It feels like a movie or something. If I didn't know better I'd say sunsets are nicer on this side of town. Or maybe it's just that everything's nicer over here. Or maybe it's Lea.

"So..." she says, turning to watch me expectantly. "You're not a stalker...."

"I swear I'm not. I was on the train and then I was here somehow. Or, I mean, I got off at Norfolk Station and started walking and ended up here. I don't even know why."

"I can tell you why," says Lea. "Because you like me."

"Oh yeah?"

"Yeah. You came to steal me away from all this."

I laugh. "You're absolutely right, Lea. I thought I'd take you away from here to a beautiful land of tenement buildings and liquor stores on three out of every four corners."

"Can I ask you something?"

I shrug. "If I said no would it stop you from asking?"

Lea smiles. "Maybe," she says. "Maybe not."

"Okay then. What's the question?"

"How is it, Marley Diego-Dylan, that you seem so shy and reserved at school, but then you get behind a set of turntables at my house and perform for kids you don't even know like it's nothing? You didn't think anything of it. It's like with your speeches—you always seem so flustered, but here with me now you're all confident and manly."

"Manly?" I ask, raising an eyebrow at her.

"You know what I mean. You're like you are right now. It's nice. I like you like this."

"I don't know why," I say. "I think maybe it's because I'm with you. Like you said before, you bring this side out of me."

Lea smiles quietly to herself. She stays quiet like that for a long time.

I stay quiet too, not wanting to interrupt her if she wants to say more. I think instead about the fact that she's always seemed so engrossed in that notebook of hers during my speeches, but it turns out she was paying attention all along. "Here's what I'm thinking," she finally says, curling loose blond strands of hair behind one ear the way she does. "What you need to do is think of your speeches as if they're not speeches at all, but gigs. You know, DJ performances or whatever. Like you should think of each flash card as a song."

I shake my head. "It doesn't work that way for me. When I get in front of people and have to speak I fall apart. English class only makes it worse because certain people get a sick joy out of messing everyone else up."

"My friends."

"I've always been bad with speeches, though."

"But how is it different speaking in front of a crowd and performing in front of a crowd? I mean a crowd is a crowd, right? You just have to get it in your head that you can do it."

"Okay," I say. "Thanks." I'm not sure I'm buying her logic, but I'm loving the fact that she cares. Or at least it seems like she cares. It's weird, really, how much she's switched up from the way she used to ignore me.

We turn onto Lea's street and I know I'm about to run out of time to ask her about it. It's now or never.

"So can I ask you a question back?"

Lea watches me curiously. "Okay...."

"Well, I've been wondering this for a while."

"Go on," she urges.

"What happened? I mean, what changed between the time you came to the restaurant where I work and now? It's like you're a totally different person. You used to ignore me. I think it's awesome that you talk to me now, but I can't figure out why it is that things changed between us, you know?"

Lea puts her head in her hands and groans.

"Should I not have asked that?"

"No," she says, "no, you should have."

"I mean, it's a fair question, right?"

"It's a totally fair question, Marley," she says. "What happened was I acted like an ass at Spazio's. I didn't mean to. Believe it or not, it wasn't about you at all. But my brother totally let me have it when we left. He said you were going to feel like I was snubbing you for working there or something."

"But you kind of did snub me."

"I know. I'm sorry. It wasn't on purpose. I was just really upset and not talking to anybody that night. It was the day Todd Bitherman and I broke up."

"Sorry to hear that."

"Don't be. I'm not. But my parents were really pissed when I told them I'd broken up with him. They're best friends with Todd's parents, and he's from this really good family or whatever, and they told me they were disappointed in me and that I should give him another chance."

"That sucks."

"Yeah, it did suck," Lea agrees. "We had a huge argument about it in the car on our way to the restaurant, and then I was just in a funk the rest of the night and not talking. I'm sorry, Marley, I should have been nicer. You didn't have anything to do with it — you were just trying to do your job."

I shake my head in disbelief. "All this time I thought you were ignoring me because I was working there and because I'm on scholarship or something."

"Yeah, that's exactly what Justin said. I felt so bad. I was hoping to have a chance to apologize when you were at my house for his party, but then my friends came over and acted all bitchy and evil. They weren't even invited. I was like, now I *really* owe him an apology. But what were the odds of us running into each other again? And then we did at the club and I said, this is it. You're going to cross the street and talk to that boy. Hanging with you ended up being the best part of the night."

I nod to show her I'm listening, but I don't say anything. I don't really know what to say. It never occurred to me that her not acknowledging me at the restaurant might not have anything to do with me at all. All this time I figured she was acting like her friends — rude and disrespectful and all that.

"What are you thinking, Marley?"

I pull my lid down lower over my eyes and take a deep breath, trying to get up the courage to say what I want to say next. Wondering if I have it in me. "I guess I'm thinking... if you don't like Todd anymore..."

"Yeah..."

I take another deep breath. Then I just spit the words out before I can stop myself. "I guess I'm sort of wondering what you're looking for in a guy. What you do like."

"Oh," Lea says. "I don't know. Someone sweet, and smart, and really cute."

"Okay."

"I like artist types," she continues, "because I'm an artist type so, you know, guys that are into music and art and dance and stuff like that."

"So you're an artist type, huh? Like that's part of your dream you're going to tell me about someday?"

"Uh-huh," she replies absently, still deep in thought about the rest of her answer. "I want a guy who's a gentleman," she says. "Todd was never a gentleman, ever. None of my boyfriends really have been. And someone romantic. And I want a guy who works. Preferably as a busboy. That's sexy to me."

My mouth drops.

"And someone tall; tall is sexy too. And I think maybe someone who doesn't drive, because I'm liking this walking thing. I definitely don't walk enough. Was that enough of a description?"

I stare at Lea, dumbfounded.

"Marley?"

"Yeah?"

"Was that enough of a description?"

"Oh yeah."

"Good. Because I'm home." She gestures toward the massive four-story mansion behind her. "And that's my mother," she says, pointing to the first-story window where a woman peeks out at us from behind the curtain.

"Okay, then," I say.

"Okay, then," Lea says back.

"I guess I'll see you at school."

"Not if I see you first," she says, winking at me before turning and rushing up the long front walk.

I watch as she reaches her front door, unlocks it, and pushes it open. She smiles at me before walking inside and shutting it behind her, and it's all I can do to catch my breath.

I turn and start the long trek back to the train station once again, but this time with my heart and my head in the clouds. The sunset looks even more stunning now that the sun is really low in the sky. Yeah, sunsets are definitely nicer on this side of town. Or maybe it's Lea. Yeah. It's definitely Lea.

I shove my hands in my pockets and pick up the pace, gazing in awe at a sky streaked with rays of deep blue and wavering purple, a never-ending sea of gold. The colors a sunset could never be. But somehow is.

* * *

After my shift at Spazio's, I go back home. But only to pack. I can't stay here anymore, not after what happened. I pack records into my suitcase, throw some clothes in a trash bag, and head out into the night again.

Even though I ignore Ma and Don as I rush through the apartment grabbing my stuff, the sight of their lifeless bodies passed out on the couch brings back all the sadness and frustration I felt before running into Lea. I try to focus on thoughts of her to cheer myself up again but can't do it. The reality that I don't have a home anymore is hitting way too hard.

I walk the streets a long time, rolling the suitcase behind me with the trash bag slung over my shoulder. I wander around as if I don't know where I'm going. I do know. Even if I haven't got a clue about a long-term solution, I know what the short-term one is.

Which is why I eventually catch a late-night bus to Hawk and Hogan's place. I have to ask them if I can crash at least some of the time.

They never lock their front door, so I walk right on in.

"Hey, it's Ice," Jewel calls out as I step into the living room. She skips over to me and gives me a big hug. Dana is sitting on the couch smoking a joint, choking down a quick shot, and looking pissed-off. Leon and another regular named Craig are sitting on either side of Dana waiting to see which way she'll pass the joint. I don't notice much more about the scene than that. The turntables draw me in like a magnet and soon I am lost in my own world, spinning away my heartache and drowning my disappointments in beautiful sound. I feel dead inside, but my music keeps me alive.

Ma and her boyfriend can't take my dreams away, not really. They can rob me, and disappoint me, and break my heart, but they can't get to my mind. I won't let them. I am going to play at Fever.

23

"SOME DJS PREPLAN AND MEMORIZE THEIR entire set for a contest. Mistake! How're you gonna memorize a whole set list to play for an audience when you have no idea who your audience is? You could hang out at the club where you're gonna play a thousand nights and still not know what'll set off the crowd on that particular night.

"Some DJs do wait to size up their audience and then spin based on what they feel their contest crowd will like from moment to moment. Mistake! It's a fucking *contest*. If you want to win, you better sit down and think out a strategy and identify your strengths so you can decide how you're gonna show 'em off. Can't do that a hundred percent on the fly, can ya? No, I don't fucking think so!"

Hawk is one of those guys who don't know much about most things, but he knows pretty much everything there is to know when it comes to spinning records. He's the last person I ever would have imagined I'd actually enjoy spending time with, yet the time we spend rehearsing has become the best part of my day.

"And another thing. I don't want you going to Fever before the competition. I want you to experience the crowd there for the first time that night."

"Okay," I say. More than okay, since I have no way of getting into Fever anyway. No way is anyone going to mistake that Antonio Gutierrez dude for me. The only reason Donnie thought that ID was legit is because he never really looked at it.

"It's crucial that you have a sense of the type of crowd you're going to spin for in a competition when blueprinting your set, but there's also a whole lot to be said for seeing a crowd with fresh eyes and feeling the energy in a club with a new imagination and no preconceptions. You need to be conscious of your crowd at all times, no matter what you're doing. Sort of like remembering to check your rearview mirror when you're driving. I know what the crowd at Fever is like, so I can take care of incorporating what they'll want to hear into your mix. This is all assuming you haven't been there before. You haven't, have you?"

"Seen it. Never been inside. But you have?"

"Um, hello? I'm one of the hottest DJs around. Of course I've been to Fever."

"So what's it like?"

"Your typical fake-ass, piece-of-shit club! Now pay attention."

Life has changed a lot since I first started crashing on the couch at Hawk and Hogan's place. For the first week after I left home, I spent half my nights here and the other half at Chuckie's.

But eventually it made a lot more sense to stay here every night. I felt like I was imposing on Chuckie's family when I was there, and Hogan, Hawk, and Jewel actually like having people around. They offered their couch to me sincerely, and even though people here party, it's nothing compared to what a true drug addict does. Besides, Hawk is the one with the pimp tables—plus he's my teacher—and since I have a goal to reach and a limited amount of time to get to it and my whole routine now revolves around spinning records, Hawk and Hogan's is the best place I can possibly be.

These days, my schedule has been breaking down more like this: Get up, spin for an hour, go to school (everyone kinda sorta got the impression I'm in college, and I kinda sorta failed to tell them otherwise), learn, go back to Hawk and Hogan's place, study, then spend time developing and rehearsing my contest set.

Hogan and Jewel have been real supportive, allowing us to pretty much transform the entire living room into a sort of rehearsal space. Hawk borrowed tables from a friend and set them up on a table opposite his own so we can work facing each other.

If it's a Spazio's night, I'm taking off for work around the time Jewel and Hawk get home from their grocery store jobs, and I don't get to spend any quality time on the tables until later.

If it's a Cream night, I get an extra couple hours and rehearse until Hawk gets home around six p.m. Then Hawk and I experiment on the tables together, and I try to incorporate whatever new beats I created at school and whatever new melodies I might have found or created during lunch — which these days is usually a sandwich in the band room — plus whatever new skills Hawk's taught me into my set. That's followed by a quick dinner of Jewel's famous spaghetti, or pizza delivery and beers (with root beer for me now that I keep a stash in their fridge). Then I take off for the club.

If it's a Saturday, I head to the library to study with Chuckie and Scuzz for a few hours before going to Spazio's. Scuzz is a smart dude, but he's always needed help staying focused, especially when we're out of school and have assignments to get done during break.

But now I think I need the joint study time as much as Scuzz. With everything going on, I never feel like I have enough time for homework, and when I do have time to focus on my schoolwork, I'm usually distracted. I'm getting straight Bs now, not an A in sight. There're B-minuses threatening my GPA in both gym and English, thanks to my daydreaming and another bad speech.

The weird thing about it, though, is for the first time in my life I don't really care much about my grades. I used to practically kill myself to get straight As because I needed to get a scholarship to a college or university somewhere far away from here, a school so great I'd have no choice but to go. It was the only way I could see myself getting away from my home life with Ma. I figured if I didn't excel in school and went right into a regular job at eighteen, I'd be trapped in her life forever.

But now that doesn't matter. What with everything that happened at home and me running away, the pressure to get a full scholarship to a faraway school is off. Besides, I can really see myself making it as a DJ now. Suddenly anything seems possible, even getting big enough to tour internationally. That's the ultimate dream, and how can I focus on it if I'm spending all my time studying for classes? I've got to give this my best shot. The worst that could happen is I end up with a job like I have now, DJing a couple times a week in a club, and find a decent restaurant job as a waiter or something.

I see Hawk working at Trader Joe's part-time and then getting to fulfill his passion spinning at the club each night and all the love he and Jewel have together and all the friends around them and I think their lives look pretty good. Hawk and Jewel are even hoping to buy a house next year.

So I'm not sure what I want to do with my future now. Which is why lately, when I'm studying at the library with my boys, Chuckie and Scuzz catch me staring into space almost as much as Chuckie and I catch Scuzz doing it. The idea that maybe I could make a real name for myself as a DJ one day gets my mind wandering.

In the evenings, on the nights I'm at Spazio's, I no longer walk to Fever when my shift is over. I don't hang out at Cream to watch Hawk's set either. Now I go straight back to Hogan and Hawk's place the minute I'm done working and try to cram in either as much homework or as much sleep as I can before Cream closes for the night and the crew shows up to take over the living room and party.

That's when I return to Hawk's tables to spin as another couple hours' worth of practice. The club crew loves it because they get to have a DJ for their after parties, and it works for Hawk because he gets to sit back and watch what I'm doing right and wrong, and both of those things are awesome for me because they help prepare me for Fever.

These last few weeks, Hawk has had me focusing on how to read a crowd. He thinks my advantage over the other DJs will be my well-rounded skill set and unique ability to introduce new types of music into dance mixes without losing the crowd. But he also thinks I can go very wrong very fast if I'm not real subtle with my genre switches. He says I need to learn to be extra sensitive to what the crowd is and isn't feeling.

So when the Cream crew shows up after the club shuts down, I test out parts of my set on them and scribble notes in a little notebook the whole time on the way people react and what I think it means. Then Hawk has each person write down what they liked the most and least about the music I played, grabs my notes, and compares the two.

This has helped me a ton because it gives me not only a nightly test crowd but a nightly test crowd of people who spend nearly all their time in clubs. If I get a strong reaction to something I play, Hawk and I know to keep it for sure or tank it immediately. It's a genius system, really. But then Hawk is a genius.

I've also been learning to spin on three tables, which is as hard as it sounds. Monitoring two is plenty without having a whole other deck spinning off to the side to keep track of. But Hawk is convinced that playing on three decks will also set me apart from the other DJs. These days everything that comes out of his mouth is about what I have to do to win and who I have to be to wow the judges and what it'll take to win the crowd over and walk away with that trophy.

There's just one thing bothering me about it. One thing I've been putting off talking to Hawk about for weeks now.

"Didn't I just get through asking you to pay attention?" Hawk suddenly yells. "I'm not trying to talk to myself here."

"I am paying attention," I lie.

Hawk glares at me.

"Okay, fine, I wasn't paying attention. I'm sorry. My mind wandered."

"Your mind *wandered*?"

I pull down on my lid and shove my hands deep in my pockets. "There's something I need to talk to you about."

"Oh?" Hawk says, looking all kinds of annoyed.

"You're not going to like it. But I need to talk to you about it anyway."

Hawk's eyes shrink to slits. "Say it already then if you're gonna say something."

"It's about your vinyl-only contract."

"What about it?"

"I understand it and I respect it. I follow it at work. But

the competition…" Hawk crosses his arms over his chest like he's warning me not to say what I'm about to say. I take a deep breath and say it anyway. "The competition isn't at work," I tell him. "I'm going to use Serato during the competition."

Hawk's whole body stiffens up as he watches me for a long time. "No," he finally says.

"Yes," I force myself to reply. "I'm using vinyl and I'm using software. I'll do everything else you tell me to do, but I've made up my mind about this."

Hawk points a warning finger at me. "Respect the art!" he shouts.

"I do respect the art, and you know it. But software is the future, whether you approve or not, and I'm going to need it if I plan on keeping up with the skills of these other DJs. Dorian already told me I can borrow his equipment for the show and even bring it over here a few times to practice."

"Dorian doesn't use Serato," says Hawk.

"Dorian does use Serato," I counter. "When he's not at the club, he uses Scratch Live."

"Bullshit!" Hawk snaps, but he quickly takes a seat and I know I've got him. All I have to do now is stand my ground. Which is only the hardest thing ever around Hawk.

"The true art of DJing is making the crowd feel good," I say. "Laptops and DJ software open up a whole new world I can't get to with vinyl. I love vinyl. But I like the latest software. I'm using both. I hope you'll understand."

"I don't understand. People cheat with Serato, using all that internal syncing shit. Where's the skill in pressing a couple keys on a computer and having it automatically match the BPMs of the two tracks for you? My mother could do that."

"I don't cheat. And yeah, there are some DJs out there who do, who can't even beat match without watching a computer screen, but there are also a lot of DJs out there who are mad skilled and use Serato to elevate their skills."

"Give me one good reason why I should let you do this!"

I take a deep breath. "Because I'm not asking you to let me, Hawk. I'm telling you I'm going to."

"One good reason," Hawk repeats as if he didn't hear me, "and you better think it through for a long time and make it really count."

"I don't need to think it through a long time," I say. "You've told me the best reason yourself over and over again. What'll set me apart from the other DJs is my broad range. I need to show off all the different skills I have. My Serato skills are part of that broad range. So let me show them off."

Hawk doesn't reply.

"You want me to win, don't you?" I say, and that gets his attention. I watch him slowly stand and walk out of the room and I know I did it. He didn't say no and he didn't say yes. But if Hawk doesn't say no to something, that's pretty much the same as if he'd said yes.

I shake my head and smile as I take a seat in the chair he just got up from. It was the comment about winning that shut him down. As the days go by I see more and more how important it is to him that I win. Hawk would keel over if I ever told him this, so I won't ever tell him, but I could come in dead last and still be the happiest person alive. All I care about is getting to finally walk into that club and play.

It's like I'm a piece in a board game, and if I set foot in that DJ booth at Fever, I win.

Contest shmontest, I just want to get there.

That is the real victory.

24

THE MOST UNBELIEVABLE THING HAPPENED TO me today while I was making yet another pitiful speech in Advanced Lit. For the first time we were allowed to do our research and write our essay on a subject of our choice: any political or religious figure we pleased. I chose Bob Marley. I thought if I picked a subject I felt really passionate about, it'd help me feel more comfortable when the time came to present an overview of my paper to the class.

I thought wrong. I tossed and turned all night on Hawk and Hogan's couch thinking of the grave injustice I could end up doing to Bob Marley's memory. That got me panicked, and once I was panicked there was no hope at all. I stood at the front of the room trying to will my hands to stop shaking as I flubbed my way through a summary of points from my essay.

Melanie and Brittany gave me their usual attitude from the front of the class. Richie and Jordan, who sat in the back taking turns pretending to cough really loud during every guy's speech except their own, were throwing me off too. As usual Ms. Beckett warned them to stop here and there, but barely.

I stared down at the page in front of me I'd written all my notes on. No more flash cards for me. I'd learned that lesson. "Bob Marley was a great political activist and um... really... into... really into the idea of peace through music. I mean of bringing peace to people through music. Around the world. To people around the world."

I looked up and my eyes fell on Lea sitting at the desk directly in front of me. As usual, she was deeply engrossed in whatever she was writing in that fuzzy pink notebook of hers and paying me no mind. And then all of a sudden she looked up. She looked directly at me and my heart lurched. She put down her pen and picked up her notebook, turning it around for me to see.

I frowned as I read it and then broke into a big, goofy grin.

In huge, block letters across the page, it said:

THINK OF THE WORDS LIKE MUSIC! YOU CAN DO THIS! COOL AND

CALM, LIKE EACH STATEMENT'S A SONG.

For the rest of my speech I couldn't stop smiling. Eventually Lea looked up again and smiled back, and for a second it felt like we were the only people in the room. I stood there in front of my class cheesing like that through the rest of my speech, preoccupied and happy.

It was the best speech I've ever given. Not to say that I broke Bob Marley down to the class in a cool, calm, collected way or anything, but being so distracted by Lea made me a lot less nervous, and the words came easier.

"Very good, Marley," Ms. Beckett said when I was done. "Much improved. Seth, will you come up and read excerpts from your paper, please?"

I returned to my desk and slumped into my seat and sat there the rest of class dazed and smiling and thinking about Lea. My heart is warm and my head is still full of thoughts of her as I practically float up the three flights of stairs to my apartment after school. It's like all my dreams are becoming reality. First my music, then the contest, and now, maybe, the girl. Not just *a* girl either, but *the* girl! It seems way too good to be true.

I face the front door and wonder if this is where the dreaming part ends.

This is the first time I've been home since I moved out three weeks ago, and I don't want to go inside. Something in the way the floorboards creak, and the gray paint chips and peels away from the walls in the hall like a decaying life, makes me want to run the other way.

But I need to make this trip back. When I left before, I just threw a few changes of clothes into a trash bag because I was so desperate to get in and out fast, without talking to Ma or Don. Now I need to get the rest of my clothes. I unlock the door and burst into the front room of our apartment, trying not to think about what happened the last time I was here. Maybe Ma did crush me, but I'll be damned if I let it show.

I look around the room in surprise. It's deserted. No TV blaring, no strangers partying, no ashtrays overflowing with cigarette butts and weed roaches... If I didn't know better, I'd think I was in the wrong apartment. No coffee table. That one throws me for a second, but then I remember Don falling through it.

It's weird to see my place looking like this. Not because of the emptiness either. It's the cleanliness that makes the whole scene strange. The apartment has a slightly odd smell to it, but overall it looks pretty good, almost as good as it does when I'm done with a weekend cleaning. Except for the fact that no one else around here ever cleans.

I'm headed to my room with the empty suitcase Jewel lent me when I hear something clatter in the kitchen. "Hello?"

"Hello?" my mother's voice calls back from the other side of the swinging kitchen door.

"Ma?"

"Marley, is that you?"

"Yeah," I say, leaving the suitcase in front of my bedroom door and going to the kitchen, where I find my mother with her head in the fridge like she's searching for something. The odd odor that was emanating from this direction gets much worse, like bleach mixed with burned grease and hot lard.

The countertop is in complete disarray. Pots, pans, spices...a recipe book lies open beside a spill of brown sauce.

"I was just stopping by to grab some things from my room," I explain, eyeing our kitchen table, which is set with silverware for two and a candlestick. "My clothes and my other pair of shoes and — what's that smell, Ma? It's awful."

"I'm making dinner," my mother replies.

"Dinner," I repeat in a monotone voice. Yeah right, like that would ever happen.

She closes the refrigerator door and turns to face me with a bottle of ketchup in her hand. "Well, *trying* to make dinner at least," she says. "So far I'm not doing too good a job of it. This is my third attempt this week." She puts the ketchup bottle down on the counter and shrugs at me awkwardly. "Smells pretty bad, huh?"

I want to answer her but can't. I drop into the nearest chair and just stare.

"I was hoping to get good at it so I could invite you over and cook for you. I had no idea all this time when you were cooking for me that it was this hard. Your father always cooked."

I nod. I can't speak. All I can do is look at her. She looks so...normal. I can't believe what I'm seeing. She's wearing makeup on her eyes, and lipstick, and she's actually dressed in real clothes, no robe or dirty pajamas. The way she looks right now reminds me of when Pop was still alive. I haven't seen her look like this in four years. "Wow."

"Are you surprised?" she asks, her mouth turning up but only halfway, as if she's not sure whether or not it's okay to smile.

"Um, yeah, of course I'm surprised," I say, continuing to

look her over. There've got to be five to seven pounds on her she didn't have before. She's still too thin and still looks worn-out even with the makeup, but her hair has been combed and the dark circles under her eyes barely show. I stand and take a couple steps toward her, wanting to make sure I'm really seeing what I think I'm seeing. "You're...clean?"

My mother nods. "Twelve days and counting."

"I..." I start to say, but my mind goes blank. She's clean. I can't even count how many times I straight begged my mother to go into rehab. It's hard to believe this is really happening.

She grabs a hot pad and pulls a pan from the oven, setting it down on the counter.

Then she stands there with her back to me for a long time.

"I'm sorry, Marley," she finally says, turning to face me. "I'm so sorry. I don't...there's no excuse. I should have... should have..." She shakes her head. "Should," she tries again, but she chokes on the rest of the words and begins to cry.

I can't explain why, but for some reason seeing her cry makes me kind of mad. Like she doesn't have the right. Like if anyone should be crying, it should be me. I'm tired of her always being the victim. I always fall for it too, always forgive her for everything. But not this time. This time she has to work for forgiveness. Twelve days is a good start, but it's not enough.

"I wasn't a good mother," she admits, wiping at her tears.

"No," I say. "You weren't."

"But I'd like to try now, if you'll give me a chance. I want to be a mom."

I look at her like she's lost her mind, but say nothing as I take a seat again, my head buzzing with her words. For years I've longed for a real mom. Someone to treat my scraped knees, attend Little League games, make brownies for the PTA bake sale. But it feels too late now. Besides, accepting the idea of Ma as a real mother sounds dangerous. Who knows how long the "real mom" would stay.

"Would you?" she asks. "Give me a chance, I mean?"

I think about all the chances I've given her already. I feel like I sacrificed half my teen years giving her one chance after another and being disappointed again and again. "I'm not sure," I answer, watching her carefully.

The doorbell rings and my mother's eyes go wide.

"You expecting somebody?"

She nods. "Michael. He's coming for dinner. He's been letting me practice my cooking on him."

"Who's Michael?"

Guilt flashes in my mother's eyes. "My new boyfriend."

"You have a new boyfriend? Already? Aw, Ma." I shake my head.

"He's not like the rest," she says quickly. "He's different from the others."

"Don't you know the men in your life are just another drug? Another addiction you need to drop?"

"Marley," she tries to protest, but I shake her off.

"No," I say, jumping up and backing away from her. "No, I can't do this right now. I have to go." I walk out of the kitchen as the doorbell rings a second time, but I ignore it and head for my room. I'm furious as I eye the jagged hole Don made in my door and flash back on everything that happened.

"No," I say again to myself. I can't be here. I have to get away from all this for good.

I pick up the suitcase and open the door to my room, wanting to hurry up and get my stuff and get the hell out. I cross to my dresser and open it and start putting clothes in the suitcase. Then I stop. I look at my dresser, startled. All my clothes are back in the drawers, folded.

I turn to look at my bed. The mattress is back. The sheets and blanket are strewn across it crooked and tucked haphazardly under one corner like the bed's been made by someone who's never made a bed before.

I close my eyes and take a deep breath, letting it out slowly.

I open my eyes again and look around. Ma tried to put my room back together.

It's the nicest thing she's ever done for me.

I cringe with guilt thinking about her asking for a chance to be a real mother and me getting angry and walking away.

But then I look at my desk. I want to look away, but force myself to keep looking at it sitting there bare. This is definitely the nicest thing she's ever done for me, but there's something really wrong with that. I should have tons of memories of Ma doing nice things for me. *Don't go soft, Marley,* I tell myself, keeping my eyes locked steadily on my desk. *She may have straightened up your room, but she's also the reason your room was destroyed.*

She is the one responsible for Pop's turntables being gone. That was the last thing I had to remember my father by, and now I can never get them back. I have to remember that. I take another deep breath and finish filling the suitcase with the things I need. Then I take one last long look at my room and walk out.

In the living room a really tall white guy with blond hair and a dress coat stands and offers his hand.

"You must be Marley," he says.

"Yeah," I say as I shake it.

He sports a designer tie imprinted with fancy checkers in different shades of green. No grungy clothes, no disheveled hair, no crazy eyes, no jittery movements. "I'm Michael."

"*You're* Michael?"

"That's right."

"You're going out with my mother?" I don't mean to be rude, but I'm in need of clarification on this one. Why would this dude standing here in a business suit, looking smart and successful, want anything to do with Ma?

He's nodding his head, though, and grinning like a love-struck fool. I've seen that look before. Every boyfriend Ma's had has worn that same dopey grin. Only difference is that this guy's dopey grin is made up of a full set of perfect teeth. Yup, he's dating Ma all right.

"Your mother is amazing," he says. "A beautiful woman. And so charming."

Charming? My own experiences with her haven't included much charm and, being that they just started dating, I'm guessing I know her better than he does. "Right," I say. "Well, I'll just go get her."

"Sounds great."

I move through the swinging door back into the kitchen where Ma is turning in circles looking for something. She stops when she sees me and watches me with a nervous, questioning look. "Do you like him?"

I shrug.

"He's a great guy," she offers. "An attorney. Can you imagine that? Me with an attorney?"

"Where'd you meet him?" I ask.

"At the happy hour at Bernie's Place."

"You mean the bar? You mean you haven't stopped drinking?"

Ma looks down at her hands and rings them together. "I'm working on it," she says, but her voice is hesitant like even she isn't sure she can quit.

"And he knows about you being a drug addict and an alcoholic?"

"*Recovering* drug addict."

"But he knows about it?"

"Yes," she says. "He knows."

I nod. "He seems nice, then," I say. "As for the rest, I guess time will tell."

"Okay," she says, her mouth turning down as if she might cry again. She goes to the oven and pulls out another pan of something I don't recognize as food. "Would you stay and have dinner with us?" she asks as she puts the pan down on the stove top and picks up the big bowl of salad she made. "I'm just going to take this into the living room. We're moving the table in there so there'll be more space."

I look down at her hands. They're shaking so hard she can barely hold the bowl level.

"Let me help you with that, Ma."

"No, I've got it," she says, smiling up at me. But then she turns and catches her heel and the bowl slips from her fingers, dropping to the floor with a metal clatter and spilling salad everywhere. She sinks to her knees and tries to pick up spilled lettuce with trembling hands, but her tears catch up to her again too quickly. *"Damn it!"*

I grab some napkins from the counter and kneel beside her to clean up the mess. Like always.

"I can't do this," my mother cries. "It's too hard."

I look up from scooping salad off the floor and we watch each other silently.

"Ma," I start to say, but then I drift back into the silence. I don't want to tell her it's okay. I'm tired of letting her off so easy. I've been cleaning up her messes all this time and there's nothing okay about it.

"I never learned how to cook," she says. "My mother wanted me to spend time in the kitchen helping her with dinner, but I was too busy running off to party with my friends. But you, Marley, you're a great cook. Look at you. Almost sixteen already and so grown up. You're such an amazing kid."

"Almost seventeen," I correct her.

"I knew that," she says quickly. "I'm sorry. I did know that, I just wasn't thinking. I guess that's what I mean. I should know that without thinking about it. I should be more involved in your life. That will be my biggest regret, falling apart the way I did when your father died. Not picking up the pieces and taking care of you. I waited too long to be a part of your life, and now it's too late for me to do that."

I wipe up the last of the salad and take the bowl back to the counter. I stand there for a long time, trying not to break down. I'm not ready for this. It's too much too fast.

I can feel her standing behind me, watching me, waiting, her eyes wide and sad and needy like a little girl's. I can't stay here. No way. Not a moment longer. "I have to go, Ma."

"You can't have dinner with us?"

I shake my head. I do need to forgive and forget, I know that. But I need more time than this. Any angle I come at it from, I hit the same wall, come across the same conclusion—this is too much too soon. Especially with her new boyfriend waiting in the next room, expecting us to walk out of the kitchen arm in arm and show him what a happy little family we are.

"I have to get going."

She takes a step toward me as I move to the kitchen door. "Please stay."

"I can't, Ma, I have to work tonight. I'll see you later, though, all right?" I start through the swinging door into the front room before she can say anything else, and approach Michael with my hand already extended to shake his. "I have to go, but it was great meeting you and I hope to see you again."

"You aren't having dinner with us?" Michael asks, looking disappointed.

"I've got work," I tell him.

Michael turns to look at my mother with stars in his eyes. "Already a hardworking man. I love that! You sure have a great kid, Roselia. You're quite a mom."

I give Ma a long look when he says that, but she won't meet my eyes. "Take care, Michael," I say.

"You too, Marley," he replies, reaching out to shake my hand again. "Hopefully we'll have more time to get to know each other next time."

"I'm really glad you came by," Ma says hurriedly as she follows me out into the hall. "I've missed you a lot, and I'd love for you to come back home if you ever feel like that's something you want to do."

I nod. It actually feels kind of good to have my mother give a shit about me for a change. Extremely strange, but good. "I'm proud of what you've done so far," I tell her. "I know it hasn't been easy for you. I just hope you finish what you started. I can't come back until you do."

"Okay," she says. "I'll try. I'll try really hard."

When I look at her again, a strange sadness fills me. She looks so small and helpless, standing in a washed-out hall of a washed-out apartment building. She looks washed-out. She isn't all that old, though, only thirty-one. Thirty-one years with nothing to show for it but a kid she doesn't really know.

I don't want this life. I feel claustrophobic here. I've got to get out. "I'll see you later, Ma, okay?"

"I hope so, Marley," she says, trailing me to the stairs.

It's so weird to be the center of her attention. My whole life I've been trying to get her attention, and now that I have it, I don't know that I still want it. "Good-bye, Ma," I say.

I turn to leave, but then something stops me before I can start down the stairs. Something I realize she's wrong about. I turn back to face her one last time. "Ma?"

"Yes?" she asks, stepping forward and trying to smile.

"You know how you said you wish you'd been a part of my life before and how it's too late now and it's your biggest regret?"

My mother's face drops and so does her gaze. "Yes."

"Well," I say, "the thing is, it's never too late to become a part of someone's life. You can still become a part of mine. If you really want to, that is."

She looks up again, her eyes filled with surprise and hope but fogged over in a thin film of despair at the same time. I leave her like that, standing there speechless in the hallway watching me go.

On the way down, the stairs seem to creak louder than before. The paint looks more badly chipped than I first thought.

My mother is wasting her whole life away in that apartment.

But not me.

No way.

I am going to fly.

25

I HAVE A DATE WITH LEA HALL! I CAN HARDLY
believe it.

A couple days after I gave my Bob Marley speech, I walked
her to her calculus class. After that we started talking every
day. The more we talked, the easier the idea of asking her out
on a date became. By the time I actually did it, it felt like no
big deal at all. I just said, "Go to the movies with me," and
she said, "Sure." I'm nervous and hopeful and excited all at
the same time. But I can't think about her right now. I have to

put my thoughts of Lea, and everything else going on in my life, out of my head when I spin.

"So what are we working on today?" I ask Hawk, eager to get started.

Hawk lights a cigarette, takes a long drag, and blows smoke across the room. "No lesson today," he says. "Just play. All four hours' worth. Since you've got Dorian's...stuff for the day, I want to see where we're at."

"All four hours?"

"What, did I stutter?"

Wow. Okay. I step behind his decks and try to silence all the thoughts running around in my head, get myself in the zone. For the contest, I'll be playing some trance, some drum and bass, some funky house, some jazz, some disco, some hip-hop, a little of everything.

I play for almost four hours straight, covering my whole set for the very first time, and when I'm done, I'm exhausted—totally wiped out. But I'm real good. I'm still working from a sheet of notes and am not totally polished yet, but there's still time. Even I am impressed.

I look at Hawk expectantly, but he remains silent, staring into space.

I watch him and wait. No way can he not have some kind of compliment, even if it's delivered beneath a veil of sarcasm. Getting through all four hours of the hardest set I've ever played is worth that on its own. But he makes me wait a long time, and after a while the silence starts to feel suffocating.

When he finally turns to me, I can't tell if he's disappointed or upset or pissed off or frustrated or what. He could be all of those things. Then again, he could be totally thrilled and just giving me one of those "Hawk looks."

All I know is that he has to say something good. I'm due at least a semicompliment. "It's better," or "Not bad," or "You've sounded worse," accompanied by a casual shrug.

"Well?" I ask.

Hawk stands and starts to pace back and forth, trying to decide what to say, I guess. Then he turns and looks me dead in the eye. He watches me silently for what seems like an eternity. Then he looks away again. Then right at me again. "You're not twenty-one," he says.

"What?"

"Twenty-one years old. I said, you're not twenty-one."

Jewel looks up from the couch in surprise.

"What makes you think that?"

Hawk's eyes narrow. "It's obvious. You look underage. You act underage. You are underage. What are you, like, eighteen? Nineteen tops?"

I drop my head with the weight of my shame for lying to him, lying to everybody at Cream. "I'm sixteen. I'll be seventeen in a month, though."

Hawk shakes his head slightly but doesn't respond. I glance at Jewel and can tell by the shocked expression on her face she didn't know. Hell, I'm feeling a little shocked myself. I'd forgotten that nobody knew. How could I have predicted I'd become friends with the people who worked at Cream when I first went there under false pretenses? Who knew I'd even get the job?

"I'm sorry I lied to you," I tell my feet. "Are you mad?"

It's a stupid question. Wishful thinking on my part. Of

206

course he's mad. Hawk is always mad and this time he has good reason to be.

He glowers at me, his eyes hard, his arms crossed over his chest, his mouth tight.

"I'll only be mad," he says, "if you lose that fucking contest."

26

MY MOTHER HIT THIRTY DAYS OF SOBRIETY last week. Thirty days! She's like a new person and, for the first time in my life, I feel like I'm getting to know her. Her boyfriend Michael actually stuck around. Go figure. He's really been there for Ma, giving her rides to and from her rehab sessions and covering the rent on our apartment.

He even convinced me to have dinner with them on Christmas Eve. After that I started bringing a pizza over on Tuesday nights before my shift at Spazio's, to thank Michael and support Ma. Tonight will be our third pizza night, and I have

Michael to thank for that. Having him around makes it so much easier for me to spend time with Ma and slowly get to know the new person she's becoming.

Things are really coming together. My music is going well, my mother seems to be pulling the whole sober thing off, and my big date with Lea is tomorrow night. I feel pretty good as I approach the door to our apartment.

Then I go inside.

And everything changes.

In the main room the TV is blaring, but no one is there to watch it.

"Ma?" I call out. "Michael?"

Nobody answers.

I walk through the swinging door into the kitchen. The oven has been left open, with a burned pan of something or other left on the top shelf inside. I pull the pan out of the oven and replace it with the pizza I brought as I eye all the dirty dishes in the sink.

The dishes piling up, the burned pan in the oven, the TV left on...Something is really wrong here. Is it Ma? Is she using again? Is she out on a binge right this minute? Is that it? There's no obvious evidence of it, but something's definitely off.

I leave the kitchen and go to my mother's bedroom. It's only a few feet away, but it takes me forever to get there. My legs move slower than I mean for them to and feel much heavier than they should as I approach the closed bedroom door and knock, already afraid of what I might find on the other side of it.

"Ma?"

When no one answers, I force myself to push the door open and flip on the light.

"Ma?"

Nothing. She's not here. So she has to be out somewhere, which could be good or bad. I walk back out of her room and that's when I notice the light streaming out from under the half-closed bathroom door. I walk to the bathroom and gently push the door open the rest of the way and *shit*! "Oh shit!"

That's all that will come out as I look down at my mother's body sprawled out facedown on the tile floor. I stare down at her in horror.

"Ma?"

She doesn't respond, doesn't react at all.

"Ma?"

I move into the bathroom and drop to my knees next to her still body, forcing myself to touch her back and then gently shaking her.

Please be unconscious, Ma. Please just be passed out.

I grab her by the shoulders and this time I shake her hard. "Ma! *Ma!*"

But her body is deadweight, and when I grab one of her hands, it's colder than it should be. Deadweight...there's a reason they call it that. I get a good hold on her and slowly turn her over onto her back, and that's when I see the syringe on the floor. "Damn it!" I exclaim as I pick up the needle and hurl it against the wall in anger. I study my mother's face. She looks bad. Real bad. Like she's been unconscious a long time.

"Ma, wake up," I plead. "Wake up, okay? Please? Don't do this."

210

My throat swells and constricts as I wrap my arms around her and try to rock her back and forth.

I feel like I can barely breathe as I pull out my cell and dial 9-1-1.

My mother overdosed.

1610 Third Street, Apartment 428.

Heroin.

I'm sure.

No, I don't think she's breathing.

I don't know if she has a pulse.

Please, please tell them to hurry.

I stare down at my mother again as my mind empties out into vacant space.

The man on the other end of the line is still talking to me, probably wanting me to check for a pulse, but I can't hear what he's saying anymore. I can't deal with this.

I'm starting to deteriorate.

Slowly at first.

But then the downfall picks up speed.

I plummet toward the bottom.

I am losing track.

Disconnecting.

I can't believe this is real, can't believe it's this bad.

How could she do this?

After coming so far...

How could she?

27

I'M SITTING IN A WOODEN CHAIR IN A HOSPITAL
room at County General. My back is stiff and achy. My eyes
are puffy from lack of sleep. My mother lies motionless in a
bed nearby.

For four days I've been here, watching and waiting. For
what I don't know. Life? Death? She has yet to open her eyes
and she has yet to die. One of the nurses told me Ma could
come back at any moment, said she's seen it happen lots of
times with heroin overdoses. She said they tend to either go
into immediate cardiac arrest and die on the spot, or they go

gradually and end up coming out of the whole thing okay. I can't tell if she really means it or if she's just trying to cheer me up, tell me what she knows I need to hear. I hope what she's saying is true. But it's hard to know what to think after watching Ma for four days and seeing her do nothing but lie here, hour after hour after hour.

While she's been lying in her coma, my whole life has fallen apart.

I'm not playing at Fever anymore. I can't even believe it, but it's true. I'm out of the contest. I'm not sure exactly how it happened. All I know is that when I called Hawk the first day, he was sorry to hear about Ma's coma. But by yesterday, my third day of not coming to practice, he was annoyed. And when I called today to tell him I couldn't come over again, he was totally pissed off.

"The contest is in *nine days*," he said.

"I know."

"This is ridiculous! When can you practice again?"

"I don't know," I admitted. "It depends on what happens to my mother over the next few days. If she wakes up, I'll come right over."

The rest of the conversation is a blur now, but I remember Hawk saying that if I couldn't commit to being there, he'd have to get someone else. I was devastated to even hear him say the words. But when I called him back an hour later, I told him I thought maybe he should. It broke my heart to admit it, but the truth is, I have no idea what's going to happen with Ma. And if someone else out there is worthy of the opportunity to play at Fever, I should give that person the chance.

Mostly I did it to let Hawk off the hook. He's invested as

much in this as I have. It isn't fair to take him down with me. I just can't guarantee that I can be there.

I go back into Ma's room after we hang up, and stand over her bed and just glower at her for a good minute. I'm the most furious I've ever been with her, and that's saying something.

But it's hard to watch your mother lying close to death and stay angry for more than a few seconds. Sixty is all I can manage. After that I slump back into my usual chair and stare at the wall for an hour. Mostly I just don't want her to die. And if giving up Fever is what it takes to keep her alive, I guess it's a sacrifice I have to make. I just hope Hawk finds someone to take my place who wants it as bad as I did. Because I never wanted anything in my life as bad as I wanted to spin at Fever.

I pull my headphones over my ears and try to drown myself in music, but every beat, every melody, every lyric, every chorus, everything feels like another knife stabbing me in the heart and reminding me that I failed, that my dream isn't going to come true after all.

I turn to stare at Ma again and shake my head in disbelief. How did we even get here? Everything was going so great. For both of us.

"Marley?" a voice calls out behind me.

I turn to see Colleen, one of Ma's nurses on the day shift, hovering in the open doorway. "Your mother has a visitor."

"Thanks, Colleen," I answer, not even bothering to ask who it is. I know it's not someone to see Ma. No one has been to visit her. Not even Michael.

I called and left him a message the night she overdosed, telling him what happened. He called me back her second night in the hospital. He kept it short, explaining that he enjoyed getting to know me and feels terrible to hear what happened. He said he cares about her a lot, but that he simply couldn't handle it.

And who could blame him, really? I don't know exactly what went down between him and Ma, but I can guess — she totally fucked up. She slipped and got high. And seeing her like that is all it would have taken.

Unlike Ma, I've had many visitors. Latreece has stopped by a couple times. And Chuckie and Scuzz have come through every day so far. Yesterday they brought some of our crew with them. Chuckie, Scuzz, Will, Jennifer, Tanika, K.C., Terrell, and Terrell's girl, Wanda, all stood around my mother's room trying to act as normal as possible.

I should feel lucky to have friends visiting me at the death-bed of what's left of my family, but I don't. I don't know what's wrong with me. *Hey*, I want to shout, *meet my mother, everyone. You can't miss her. She's the one in the coma.* I am embarrassed and ashamed, and ashamed to be embarrassed.

And all the while there are shadows moving in and out of my head: nurses who fix the other bed in the room so I can stay through the night, the occasional doctor who says so many words that explain so little, and stranger after stranger after stranger passing by the open door.

"Marley?" someone calls out, and then I'm turning to see a shadow I know filling the doorway.

"Hey," I say.

"Hey," she says back.

I stand as she enters the room and try not to look as shocked as I feel to see her.

I don't know which is more surprising — the fact that Jewel

is here or the way she looks. I hardly recognize her. Pretty much all her wildness and flare have evaporated. A black bandanna covers her multicolored hair, her face is makeup-free, and her clothes are plain—a black pullover sweater and a basic pair of blue jeans. Even her green nail polish has been removed.

"How's it going?" I ask, and the words sound really strange, like I'm trying to pretend we're at her place hanging out.

Jewel responds with a weak smile as if she's not quite certain what to do or say. It's a strange sight coming from someone always so sure of herself. As she eyes the hospital room around her, her fingers strengthen their grip on the straps of a massive purple purse.

"I'm surprised to see you here," I say, and immediately worry she'll take it wrong. "What I mean is, I'm glad you came."

Jewel stares at Ma's body lying comatose in the bed to her right. "I can't even begin to tell you how sorry I am," she mumbles.

"Thanks."

"Is she—"

"Sleeping," I say, which is a half truth, I guess. I don't add that nobody's sure if she'll ever wake up. Jewel doesn't look like she could handle that much reality right about now, and I don't want her to bolt.

"So she could have died, huh? If you hadn't shown up?"

I nod, looking over at my mother's bed, at the standard hospital sheet and blanket set that cover her body and the high-tech machines that keep her connected to life. Jewel looks completely spooked. Like if I don't get her out of here soon,

216

she might have a nervous breakdown or something. "So you want to grab a bite to eat? They've got a cafeteria on the second floor that's almost okay."

"Oh, please!" she says, unable to hide her relief. "That would be great."

Since neither of us is hungry, we just find a table and sit, her with a cup of coffee, me with root beer. Jewel forces a smile. We sip our drinks. The silence is long.

"What's going on with school?" she asks. I know she's just stalling, trying to avoid mentioning Fever, but I get it. I'm not sure if I'm ready to talk about it either.

"My school's been real nice about everything," I tell her. "They've already arranged for me to do makeup work in all my classes when I get back. Whenever that is."

"That's great."

"Yeah, it kind of is. What with everything I had going on, my grades were slipping. This way I'll have a chance to get them back up. It's sort of a relief."

"Good," she says. She tries to pull off a pleasant smile, but faking stuff doesn't really work on Jewel. "That's good," she says again.

I nod.

Jewel takes a sip of coffee and sits quietly for a moment. "What on earth happened?" she finally blurts out.

"With Fever?"

"Yes, with Fever!"

I shake my head. I don't even know where to start. I'm not even sure I can explain it. "What did Hawk say?"

"Not much. He's been grumpy and sulking for three days. Then I come home today and he tells me you're not playing at Fever anymore? Says he's found someone else already. That the guy is coming over tonight. What the hell, Ice? It's so awful I don't even know what to say."

I fiddle with my straw and stir the ice around in my drink. "It's my fault," I tell her. "I did it. I told him it was okay to get someone else. I didn't know what else to say. I couldn't leave my mother. If I hadn't left her in the first place, none of this would've happened."

Jewel leans back in her chair and sighs. "It's horrible what's happened. I hate that it had to go down like this. You worked so hard and got so close. But I understand. And I think it's important for you to be with your mom right now."

"I'm all she's got," I say.

"Do you think she'll be okay?"

I stare down at the linen napkins preset on every table whether you're there to eat or not, at the heart-covered coffee mug in Jewel's hands, at the tall plants placed intermittently around the room. It all seems wrong somehow. Like they're trying a little too hard to make the place feel homey when really it's just a lousy-ass hospital cafeteria. "They're saying they think she'll probably come out of it. But sometimes it's hard to tell if they're being totally straight with me. It's like they're telling me she'll probably be okay, but I feel like maybe they're holding stuff back because of me being a minor and all."

"Are *you* okay?"

"I'm hanging in," I say. "I'm a little tired. It's been kind of tough."

It's been horrible, actually.

I think back to the night my mother OD'd. To the way the

218

ambulance reached the hospital and Ma was whisked away on a gurney without anyone explaining anything to me.

A hospital employee grilled me with questions.

What happened?

How old is she?

Is she married?

Do you have siblings?

Who over eighteen can come to the hospital?

We need to speak with an adult regarding your mother's condition.

What about her family?

Have you been in touch with them?

Do her parents live in the area?

Do you have any relatives nearby?

I didn't tell them she ran away from home when she was fourteen. Or that she hasn't spoken to her family since before I was born. It seemed wrong to. I think her mother may live somewhere not too far from here, but I've never gotten the chance to meet her and wouldn't have the first clue where to look. I don't even know her name.

"No," I said. "No family. No friends. She has no one."

No one to sit with her, no one to care if she lives or dies. Only her. All alone like she must have been in our apartment those last few days. But that's okay because I won't let her wake up alone. I won't leave her alone ever again.

I gaze across the room at a group of exhausted-looking doctor types loading up on caffeine and sugar. The mere sight of them makes me feel even more tired.

At a table two away from ours an old man attempts to comfort a sobbing woman who looks to be around Ma's age. They are the only other people in the cafeteria besides us and the doctors. "I really blew it, huh?"

"No, Ice. You didn't blow it. And as for Hawk, I want you to know that he's devastated right now. He'd never admit it to anyone, but he is. He doesn't want someone to take your place. He probably only said that to try to trick you into coming over. When that backfired on him, he had to hurry up and find someone else just to prove that he could. He's only acting like a jerk because he cares so much. You'll get your chance again though. It'll happen for you. You're too talented for it not to."

I stare down at my drink, play with the straw again. It's hard to stay focused. I am so completely exhausted.

Jewel reaches across the table and rests her hand on top of mine. "It's a sucky lesson, but you'll learn it more and more as you get older, and that's that everything happens for a reason. We might not know what it is at the time and some reasons we'll never find out, but there's a reason for all this. You're gonna be okay."

I nod, grateful that someone understands it because I sure as hell don't.

"You know," she says, "they say even though someone is unconscious, they can feel your presence. Your being here is helping her. And if you ever wanna try it, I've heard that talking to people in a coma is one of the best things you can do. Like they can hear us or something. Maybe you should try that. But no matter what you end up doing, you need to remember that you are not responsible for what happened to her. You didn't put her here, Ice. In fact, you saved her life."

Yeah. Deep down I guess I know that. But at the same time

220

I wish more than anything that I'd been there when she relapsed.

Jewel stands and moves to my side of the table, bending down next to my chair so we're face-to-face. She pulls off my lid so my eyes are exposed and stares into them with crazy intensity. Jewel-style intensity.

"I totally fell apart when my mother went into the hospital," she tells me, "and that was only to have her tonsils removed. I can't even imagine what I would be like if I were in your shoes. You're a very strong person, Marley." She touches my cheek for a moment, and I realize she's never called me by my real name before.

"This is so unfair," she says. She leans in and kisses me on the forehead. "But the thing is," she whispers, "life is unfair. Shit happens. There's nothing you can do about it but your best. And you're doing that."

"Thanks," I manage as I watch her pick up her purse and coat. She gives me a sad smile and a wave before turning and walking away from the table.

I don't see her out. I know Jewel, and she wouldn't want me to.

Instead I sit back in my chair.

I listen to her heels as they *click-clack* through the cafeteria and out into the hospital hall.

And my heart feels unbearably empty.

28

IT'S BEEN FIVE DAYS SINCE MY MOTHER FIRST
went into a coma. I've missed school. I've missed shifts at the
club. I've missed work at the restaurant. And in a week I'm
going to miss out on the biggest opportunity of my life.

I stare down at a table in a cafeteria I've become way too
familiar with. Chuckie and Scuzz sit across the table from me.
I can't bear to look at either of them.

"Damn!" Scuzz exclaims.

"Why'd you do it?" says Chuckie. "Why'd you tell Hawk
he could get someone else? Fever meant everything to you."

"I had to," I tell them. "I need to be here for Ma. I don't know what's going to happen to her."

"I don't get it, Mar," says Scuzz. "She's been such a shitty mother to you. Why do you have to be such a good son to her? It just felt like for once you were getting what you deserved. You were doing big things with your music and getting away from home.... And even with all that, she still found a way to ruin everything for you. That pisses me off. I'm tired of seeing her do you like that."

"I know you guys don't totally understand," I say. "But you have your mom and your sisters, Scuzz. And Chuckie, you have your mom, and your dad, and your brother.... You have real families. When my father died, I felt like I lost that. My mother's a nightmare most of the time, but she's the only family I've got. I want to see her come out of this and be okay again. She was trying really hard to fix things. She was sober for at least thirty-three days. That never happened before."

"I don't care," Chuckie snaps. "Trying or not, she still blew it for you. This was your big shot, Marley. She always ruins everything. We're your best friends. We've been watching her destroy your life for years now."

"I know," I say. "You're right, I fucked up." I put my head down on the table and close my eyes. "I'm just so tired of everything. I don't know what to do anymore."

"It's all right, Mar," Scuzz says, reaching out to squeeze my shoulder. "You're gonna get through this. And she's gonna be fine. She always is."

I lift my head and look across the table at Scuzz and Chuckie. "I know you mean well," I tell them, "and I know that you're right about everything. But it'd really be great if we could talk about something else for a while. Anything other than my mother and her overdose and this hospital and the contest. Please."

"We can do that," says Scuzz.

"Sure," says Chuckie. "We only want what's best for you."

"I know."

"Why don't you tell us about your girl? About Lea."

"There is no girl," I say. "We didn't even get to go on our first date."

"She been to visit?" Scuzz asks.

I shake my head. "I've talked to her on the phone a couple times, but no. I can't ask her to come to the hospital. It's still so early on, you know? We were only starting to get to know each other."

"Really?" says Chuckie. "Because Lea doesn't feel that way. She told us she was coming."

"You talked to her?"

"At school. She came over and asked how you were doing. Said she was planning to visit. She's nice."

"I like her too," Scuzz agrees. "She's not what I expected at all. And I think she really digs ya."

I nod and try to smile. Lea made a point of talking to my friends. She even said she was going to come see me.

And she does.

She appears in the doorway of my mother's room that very night, wearing a short blue dress over jeans and gazing steadily at the floor the same way Jewel did.

"Hey," I say.

"Hey," she says back. "You okay?"

I nod. "Hanging in."

Lea looks from me to my mother, then back at me again. "I hope it's all right that I'm here. I wasn't sure, but then I talked to your friends and they said I should come, so I did."

"Thank you," I say. "I love that you came. I should've invited you to when we talked. I just didn't want to put you in a bad spot or anything."

Lea forces herself to look over at Ma again. "So she's doing the same, then?"

"Yeah. No change."

"I'm sorry."

"Yeah," I agree. "Me too."

"I really miss seeing you at school."

"Oh yeah?"

"Yeah. I guess you have no idea when you'll be back, huh?"

I shake my head. "I don't have any idea about anything anymore. I'm sorry about our date and everything. I really wanted to take you out."

"Don't worry about it," Lea says. "You just focus on you right now, all right? You get your mom better. That's what matters. If it's meant to be for us it will be, you know?"

"Sure," I agree.

Lea's phone beeps and she pulls it out to read a text. "I have to go. Believe it or not, Melanie was my ride here."

"Melanie *Jergens*?" I scoff. "You're kidding. She brought you to the hospital to see me?"

Lea shrugs. "Not like she had a choice. But that was her texting me to hurry up."

"Okay," I say. "Can I walk you out at least?"

"'Course," she says, smiling. "That should be interesting."

I walk her down the hall to the elevator where Melanie,

Brittany, and another snotty Have girl named Veronica are waiting, looking more annoyed than usual.

"Hey," I say, smiling the hugest smile I can manage.

"Hey," Brittany and Veronica mumble back unenthusiastically.

"Let's go, Lea," says Melanie. "Like, right now."

"*Okaaay*," Lea tells her. "Jeez." She turns to me and winks and we both crack up laughing.

Lea reaches in her purse and pulls out a long tube with a silver bow on top. "It's just a little something," she says, handing it to me. "No big deal."

"Thanks," I tell her.

Brittany presses the Down button for the elevator to hurry things along.

"Don't you guys want to say anything to Marley before we go?" Lea asks her friends. "You promised."

Melanie turns to look at me. "Marley," she says, "we just wanted to tell you that we're really sorry. You know, about your mom and all."

"Yeah," says Brittany. "It really sucks."

"Thanks," I say. "I appreciate that."

Lea turns to me and reaches up to hug me then. "See?" she whispers in my ear, "I'm working on them. We'll all be hanging out together in no time."

"Yeah right," I say, laughing and hugging her tight. It's the first time I've ever really touched her, and it feels amazing. She's wearing that flowery perfume again, the one she had on at Spazio's. I never want to let her go. I wish I didn't have to. If only that elevator wouldn't come. Ever.

But it does. We let go of each other and I have to watch

helplessly as she steps inside with her friends. A bell sounds, warning the passengers that the elevator doors are about to shut and simultaneously warning me that I'm letting the most amazing girl in the world slip through my fingers.

We watch each other until the doors close.

And then she's gone.

Just like that.

I slowly make my way back to Ma's room, wondering how things got so screwed up.

I feel like I set up a stack of dominoes, each representing a really good thing going on in my life, and then my mother knocked her domino over and it started a chain reaction. When I reach her room I take a seat in my chair and pull the top off the cylinder Lea gave me. Inside is a rolled-up piece of paper. I pull it out and unroll it, and then I feel truly heartbroken.

It's a painting. Sort of a side view, but I recognize my hat and my headphones right away. I also recognize Fever.

I can't believe she did this. Lea painted me sitting across the street from Fever, watching the crowd.

In the bottom right corner of the painting in black lettering are the words *Marley's Dream*, and underneath the title Lea wrote her name in pretty cursive. Her signature. Her autograph. As soon as I see it, I know—this is her dream. She wants to be an artist, a painter. She's good too, real good. I stare at my likeness sitting on the sidewalk across from the club, at the sandwich on a bag beside me, at the can of root beer.

But how? How could she have remembered that night in so much detail? It's the most beautiful gift anyone's ever given me. I lean back in my chair and stare at the painting. And I know it in that moment—I'm in love with Lea Hall.

I feel like I'm floating on a cloud and sinking to the bottom of the ocean at the same time.

Because I love her. But something tells me I'll never actually get to be with her.

29

TONIGHT, I HAVE A HORRIBLE DREAM. I WAKE WITH a start to find the hospital room chilly and dark, lit only by the flickering light of the TV. An infomercial. I stare at it for a moment, too weary to get up and shut it off. Too busy swimming in shock from the dream I just had, which lingers with me even now, muddling my thoughts and making my eyes throb.

In the dream my mother overdosed and lay unconscious in a hospital bed. Then a doctor came in to inject her with that last little bit of heroin she would have needed to finish herself off. I begged him to stop, but he couldn't hear me. I grabbed my mother and shook her hard, screaming at her to get up, but she couldn't hear me either.

I wake up like that, screaming, "Get up, Ma!" But there is no doctor in the room, and Ma is still lying in her bed comatose.

My shirt is damp with sweat and eventually makes me shiver in the overly air-conditioned room, forcing me to find the energy to get up. I check the time. It's only 9:20 p.m. I've completely lost track of when I should be awake and when I'm supposed to be sleeping.

I turn off the television and grab my iPod, hoping to find a song, any song that'll release the tragic feeling overloading my veins. It used to be whenever I was feeling nervous or stressed, I could always count on music to help me relax. When I was pissed off, music calmed me back down. When I was depressed, music cheered me back up. When I was happy, I could always find songs that expressed how good I was feeling.

Certain songs even had the power to make me feel safer. Protected. Hearing the right song in the right moment is like being in a cocoon. Like being in a shell no one else can get inside, a shell I can curl up and totally lose myself in.

But not anymore. Not since I blew my chance to play at Fever. Now every song I play feels bland, and every time I start to lose myself even a little, I get hit by a flashback from that dream: an image of my mother giving up or of that face-less doctor leaning over, ready to inject her. I pull my head-phones off in frustration. I can barely breathe, I'm so upset.

I walk over to Ma's bed and kneel beside her body. I close my eyes and think of my father.

Pop, please help me.

I don't know what to do anymore.

I can't fix this on my own.

Why did you have to leave?

I slowly lay my head down against my mother's stomach and stare at the emptiness of the dark room around me. *Why did you leave us, Pop?* I silently ask again, but the words feel wrong. Like I'm blaming him for something and I'd never blame him, not for anything. He was the best father a kid could have. He was just walking home from a long night working at the shop when that car hit him.

Losing him felt like the end of the world. And now Ma did this. I may not be close to her like I was with Pop, but she's still my family, and I can't afford to lose her too. I lift my head and force myself to look at my mother's unconscious face. Then I do something I've thought about doing since Jewel first mentioned it but haven't had the courage to do until now. I talk to her.

"Ma?" I say, my voice hesitant at first. "Ma, I'm so sorry."

And the next thing I know I'm talking like crazy, the words spilling out of me in a waterfall of honesty and rawness and sorrow. It's like the words are real painful to speak, but also like I've been holding them in way too long, and now that I'm finally purging them, they're coming out of me all at once.

"Ma, I'm sorry for all this you're going through," I say. "But right now I really need you to hold on. I know how much you wish Pop were still here, and I know it's hard now that Michael is gone. But I'm still here. I'm here and I really need you to be here too."

I reach out and slowly take hold of her hand. It's limp but warm and surprisingly soft, like the hand of someone who has been taken care of her whole life. Someone who has never experienced a moment of heartache or suffering. Someone my mother could never be.

"I want to tell you something," I whisper. "My friends? They think I should've walked away from you a long time ago. They never understood why I stuck it out, why I supported you even when it was clear you wouldn't stop using. I've explained lots of times that I did it because you're my family and I'd rather sacrifice to keep a roof over your head and know you're safe at least some of the time than have you living in the streets and being afraid for you all the time.

"But what nobody ever knew was that I also stayed because I secretly believed in you. I always knew there was a chance you could get clean. You just had to want it.

"Then all of a sudden you did. You got clean all on your own. It was awesome and I was so proud of you and you can still have it, Ma. You can get clean and sober, like for real, like for good. I know that now. I've seen how strong you can be. Think how far you could get if you let me help you. I can take care of you. I'll find you the best rehab there is, a real residential treatment program. And then, when you come back home sober, we can take care of each other. All you have to do is give it a chance. Just wake up. *Please.*"

I know I'm gripping her hand too hard now, my fingers squeezing hers too tightly, but I can't let go. I'm desperate. I've given up everything to have this one happy ending. I need this so badly.

"I wish I could have told you stuff," I say. "I wish I'd let you know how much having dinner with you and Michael those three times meant to me because it really meant the world to see you like that. I loved those dinners. And I do want you in my life, Ma. I really do. So please come out of this. I'll move back in and everything. Just come back, okay? I really need you to come back now and be my mom."

I feel ashamed when the tears break through and I'm not sure why. They well up in my eyes and spill over onto my cheeks and drip off my chin. They've built up over years of secretly wishing for something I could never have. They're way overdue. But there's no relief in them. They feel awful. Wimpy. Helpless.

I wipe at my cheeks with the back of my sleeve and kneel there beside my mother's body in silence for a long time. I find myself thinking about what a trip life is. I don't think I'll ever understand how it can be so cruel and sad and unfair, yet so beautiful at the same time. My mother is lying unconscious in a hospital bed. Yet this is the closest I've ever been to her—the first time I can remember wanting to touch her or hug her. The first time I've told her everything.

I press my hand to my forehead and feel all the broken pieces that run over themselves like records haunted by the tiniest little scratches. No matter what I do, no matter how hard I try, I can't seem to get past that one, single, damaged note.

30

I DON'T REMEMBER FALLING ASLEEP AGAIN THAT
night.

But I wake up in the wooden chair to see hospital staff surrounding Ma's bed. I pull off my headphones and slowly stand.

"Marley?" someone calls out. "Marley, we need to go."

I stare at Nurse Colleen in confusion. "What do you mean?"

"We need to leave the room now," she says.

"Why?" I ask as I try to see past her. I have to see Ma, have to know she's all right.

"We need to go," Colleen tells me again.

"I don't understand," I say as I slide down into the chair again and stare at my mother's bed, stare at the doctors examining her. "What's happening?"

"I'll explain in a minute," Colleen says, and then I'm being pulled to my feet by a huge orderly who helps Colleen lead me out of the room.

I study the expression on her face and then try to see over her shoulder, look back into Ma's room. "My mother . . ."

"I know."

"I need to get back in there."

Colleen shakes her head. "No, Marley. Not right now."

I try to move past her, try to go back to the room.

"You can't see her right now," she says.

And then it feels like everyone is talking to me at once. Nurse Colleen, and the orderly, and another nurse I don't know. "I don't understand," I tell them. "I don't understand. I don't understand." I just keep saying it over and over as I try to get past the people talking to me, try to get to Ma. "She's okay. I just need to see her."

"She's not okay," says Colleen. "You can't be in there right now, Marley. I'm so sorry."

"But I can . . . help her. . . . I can . . ." I start to feel dizzy as someone pulls me farther from the room and gently lowers me into another chair. I stare at the door to Ma's room. "She was okay last night."

"She hasn't been okay since she got here," the other nurse tells me.

"I don't understand," I say as I watch the doctors and nurses walk out of my mother's room one by one, their faces grim, their heads shaking.

Ma's doctor breaks off from the group and walks over to me. He wears a sad smile and speaks in a gentle tone, but his words are harsh. Horrible phrases sting my ears— "probable brain death" and "waiting for an EEG" and "second opinion before confirming."

"But I thought she was supposed to pull through," I say.

Dr. Fehrman shakes his head. "I'm very sorry," he tells me. He's apologizing even though he doesn't have the test results yet. I realize he doesn't need them.

He knows.

I know too.

She's gone.

She left me.

My mother just up and left.

Colleen kneels down and puts her hand on my knee. She tries to say something comforting, but I can't let her do that.

I can't let this be real.

"I'm so, so sorry, Marley," I hear her say, but I won't listen. I can't hear. I can't understand.

I don't have the strength left to understand something like this. Not this. This can't happen.

31

THE RAIN STARTS THE DAY MY MOTHER DIES. IT pours down in ugly gray sheets over everything. For days I watch it. There is no thunder, no lightning, no hail, no great wind, just a constant, steady downpour.

Lying in the bed in Chuckie's spare room, I wake up to it and fall asleep to it, but mostly I just stare out the window at it and think of Ma. I think about how I'm never going to see her again. I think about how I don't have a family anymore.

And then the darkness comes. Everything closes in and stays that way and my brain and heart both crumble to pieces. After that I can't think at all, can't feel anything but despair.

Somewhere in the darkness Chuckie's mom brings me cream of chicken soup with Ritz crackers. "You have to eat, Marley," she tells me. But seeing what a good mom she is only makes it hurt more.

"No, thank you," I say, and put my head back down on the pillow and close my eyes.

There are talks of a funeral that someone is planning. "Your grandmother," I hear Chuckie say, but that can't be.

Most of the time when Chuckie and his family speak to me, the words feel more like memories from another life I'm not really living. Nothing feels real. I look out at the dark, cloud-covered sky and wonder if I'm merely caught in another nightmare like the one I had at the hospital. I wait for the moment when I'll wake with a start to find Ma lying in her hospital bed alive, but the moment never comes.

When Chuckie's mother presents me with a black suit and tells me I have to get ready for my mother's funeral, I refuse to go. I tell her I can't deal, that it's too much. She tells me going will help me say good-bye. That I'll always regret it if I don't.

But I can't do it—can't even bear the thought of facing the outside world let alone facing my mother's grave. Will she have an open casket? Will she be buried next to my father? Will anyone even show up?

Will a preacher stand in front of a church spurting the truth about her life or make up some BS story about how kind and giving a person Ma was and how much she accomplished? How do they do eulogies for heroin addicts who've stolen from or abandoned everyone who ever cared about them? Is there a special prewritten script they pull out and use whenever there's an OD funeral?

These are all questions I don't mind not having the answers to. I pull the covers up over my head. It's just not worth it.

"Marley, please," Chuckie's mother pleads, and I feel horrible to tell her I can't go, to make her life more difficult after all she's done for me.

"I can't," I say again. "I'm sorry, Mrs. Wu. But it's not like it really matters if I go or not."

"All right," she says, before collecting the untouched plate of spaghetti she brought me earlier and carrying it out with the suit.

Not a minute later Chuckie's father comes barging in and literally drags me out of bed. "You will go to the funeral," he says. But really I'm grateful to him for making me go instead of leaving it up to me to decide. When I tell him I'm not comfortable wearing a suit, he helps me find a blue pullover sweater and gray slacks to borrow instead.

The service is short and sad, just like Ma's life.

Surprisingly, nobody argues with my request to sit in the back row and wear Chuckie's sunglasses. I hide there, watching the backs of twenty-five people's heads but not really seeing even that much. I'm physically in the church, but my mind is still lying in bed at Chuckie's house drowning in darkness and wondering how only three days could have passed in the outside world since Ma died.

Then Chuckie and his dad are helping me to my feet, and his mom is announcing that there will be a receiving line so people can offer their condolences. Chuckie and his parents and his younger brother stand just outside the church doors and position me in the middle of their line. I stand there in my darkness and reach out to shake the hand of whoever approaches me.

But the first person to approach is Scuzz, with his mom and sisters. Then Latreece is enclosing me in a massive hug. Latreece is followed by Will, and Terrell, and Juan, and Jennifer, and Denise, and K.C., and Tanika. I am grateful for the familiar faces that came to support me, to remind me there's a life out there I still have to go on with and that they're here to help me do that. Seeing the people I love is beautiful and powerful and the reminder I needed of how lucky a person I really am.

But no one seems to be here to say good-bye to my mother. It's just like it was at the hospital, and the thought that nobody who actually knew and cared about Ma came to say good-bye to her is really sad. I see Hogan, and Greg, and Rick, and is that Dana sitting on the stairs smoking a cigarette? Even Dana came?

I see some of the other DJs from Cream — Dorian, and Jay, and Bob O. — and some of my Spazio's co-workers, and a really tall white guy with blond hair. I do a double take on the guy and watch until he turns toward me. It's Michael!

When he reaches me I can see that he's been crying. His suit is wrinkled and he looks like he hasn't slept. I look up and offer him my hand. "Marley," he starts to say, and then he just breaks down, sobbing hysterically.

I lean in and place a hand on his shoulder. "Please don't," I whisper. "You didn't do this to her. We tried so hard. That's all anyone can do."

Michael takes a deep breath and nods. "You're right," he manages. "But maybe I gave up too soon. Maybe I should have stuck it out, kept trying."

"Maybe," I say, "but it wouldn't have changed anything."

"No. I guess not." He sighs again, but this one is more a sigh of relief. "Thank you, Marley. You call me anytime you need anything, okay? Anytime."

I nod and drop my gaze back to the sidewalk, wondering how I'm going to get through the rest of this. How I'm going to face the next person and the next. My mouth aches from all the fake smiles. All the forced words. I just want to turn and run away.

"Marley?" a voice asks hesitantly. I look to the next person and can hardly believe what I'm seeing. I stare him up and down in shock, trying to take in his waiflike body, his sunken eyes, his fidgety movements.

"Don."

Don, who snatched my last memory of my father right out from under me. Don, who helped my mother down the road to this fate. That same Don steps forward and holds out his hand. I stare at the hand he offers me for a long time. I know him holding it out is about a whole lot more than me shaking hands with him. It's about him asking for forgiveness and wanting me to give it to him.

I stand there staring at his extended right hand and thinking about all the things it represents. I think about taking my own right hand and wrapping it around his bony neck and bringing the left one up to join it and strangling the shit out of him.

It takes all I have to even lift my arm, but I do it and I

shake hands with that dope fiend who looks like he's only a couple weeks away from ending up in a coffin himself and I forgive him. I let it go.

"Thanks," he says, nodding to me and quickly moving away. I don't know the three people who shake my hand next, but I know by the look of them that they're also friends of Ma's. Seeing them makes me feel oddly better. Maybe twenty out of twenty-five people at her funeral are here for me, but five still came because of Ma and that counts.

And then I see Jewel. She looks the same way she did at the hospital — no makeup, no colorful outfit, no wild hair. She holds out her hand and I take it.

"I wanted to tell you how sorry me and Hawk are for your loss," she says quietly.

"Thank you, Jewel. It means a lot that you came."

She leans in and kisses my cheek. "It didn't work out with the other DJ," she whispers. "He and Hawk couldn't get along. Hawk isn't taking him to Fever."

I nod to her in reply as she lets go of my hand. She waves awkwardly to Chuckie and his mom and then rushes off to catch up with the rest of the Cream crew.

I don't recognize the next two people who walk up. More people Ma must have known. The woman is older, in her fifties or sixties maybe, and the man at her side is practically holding her up. Her face is covered in heartbreak.

I offer my hand to her, and she takes it and clutches it tightly in both of hers and stares at me long and hard, like she's studying me or something.

"Hi," I offer, "are you a friend of my mother's?"

The woman leans forward, touches her forehead to my

hand, and begins to cry. I look down at her in confusion until the man with her steps forward.

"Marley," he says, "my name is Raul Diego."

I stare at him, and then at the woman, and then at him again.

"Do you know who I am?"

I look down at the woman's bowed head. She's still crying softly, still clutching my hand. "Are we...related?"

The man nods. "I'm your uncle. Your mother's younger brother." I open my mouth to respond, but no words will come. I just watch him in shock. "And this," he says, gesturing to the woman who is now looking up again and holding my hand to her heart, "this is your grandmother."

I don't know exactly what happens right after that. It's as if the world stops turning for a moment, and everything is still.

"Marley," my grandmother cries out, my *grandmother*. "What a handsome young man you are," she says. "My grandson. My beautiful grandson." And then her tears become hysterical.

She pulls me to her and hugs me tight and I can feel her body shaking and her face wet with tears and it's all too much. Raul steps forward and wraps his arms around me and my grandmother, and then I totally lose it. I start to sob, just sort of break down. I can't believe they're really here, that this is really my family.

We all stand there hugging and crying and I really keep at it, the tears falling for what seem like ages. It's the first time I've cried since my mother died, the first time I've actually let any of it out. "It's okay, Marley," my grandmother whispers, and her voice is like a song, soothing and warm. "I'm here now. We're here now. You cry for your mom. It's safe now to cry for Roselia."

And I do. We all cry together. Me and my uncle and my grandmother.

Meeting for the first time ever.

I have a family.

THE NEXT DAY CHUCKIE WALKS WITH ME TO MY
apartment to get what's left of my stuff.

It's creepy to be back. I won't go into the kitchen or my
mother's room, and I don't even want to be near the bathroom. I go into my room and sit on the bed and gaze at the the
bare metal desk where Pop's Technics used to sit.

"You guys were right all along," I tell Chuckie, who stands
in the doorway to my room. "I should've walked away from
her a long time ago."

"Naw," says Chuckie, "I changed my mind about that. I think you did right by her."

I shrug. I'm not so sure. "Fever would've been tomorrow night."

"I know."

"Can we go out tomorrow night? You, me, and Scuzz? I don't want to think about it, you know?"

"We'll find something to get into, keep you distracted. Just don't beat yourself up about it. You're a good person, Mar. You're good to everybody. Don't fault yourself for being good to your mother."

I figured there'd be a bunch of stuff I'd want to take with me, but there ends up being hardly anything left here that I want. The little there is all fits in my pack. "I won't ever come back here," I tell Chuckie. "Never again."

"Yeah," he agrees. "Good."

I take one last long look around me and then walk out of my apartment for the last time, descend the three flights of stairs, and walk out the front door of my building for good.

"You think I could meet you back at the house?" I ask Chuckie as we start down the street.

Chuckie frowns. "You okay?"

"Yeah. I just feel like I need to walk for a bit. Clear my head."

"Okay. I'll see you back at the house, then."

Chuckie and I grip hands, and then I turn and start off in the other direction. I pull my pack over my shoulders and pick up the pace.

I turn the corner and start to jog as thoughts flash through my mind of all I've been through, all I've given up. Suddenly

I feel furious. I'm angry as hell at Ma for ruining things for me. But the anger toward her turns into anger at myself. I feel disgusted thinking of all the things I gave up for her. More than anything, I'm disgusted about Fever. I should've held on to that no matter what. I worked so hard, wanted it so badly.

The more angry I feel, the faster I run. Soon I'm sprinting like crazy through the streets, past the crack addicts and the liquor stores, and the crappy apartment buildings that people feel so good to live in because they represent that step up from the projects. I run alongside the train tracks, block after block, crossing under the section where they ride high above the ground. I've covered a good seven or eight miles at least. And I keep going.

I run until I am dizzy and out of breath. Then I run some more: five more blocks and around the corner and around another corner and down another block.

I hit Hawk and Hogan's building and rush up the stairs and burst into their apartment like a desperate man. Like a desperate boy who's been pretending to be a man because that's what it took to follow his dream. A boy stupid enough to let that dream go after all he's been through.

Tell me it's not too late....

Tell me it's not too late....

"Tell me it's not too late!"

Hawk looks up from the couch, where he's sitting reading the paper. His face transforms from surprise, to confusion, to fury, but he controls it well, forcing a calm expression.

"Late for what?" he says, as if he has no idea what I'm talking about.

"The contest," I say. "Tell me it's not too late, please!" I pause for a moment to catch my breath before pleading some more. "Please, Hawk. I'll do anything you ask. I should never have dropped out. I know that now. But I need another chance. It's all I've got left."

Hawk eyes me carefully over his paper. "The contest is tomorrow night," he says.

I study the beige-colored carpet fibers beneath my feet. "I know it's tomorrow night."

"And?" he asks expectantly. "Look, it sucks the way everything went down with your mom; it really does. But the way it went down is the way it went down. There isn't anything else."

So that's really it then. It's really over. "Okay," I say. "I understand. I figured as much, but I had to try. Thank you for everything, Hawk. I'm really sorry it didn't work out, but really thankful for everything you've taught me."

"Okay," Hawk says. He watches me for a moment longer before going back to reading his paper, and I realize it's a sign for me to go.

"Ice?"

I turn to see Jewel at the other end of the hall coming toward me. "Ice! You're here! Oh, I'm so glad you're here. Are you okay?"

"I'm okay," I say. "And thank you so much again for coming yesterday."

"Of course," she replies.

"I came to ask Hawk about the contest," I tell her. "I was hoping there was a way to get me back in somehow. I still want to compete. But I understand it's too late. I just had to know that I tried, you know?"

Jewel beams as she moves into the room. "Well, that's great!" she exclaims. "Isn't it, baby? He still wants to compete. It's what you wanted." Hawk pretends to be deeply engrossed in his paper. "Baby? Say something!"

"What am I supposed to say? I already called and told them I wasn't bringing anyone, and even if I hadn't, there's no way he'd be ready in twenty-four hours."

"Thirty-two," I correct him.

"Thirty-two hours is a long time," says Jewel.

I step out of my desperation for a moment to survey the scene. Jewel is definitely on my side. That's worth more than gold!

"It doesn't matter how many hours there are," Hawk says. "He quit. He's out."

"His mother was dying. Anyone would quit under those circumstances."

"Most people probably would, yeah," says Hawk. "I told him I think it sucks what happened. It sucks a lot. But what else is there to say? When it comes to the Fever DJ Battle tomorrow night, he's still out."

Jewel's face transforms into something almost monstrous as her arms intertwine across her chest. She speaks to Hawk in a slow, purposeful way. *"So get him back in, then."*

Hawk eyes Jewel with a crazy stare. "What!"

"You heard me. Fix this."

"And how am I supposed to do that? With my magic wand? He *quit*!"

"You know exactly how, Hawk Rosen."

Hawk stares at her in confusion for a moment. Then all of a sudden his face lights up like he's just realized what she's talking about, and the confusion turns to anger. "No way, Jewel!" he snaps. "Don't even think about it!"

"Stop being so stubborn," she says. "Let go of your pride; it's been long enough. Call up Lord. Have him pull whatever strings need to be pulled to get Ice back in the contest."

"Call Lord? Are you crazy? How can you even say that to me? Do you have any idea what you're asking?"

"Of course I do. I was there, remember?"

"I would never give that prick the satisfaction! Ever!"

Jewel sighs heavily as she kneels in front of her boyfriend. She gently pulls the paper from him, tossing it aside. She clutches both of his hands in hers. "Hawk," she says, "everything in life happens for a reason. Ice coming to work at the club, and then the contest happening and your being put in the perfect position to coach him, and then his mother getting hospitalized so he'd have to drop out? Even the guy you tried to get to replace him didn't work out. None of it is a coincidence. All of this happened to get you to call Lord and finally make amends. Do it. Help this boy. His mother *died*, Hawk. Do you have any idea what that must be like? Because I sure don't. And did you know his father died too, in a car accident a few years ago? He's sixteen years old.

"I could understand you saying screw it if he was just some scrub who slacked off and dropped out because he didn't feel like keeping the commitment. But Ice isn't like that. He would have done anything you asked of him. He got hit by a horrible tragedy, Hawk. Life is cruel sometimes and it was just extremely cruel to him. But you can help him. All you have to do is suck up your pride and make amends. Have forgiveness toward someone you should've forgiven a long time

250

ago anyway. Baby, I swear if you do one thing right in your life, help this boy. Do it because it's the right thing to do."

She gets up again and takes a seat beside him on the couch. "Hawk," she says, "do it for you. This isn't just about his dream; it's about yours too. You can't afford to be angry anymore. Not when something this important is at stake. Ice playing tomorrow night is something you want too, remember? So make the phone call to Lord and get him back in."

I can't hold it in anymore. The last thing I want to do is interrupt, but I have to. "When you say Lord, are you talking about DJ Lord? From Fever?"

"He was Hawk's partner," Jewel explains, still watching Hawk closely. "DJ Lord, whose real name is Jessie Forsythe, and Hawk landed this gig together at Fever. They used to DJ as a pair, you know, spin in unison on four tables? That was their thing and they were really popular. Lord ended up stepping on Hawk to get ahead. Hawk got screwed out of his job because of Lord, and he's never forgiven him for it."

The pieces start to fall into place. Everything begins to make sense. Hawk's bitterness. His hatred for Fever. I'd caught all the negative comments he'd been making about the place.

Jewel eyes Hawk carefully, meaningfully. "Until today." She gets that determined look again as she crosses her arms back over her chest. "When he's gonna suck up his pride at losing his spot at the best club in town and call Lord for a favor that Lord will be grateful to do for him."

She turns back to me. "Lord's tried to apologize many times over the years. He's admitted to Hawk that he lied, and he's even told the management at Fever what he did, but

Hawk won't forgive him because it took him so many years to do it. I understood his anger; I felt it too. But it was a long time ago." She wraps herself around him, speaking gently. "Now is the time to accept that apology, sweetie. To get this boy back in the contest. Can't you see? You and Jessie were so young then. That was eleven whole years ago, and this DJ standing before you now had nothing to do with any of it. Ice is so young and such an amazing talent. You told me so yourself. All his dreams are ahead of him. But yours can be too, Hawk. If you'd only let them be. It's not too late.

"The way I see it, Lord has been at that club for ages. He's glued in place. You were always more talented and you can still go places, travel, tour, guest DJ. Your music is beautiful. You only need it to be heard and discovered. If not to help this boy, at least do it to have your music played during his set. Hell, find some reason to do it. Move on. For his dream and for yours. This is the time. So fucking do it, Hawk!"

It's some speech, that's for sure. I feel drained. Mostly because Hawk isn't going to help me. Even if he really wanted to he wouldn't. His pride is too massive.

I don't know what else to do. I feel like I have to get into that club somehow. I have to make this right again. After all those nights sitting across the street with my tuna sandwich and my root beer, it has to happen. I have to get it back, but I don't know where to go from here. "I should've never quit when my mother got sick," I hear myself say out loud. "I should've known better."

"No, Ice," says Jewel, standing and crossing the room to put her arm around my shoulder. "Don't let anyone make you think that. If you hadn't devoted yourself to your mom when you did, you would've missed out on the final days of her life. Don't regret any of this, you hear me? Don't you dare because—"

"Oh my God, shut up!" Hawk yells. "Just shut the hell up! Both of you. I can't take it anymore." He stands abruptly, tosses down his newspaper, and stalks out of the room.

"Hawk?" Jewel calls after him. "Hawk, you come back here! We need to talk about this some more. Hawk? *Hawk!*"

Hawk turns back and points his finger at Jewel. "No!" he says. "No *you*..." He points his finger at me. "Both of you. Get out of my face. For real."

"What are you even acting angry for?" she yells down the hall as he turns and walks into their room. "You have no reason to be mad right now!"

Hawk slams the door hard behind him. Jewel and I look at each other, and she shakes her head as if to say she's sorry. The bedroom door swings open again, and Hawk steps back into the hall looking beyond furious.

"No more!" he yells. "I'm done with it, you hear me, Jewel? Done! Cut the sad looks, and the guilt trips, and whatever it is you're planning to say about me while I'm not in the room. Stop the insanity. I'm pissed as hell at both of you right now for making me do this. At least let me have some peace and quiet around here. I deserve a moment of peace before I call up the biggest asshole who ever lived and ask him for a favor!"

33

IT'S LIKE ANY OTHER NIGHT AT FEVER. I SIT ON
the sidewalk across the street. I unwrap my tuna fish sandwich. I flip the top on my can of Mug and take a sip of cool,
foamy root beer, letting it slide down my throat sweet and
smooth with the slightest bite along the way. It's like any other
night.

Across the street the club is swarming. The men sport
spiked hair frozen by an endless stream of hairspray, waxed
eyebrows, and collared shirts with the top buttons left undone.
The women have molded every strand of hair into place.

Their tops are super skimpy, covered in plush velvet and shiny satin. Their pants are tight, their skirts are short, their boots are tall. Cleavage bursts out in every direction, and all I can think is that Lea is more beautiful than every one of them.

I polish off my sandwich and chug the rest of my root beer. My heart is pounding like crazy, but it's a steady beat, reminding me of what I'm about to do but not causing me to panic. An easy reminder. *Badoomp, badoomp, badoomp* ... I crumple my wax paper and stand. My new competition time is midnight. It's 11:35. It's time.

I take a deep breath and do something I've always wanted to do but never had the courage to before. I step off the sidewalk into the street. Then I take another step, and another, and another, until I'm walking steadily across and stepping onto the sidewalk on the other side.

It is the closest I've ever been to the club and feels more like stepping onto another planet than onto the opposite side of the street. The energy of Fever buzzes around me like an electrical surge. It picks me up and carries me along with it, filling me with its excitement and causing my heart to beat harder. *Badoomp, badoomp, badoomp* ...

The line forming behind the red rope is huge tonight, much larger than usual.

"What's going on?" an arriving couple asks.

"Big DJ battle going on tonight," someone answers. "The best up-and-coming in the city are supposed to be here."

The best up-and-coming in the city. Could that be me? Among the best up-and-coming?

"Aye! Ice!"

I turn to see Hawk dressed in his usual T-shirt and jeans, looking like his typical self. I've chosen to wear regular clothes too. I might look underdressed for a place like this, but at least I'll be comfortable when I spin.

"'Sup, Hawk." I move up to where he's standing off to the right of the line. He shakes my hand firmly, like we've just closed a major business deal or something.

"You okay?"

"So far."

"Been here long?"

"I've been across the street for a couple hours."

Hawk frowns. "You didn't go inside and listen to your competition, did you?"

"You told me I couldn't watch anyone before me, so no."

"Good. How do you feel?"

"Nervous."

"Better get over that quick." Hawk grabs me by the arm like people do little kids when they're in trouble and leads me over to one of the huge bouncers at the entrance. "Mick, this is DJ Ice. Ice, this is Mick."

The bouncer, Mick, crosses his sausage-like arms over his bulky chest and studies me. "You look familiar, Ice. You play here often?"

Hell yeah, I look familiar. I sit across the street from him practically every night. But I only shrug at the guy in response. I can hardly think let alone get into any unnecessary conversation. He shrugs back, and then I look on in dead shock as he reaches over and unhooks the red velvet rope that holds the crowd at bay. He ushers Hawk and me in before all of the people waiting in line, then latches the rope again.

Now, I'd love to pretend like this is no big deal. But the truth is, this is a totally key moment. Here I am, me of all people, skipping the line. Little ole' nothing me, a skinny teenager who sits across the street eating sandwiches under this same huge bouncer's observant eye and works as a busboy down the street, cleaning up after the people who normally pass up the line.

"Are those two of the DJs?" I hear someone ask.

"Maybe," someone else replies. "They look like DJs." And I can't help but smile.

These are the last words I hear before being whisked into darkness.

I follow Hawk down a narrow hallway with dim blue lighting along black walls that vibrate with deep bass sounds from somewhere up ahead. And there is the beat of my heart again, pounding a little faster now. *Badoomp, badoomp, badoomp...*

"Come on," Hawk orders, "hurry up!"

But it's hard to hurry when I'm trying to take in and remember every detail.

We pass a window on the left and Hawk pauses, leaning into the booth to give the redhead sitting inside a peck on the lips. "That's Judy," he says as we continue on. "She sells the tickets and handles the cash."

"How long has it been since you worked here anyway?"

"Long enough."

"And all the same people are still around?"

"Lots of people work here for years," he says. "Others don't."

At the end of the hall we come to a small room bathed in soft red lighting. Three more bouncers stand in the center of the room with a set of steel double doors directly behind them and a staircase on our left that leads down into darkness. That same pounding bass travels up to us from downstairs, but it's much louder now. I can feel it in the tips of my fingers, in the soles of my feet, in the edges of my eyelids. It swirls in my ears and calls to me in a sweet whisper. "Marley...Marley...Marley..."

"Sorry, gentlemen," the smallest of the three bouncers says. "Gotta meet dress code to get inside. No jeans, no sneakers, no baseball caps, no team jerseys. No exceptions."

"This is DJ Ice," Hawk explains smoothly, motioning to me to show my invitation. "He's spinning tonight." These are the first people at Fever he doesn't seem to know. I hand my invitation to the bouncer, who looks it over carefully before speaking to someone through a mini mic hidden on the inside of his shirt. He presses a finger to his ear for a moment, then nods.

"One sec," he tells us.

I take my invitation back and we step aside to wait while a group of five enter the room and hand little movie theater–size tickets to the other two bouncers who stamp their wrists while the smaller one stands back and observes. He opens one of the steel doors for them and the little room fills with music as the people walk inside. Bass rattles the reddened darkness around me and my heart beats in time with it. *Badoomp, badoomp, badoomp...* This is really going to happen.

"Hawk?" someone calls out. We turn to see a tall, slick, sophisticated-looking blond guy, with a perfect tanning-bed tan and the whitest teeth I've ever seen. "Well, I'll be damned. I don't believe it. How long has it been?"

258

Hawk doesn't look the least bit excited to see the guy, and for a moment I wonder if there's bad blood between them. Then I remember that Hawk never looks excited to see anyone.

"Trevor, DJ Ice. Ice, Trevor," he says in a monotone voice. "Trevor's the lead floor manager."

Trevor offers his hand for me to shake. "Glad to have you with us, Ice. Welcome to Fever."

"Thanks," I say, trying to sound casual to mask all my jumbled-up nervousness and excitement at the idea of being welcome here.

"You've been with us before, I'm sure."

"Been with you?"

Hawk glares. "He's asking if this is your first time at Fever."

"Oh. No, I haven't. I mean, yeah, first time."

"Wow! Don't get too many first timers when you've been the hottest club in the city for over twenty-five years. Well then, an even mightier welcome is called for, isn't it?"

I smile in reply. It's hard to focus on him with my heart beating as fast and hard as it is and all.

Trevor looks like a blond version of Donnie, except even more carefully coifed and slickly dressed. Unlike Donnie, he's really cheesy. Unlike Donnie, he also seems genuinely nice. "We're running about twenty minutes behind, so the DJ before you is just finishing up his set and then we have to switch out his stuff for yours, which'll take a few minutes too."

"Okay."

"But that means you have enough time for me to give you a tour of the club if you wish. I'd love to show you around, let you see why Fever is the best of the best."

I look to Hawk for direction. Hawk nods. "Thanks," I say, "that'd be great."

Trevor turns to one of the bouncers. "George, hit me up on the radio when we're ready for Ice on the main stage, will ya?"

"Sure thing, Trevor."

"Fantastic!" Trevor turns back to me and Hawk and smiles. "Follow me," he tells us before stepping down into the darkness of the stairwell.

Okay, now, in my dreams, Fever has always been one level. In reality there are three. I've also always imagined one dance floor when in fact there are several. We descend the flight of stairs to the first, which Trevor refers to as the Elbow Room. Curved couches border the room on two sides, a bar runs the length of the third, and a DJ mixing on a small stage makes up the fourth. That's another shocker—Fever doesn't center around DJ Lord at all, but in fact has six other star-caliber resident DJs. All the other slots are filled by different guest DJs every week.

We pass through the Elbow Room into the Billiard Room, where a bar takes up about a third of the space and eight pool tables take up the rest. People are playing on all eight tables.

At Fever even the pool games look exotic. I've played plenty of pool and watched plenty of other people play pool, but it never looked quite like this. It's the blue-tinted lighting and the club music and the sounds of brand-new, shiny billiard balls colliding sharply that make it all seem so sophisticated and alluring. But really it's the people playing.

Cream seemed glamorous and exciting the first time I walked in, but I got used to it. Eventually I felt like I belonged there. I can't imagine ever getting used to the scene at Fever.

The way the people move, the way they talk to their friends, the way they flirt with strangers, and hold their drinks, and lean against the pool tables, and seem to use the music pumping in from the Elbow Room as their own personal soundtrack. I suddenly feel very sixteen.

From the Billiard Room we move into a third room with a large dance floor and swirling disco lights covering the ceiling from end to end. Small round platforms with poles in the middle have been placed around the room for people to dance on, and a long stage runs the length of the back wall. About twenty or so people are dancing on the stage, with maybe another thirty spread around the dance floor and on all the little platforms.

The feel of the people in this room is a little more like Cream. The vibe here seems to be more about having a good time than looking good the way it seemed to be with the people in the Billiard Room. Still, though, Cream is like the minors compared to this—like the spot the cool crowd hits for warm-up drinks before entering the major-league stadium for the real game.

The DJ is set up in a separate room above that looks out over the dance floor. I can just make out the top of his head bobbing up and down in the little window. Opposite the stage is another bar running the length of the room. This, according to Trevor, is the Star Room.

We climb two flights of stairs and Trevor shows us the VIP Room, which is made up of purple velvet couches and dark glass coffee tables. The walls are painted a bluish purple color, making this the only room in the club that isn't black.

Platters of fruit and desserts cover a long table against one wall, and this room also has its own DJ and bar. There are only around fifteen people here and at least half of them are drinking champagne. All of them look untouchable, as if they might snub you at any second just for looking at them. They've got their own world here and move with body language that seems to say no one else is worthy without actually saying it. They're like an adult version of the Haves.

A huge floor-to-ceiling window looks out over the main room, which is referred to, of course, as the Fever Room. Descending a spiral staircase puts us directly onto the main dance floor.

The Fever Room sits beyond the set of doors where those last three bouncers were checking tickets and is the room people normally enter directly after paying. It's like nothing I've ever seen. This is where the true clubbers go. There are still some people here who seem to be all about looking good and getting attention, but you can tell the moment you take in the massive crowd that most of the people only care about partying.

The room itself is an enormous open space with suspended cages for the Fever Go-Go Dancers to perform in. Disco balls and spotlights hang from the ceiling and walls, and a small, circular stage occupies the center of the room. The stage stands at least ten feet above the crowd and actually rotates in a slow circle. The main floor surrounds it, and two massive bars take up either side.

I look around me in awe. No wonder Donnie OD's on booze and girls every night. He has to keep himself from getting depressed that he doesn't have this! "I had no idea...."

"Well, now you do!" Hawk snaps.

Trevor guides us around a group of tables bordering one

side of the room. Each has a large silver rhinestone-covered combination booth/couch curving around one half so people can sit and socialize. We make our way to a table that sits alone on a second level. The table itself is twice the size of the others and is clearly meant for VIPs so they can sit a step above the rest of the crowd.

Trevor presents us to the table. "Everyone, this is our next contestant, Ice. Ice, this is Lord. He'll be the voice you hear introducing you to the crowd tonight."

DJ Lord looks up at me from under long, dark bangs that completely cover his eyes even though the rest of his hair is cut short. "How ya doin' tonight, Ice? You ready for this?"

I nod in reply, my heart pounding like the wheels of a subway train rumbling across the tracks. *Badoomp, badoomp, badoomp...*

"Next to Lord is Steve, and that's Pete, DJ Smooth, Julian, and last, but most definitely not least, Katie Green, better known as Femme Fatale." I figure these are the other five DJs who got to pick contestants. They all greet me and then Hawk, who already seems to know everyone. Girlfriends and friends are also mixed in at the table but aren't introduced.

Trevor pulls out a walkie-talkie and talks to whoever's on the other end. "Okay," he tells me, "we've got the congas Hawk requested, and your equipment and records are already up there as well, so you're all set."

"Up there?" I look up at the huge circular stage, and my mouth drops. "That's the DJ booth?"

"It spins at a snail's pace," Trevor assures me, putting an arm around my shoulder and guiding me toward it. "You'll forget all about it in no time."

263

"Wow!"

I soak in different energies from the people we pass as we move through the crowd and across the dance floor: all the happiness and disappointment and heartbreak and hope and laughter....

Music from a DJ in the Star Room pumps through the Fever Room speakers so the crowd has something to dance to between contestants.

"You ready?" Trevor asks once we've reached the base of the circular stage. An aluminum ladder angles against one side. My eyes follow it up to the top, one rung at a time. A door sits to the right of the ladder, which, according to Trevor, leads to a small lift inside the stage. The lift is used to haul up equipment and remains stationary while the rest of the stage moves around it.

The ladder is primarily for the DJs so they can climb up and down quickly without all the hassle of the lift. I can't even imagine how many different DJs must have climbed that ladder and stood up there, some of them famous guest DJs visiting from all over the world. I grip the ladder and watch the stage above through determined eyes. "Yes. I'm ready."

"Excellent!" says Trevor. A heavyset guy in a sweat suit with long, stringy, light brown hair and wire-rim glasses pulls out of the crowd and Trevor puts his arm around the guy's shoulder like he did me. "Right on time, Lenny. Ice, this is Lenny, your sound engineer. He'll show you the lay of the land up top."

Lenny nods a greeting and motions toward the ladder that I'm now gripping circulation-tight. When Trevor offers his hand, I let go long enough to shake it, then grab the ladder again. "Good luck to ya, Ice," he says, flashing his gleaming-white smile.

"Thanks."

He turns and shakes Hawk's hand. "Good to see ya, Hawk. Don't be such a stranger." Someone calls to him over his walkie-talkie and he moves back into the crowd.

"After you," Lenny says, motioning toward the stage. I take a deep breath and begin to climb.

Stepping onto the massive DJ stage feels more like step-ping onto a carnival ride, like a merry-go-round in slow motion. As I look around, I feel like I'm being closed into a Ferris wheel and pulled up into the air off balance, with my insides scrambling as I rise up over the top and come to a sud-den stop, swinging back and forth as I gaze over the side at the view. That's how this feels. Like being picked up off the ground, having your stomach churned, rising all the way to the top, then being kept there slightly off balance, gazing over the side at the massive dance floor below.

"This is it," Hawk is telling me, "end of the line. Remem-ber, no matter what happens tonight, *do not fuck up*. Do and I'll kill you."

"Okay," I say, but my heart is pounding so hard and I'm feeling so amped, it's hard to even speak. *Badoomp, badoomp, badoomp*...And I wonder if he's feeling the pressure too. His rep is riding on me now. After all the negative crap he's spewed about my skills, he turned around and believed in me enough to let me be the one to redeem him at the club where his career went south. Even made partial amends with his for-mer best friend to do it. Now, that is some deep shit.

I'm facing five other DJs, every one of them more experienced and seasoned than I am. I know I can't win. Under normal circumstances I would've worried about how good they are and how the three that've already gone ended up doing. But frankly I don't care. I never did. It's being here that matters. And my one goal, now that I've made it, is to stand tall and impress the judges and the other DJs enough to restore Hawk's name. It's the only way I can ever come close to repaying him for everything he's done for me.

Lenny goes over some of the technical sound engineering stuff, which is complex and complicated and goes way over my head but does give me an overview of the kinds of things he can do to help me and the types of requests I can make of him. He wishes me luck.

The music pumping in from the other room has stopped now and the crowd stands around socializing. Waiting. For me. There are so many people packed around the dance floor on every side. Many more than I ever imagined there could be. It's like wall-to-wall bodies.

"Dump the jitters," Hawk is saying. "You can't afford them anymore."

I nod slowly to show I understand, not that I really have any control over what I'm feeling now anyway. I'm not even sure I'm still nervous. I don't know what I am: excited and amazed and surprised, I think, but mostly just overwhelmed.

"I need you to forget all this going on around you and get your head around what you're about to do. Remember what I said. You can't have your set a hundred percent prepared, because you have to be able to adapt to your crowd, and you can't wing the whole thing either because a contest requires rehearsing, strategizing, putting some thought into the development of your set. It's all about sounding spontaneous but polished. You are both.

"You've got four solid hours' worth of quality and creativity to give this crowd. Now it's up to you to mix it up. Select forty-five minutes' worth of the best music you can from those four hours. Start with the two records you've always started with. From there, feel out your crowd and move in whatever direction they take you. Let them guide you. Go with your instincts. Spin the best you ever have. Cuz if you screw this up even a little, I'll break your neck in two. Then I'll kill you. Remember—"

"I know. Don't fuck up."

"You're goddamn right."

Hawk turns and moves to the ladder.

"Hey, Hawk," I call after him.

"What is it?"

And that's when I finally say all the things I've wanted to say to him. Except that I only actually say two words. Hawk hates sappy, so I simply nod to him, my eyes humble and appreciative.

"Thank you."

Hawk's gaze moves out over the crowd. He gives a slow nod of his own, but it's directed more to them than me. "You deserve it, I guess." He lets out one of his typically bitter laughs. "I mean, look at you. No matter what life hits you with, your ass keeps on fighting to get where you need to be.

"I'm gonna fight to get back everything I had and then some. I figure if a newbie like you can keep on keeping on no matter what, it's definitely not too late for me. So should you be thanking me for all I've done for you? Hell the fuck yeah! You better thank me. But maybe you aren't the only one who feels thankful."

Hawk turns his back on me then, stepping onto the top rung of the ladder and swinging his other leg over the side, but stops long enough to call out to me once more before climbing down.

"You've earned the right to call yourself DJ Ice," he says. "All you gotta do now is kick some serious ass."

Hawk's words linger with me long after he disappears down the ladder and I find myself staring at the spot where he stood and thinking back to that first day at his place. When he caught me on his tables, he made it clear he didn't think I was a real DJ. I was a joke to him and he let that small fact be known in a big way. So to hear him say I've earned my name means the world.

I watch for him to reappear down on the dance floor and finally spot him making his way across the room to sit with the other DJs. Somehow, his words are exactly what I needed to hear because I feel truly ready now. I'm eager, even.

No more lessons. Hawk is gone. It's my time now.

I pull my headphones over my ears. They're not hooked into the decks yet, but into my iPod. I shuffle to the song I want and look back out over the crowd again, eyeing the room in amazement, turning full circle to take in every inch of it as Drake's "Greatness" fills my head and hypes my senses. I turn my attention to ordering my records, pulling up my playlist on Dorian's laptop, checking my needles, and adjusting my mixer settings how I like them to be.

"You ready?" Lenny asks.

"Yeah. I'm cool."

"Hey!" a girl's voice belts out from somewhere out in the crowd below. "*Hey!* Down here! Ice! Down here!"

It doesn't take long to spot Jewel, whose hair is now streaked with dark blue to match the funky lace dress she's got on. She looks as beautiful as ever as she waves a piece of cardboard in the air that says DJ ICE RULES!!! across it in big, colorful letters. "You're the best, baby!" she yells.

I can't see them, but I know my boys are out there somewhere too. Chuckie, Scuzz, Will, and Terrell all got to skip the line and get in free on my guest list. *My guest list*... Even Rick and Hogan switched their shifts around at the club so they could be here.

I look for Hawk at the DJ table in the back, but people are swarming it now.

"All right, everybody," a voice suddenly booms overhead, "let's see how loud we can get. Because DJing from our main stage is our fourth contestant. Show your support and help me give a warm Fever welcome to Deeeeejaaaaay *Iiiiiiiccccce*!"

Now, meeting Lord wasn't much of a thrill. There was so much to take in at once I couldn't really focus on any one thing. Besides, he's such an average-looking guy. Average height, average build, average clothes. The only thing interesting about him at all is those signature bangs of his, and I've seen those plenty of times from across the street. No, meeting him wasn't exciting at all.

But having him introduce me? Now, that's special. *The* DJ Lord is introducing me to *the* crowd at Fever. That's when the reality truly sets in. I have arrived. I've really made it.

It's pretty unreal. I've only dreamed about this down to the detail. The best part is, every one of those details is better in person.

Hundreds of eyes stare up at me as the crowd cheers in response to Lord's introduction.

Since I know I can't compete on the level of the other DJs, I've decided to ditch all the stupid little things I'd do if I were competing for real and do what I want. Hawk won't care as long as I perform well within the choices I do make. And I will. I can already feel it.

I look down at the people spread out below and surrounding the stage, taking it all in and then some, letting them keep on with their applause until they get bored with it and quiet down to a mumbling state as they wait for me to do something.

There is color everywhere. In their faces, in their clothes, in their surroundings, in the spotlights. My heart pounds so hard I'm surprised no one else can hear it. *Badoomp, badoomp, badoomp…*

The colors pixelate, swimming before my eyes like so many tiny, swarming insects. Black touches the fringes of my view and slowly takes over, spreading inward until only a few colored cells remain and complete darkness takes over. Pitch-black nothingness inhabits the area where all those people once stood. Now there is only empty space.

The noise around me disintegrates and I breathe in the silence. Nothing else exists but the space immediately surrounding me and the still air and my vinyl lined up in Hawk's trusty crate. As my first record falls into place on the left turntable, I pick up the closest mic and tap it to make sure it's on.

Talking to a huge crowd happens to be the last thing on

earth I want to be doing, but there are words that need to be said. Even if I have to force them out.

"This set I'm about to play," I say, my voice echoing amid the black abyss, "is for my father, Rodney Dylan."

I put the mic back on its stand. And then there is nothing left but the emptiness. That and a sample of voices so soft they're barely audible. I gradually increase the volume and let the voices grow and grow, slowly overtaking the emptiness with a single word that sings out over and over again, exploding from every speaker before I pull it back, fading it out a little more each time someone sings it like an echo that booms in the darkness, then fades away in an evaporation that vibrates through vacant air.

"Music, music, music, music, music, music, music, music, music, music, music."

It's an eleven-note count of samples I took of voices from eleven different songs each singing the word "music," and just as quickly as the voices rise to full volume, I fade them away into nothing. Then I drop them again, letting them boom and fade, boom and fade.

"Music, music, music, music, music, music, music, music, music, music, music."

Whistles and shouts rise up out of the darkness, but I barely hear them as I drop the voices a third time around, this time distorting them into unintelligible sound as they fade away and adding keyboard notes I recorded during lunch one afternoon at school. The keyboard notes become full chords that float beneath a long, fluid little tune that repeats itself over and over as the voices continue to sing that one beautiful word again and again like mist settling below a sleepy gray sky.

"Music, music, music, music, music, music, music, music, music, music, music."

And then. At last. I add THE BEAT—an even-paced dance rhythm blending into the voice and keyboards with ease. This is my ode to the DJ world, to the eternal love I feel for that indescribable, unattainable miracle they call music.

I let the beat take over, pulling the voices and replacing them with another string of sampled sounds off a favorite track of mine called "Hole."

That's when the color returns, appearing in random drops that focus my right side and then my left before expanding into all the empty spaces in between as the crowd returns to my peripheral view. I allow myself to look up from my work long enough to see them in full focus, bodies moving, listening, starting to sway on a packed dance floor as people wait to see what I'm made of.

Everyone has a moment in life, a space and time when everything is theirs and goes exactly the way they want it to. I am in the midst of mine. In my whole life I have never been happier, freer, or more sure of myself. This is the only flawless experience I've ever known, and I don't plan on missing one single beat of it.

I move into my Brazilian set next. It's an ode to my teacher; and Hawk's friend Jobe's live conga playing adds the perfect touch to Hawk's favorite original composition now being played in front of a live crowd for the first time. I end up mixing Hawk's work into a composition of my own he helped me create called "Plenty More Where That Came From" and let that take over the room.

The crowd reaction to my addition of a live musician is

overwhelming and unexpected, and they cheer all over again when Hawk's other friend Marty steps onto the circular stage and joins in. Marty's sax sings throughout the club in long, soulful notes as the congas continue to add a sense of culture, inducing people to move from deep within.

My head bobs in a way I can only describe as more confident than it ever has before as I absorb the crowd's energy and try to mind read their desires. At school, at Cream, at Spazio's, even with my friends, I've never felt like I belonged so completely as I do in this moment here at Fever on this rotating stage. I'm taking over the whole damn club.

The next part of my set is made up of random mainstream rap lyrics laced over R & B melodies each taken from a rap song, then swapped up so none of the rap lyrics match their original R & B melodies. It's like a mash-up, except without that typical mash-up feel where someone combines two songs and people go, *yeah, that's cool*. I want them to walk away from my mix convinced the songs I combine should've been used together all along. I don't even want people to be able to remember how they sounded apart when I'm done. And that's exactly what I do.

This is also the part of my set when I move onto the third deck and spin on all three, holding my breath as I do, since I'm only capable of mastering three turntables at once for a minute or two. This is the part I was most worried about. I'm just not all that confident with a third deck spinning. I thought about skipping it and not even risking the chance of screwing up once I was on the ones, twos, and threes, but Hawk really wanted me to fit it in somewhere. I end up abiding by my mentor's wishes, and the confidence I'm already feeling spills over onto that third deck. I feel like I could mix on three turntables for the rest of my set if there wasn't so much more I wanted to do.

People shout and whistle, calling out to let me know they're appreciating the pounding, swirling sound I'm creating and I can't believe how easily their movement can join our energy together, doubling it as the beat doubles before dropping hard. The crowd is packed in so tight that people are having trouble finding enough room to dance. I watch the expressions of pleasure on the Fever crowd's faces and fall in love with the feeling.

This is where I choose to mix in the voice-over Scuzz did for me of a Langston Hughes poem called "Dream Deferred." Scuzz has the lowest, smoothest voice of anyone I know, and girls melt when he speaks to them. When he recorded the poem he really got into it, lifting his voice in all the right spots and pausing over words for emphasis the way the real poets do.

Spoken word jumps like pop rocks over my music, which now consists of John Coltrane jazz playing over a pulsating techno beat, with some scratching thrown in to show off my full range. My mix floats on air and shakes the rotating floor beneath my feet, and I can't help but beam with pride at the smooth blend of sounds and words. The poetry has the reaction I'd hoped for with the Fever crowd. They seem way hyped that I've added a poem to my mix. There won't be anyone else doing that tonight. But I'm not done yet. Far from it.

While the crowd is busy shouting for more of the jazz/poetry mix, I'm moving into my house set. Latreece climbs up onto the stage and gives me a prideful squeeze before grabbing a mic and beginning to sing, lacing her voice over my mix of upbeat, dizzying energy. Her deep, emotion-filled notes cry out across the crowd and multiply over themselves, expanding throughout the massive room until the walls reverberate from the outside in. *"Mmmmm, woa, woa, woa-aah..."*

I add a high violin sample and a light, pulsing beat, letting them dance within the record as Latreece plays with a scale of deep, heartache-filled notes improv style above it. *"Heaven....Oooooh, heaven!"* I ask Lenny to switch up the effect on her microphone so each note delivers an echo.

"HEAVEN...heaven...heaven....Oh...oh...oh...oh...oh."

Spotlights spray rainbow patterns that swirl in mini circles over the room and across moving bodies that appear and disappear as the stage turns its way around the club. I close my eyes, but even with them closed I can still see people dancing in patterns of light. I can picture Pop standing somewhere down there in the middle of the crowd, alive and loving and laughing. I can see Ma standing beside him, drug-free and happy and lost in my music. Imagining my mother finally being free of her pain helps lift me out of my own. Being here, standing on top of the world, lifts me.

Latreece's voice floats through the club over and over like the swirling colors of the music itself, like the swirling colors of the spotlights, like a swirling, colorful dream, floating on a dream, submersed in a dream.

"He-e-e-e-e-e-aaaaaaaaaven..."

And it is heaven. All of it.

The tracks themselves become dreams, spreading over the club like wildfire and filling every crevice like melting butter; and when I drop a deep, pounding bass into the addictive melody, the rainbow patterns become pink, flickering strobes.

Smoke creeps in, spreading across the dance floor and proving Lenny really knows what he's doing because the timing couldn't be more perfect.

Hell, the whole night feels perfect, and all the while I am here, not dreaming but really, actually here, standing amid a massive crowd of people and bathing in their happiness. It's so crazy the power that music has, the way music can make people feel. Whatever it was they were doing before they came here—trying to focus in some boring class, working long hours at their job, changing dirty diapers, sitting in standstill traffic—whatever struggles and disappointments they might have experienced today, I have sucked all their worries away and replaced them with euphoria.

My own euphoria has brought me to another level, a completely different plane. Kind of like when you have the most incredible dream right before you fall asleep and your conscious mind still has control and everything turns out the way you want it to.

My music is my drug: one I will always fiend for, a natural drug that'll always be more powerful and beautiful and pure than the one that killed my mother. Nothing feels as good. The energy and the control of sound parallel that feeling I get when I'm riding with Scuzz and Chuckie and someone says something so funny and we all crack up laughing. It mirrors the thrill of seeing that one special girl I've wanted for so long look into my eyes as her sweet lips form a smile meant only for me.

It feels like these moments and so many others blending together on the ones and twos and replaying inside my head, above my melodies, outside my drumbeat, around my heartbeat.

Every part of me explodes and shouts at the world, and when the people hear me cry out to them through music, they seem to understand, cheering and moving within an expanding freedom they can't control and wouldn't want to even if they could.

I am consumed by the power of this place, its glimmering beauty, sparkling in so many different forms it's blinding.

But I squint my eyes and take it in all the same, playing on and on into an endless night.

And so goes the dream....

And so goes my life....

For as long as I live,

I will never forget this.

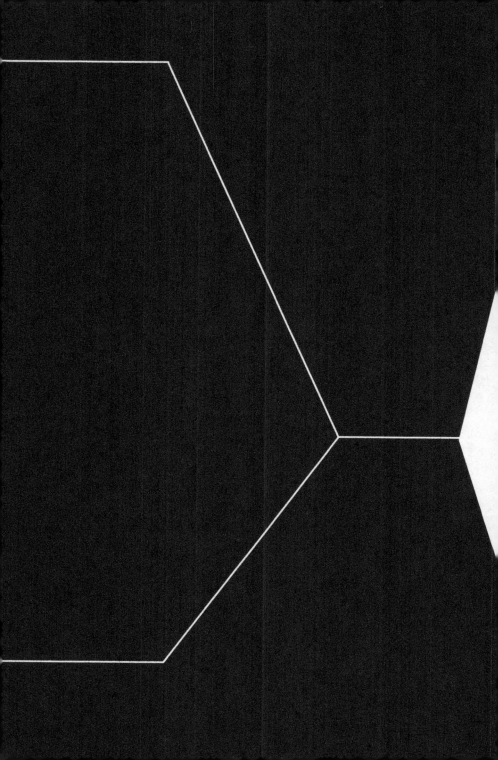

IN THE BEGINNING

ONE DAY, WHILE I WAS SCANNING RECORDS ON the massive bookshelf at Hogan and Hawk's place, I stumbled across this real cool track called "Out of Blue Comes Green." I've been spending lots of time on it, experimenting and mixing and so pumped to be working on something new. I'm not going to mask it like I did with my remix of "Angelia," but instead add layers, complement it, but still let the original tune sing through.

The thing I dig most about the song is definitely the lyrics, especially the stuff the lead singer says about the things he doesn't have the power to change because they aren't problems to solve but fixtures of life that can't be chosen or altered.

The way I see it, the blue is the stuff you can't control, life's major heartbreaks and struggles, that feeling of devastation so massive and brutal it inflicts permanent damage on the heart and the spirit that can never be undone and will always be there, stewing somewhere in a corner of your mind like deep scars you'll have with you your whole life.

The green you also can't control. But that's the part that reminds you life is worth living. It's not the here-and-there type of good stuff that happens every day either. The green is the stuff that comes in huge doses that slap you in the face when you least expect it and brings a light to all that you are through growth, and bravery, and goodness, and love. It's the stuff that picks you up when you're at the bottom and makes you keep on going even when you're sure you can't. That's the green.

The song reminds me of my life lately and the way things that happen can devastate you so badly but then turn around and totally surprise you by growing into something unexpected and astounding.

Of course, I could be wrong. I mean, who knows what the song is really about except whoever wrote it? But that's one of the many things about music that's so great. You can interpret a song and relate it to your life any way you want.

"So how do you feel? Are you nervous? Anxious? Excited?"

I drop out of my daydream and back into the here and now, where I am not working on my new song at all but on the train with Lea.

I shake my head. "Honestly, I don't know. I guess I'm overwhelmed mostly."

Lea nods.

"It's like getting the best birthday present ever, you know?"

"Maybe," says Lea, "but you haven't seen my present yet. It's pretty damn good too."

Lea smiles at me and I put my arm around her and pull her close. I still can't believe we're finally on our first date. It felt like it was never going to happen, but we're here. She rests her head on my shoulder and I can feel sparks of electricity shooting through every inch of my body. I gaze through the train windows to chill myself out, watching the outside world where life carries on, constantly moving, spreading out in every direction as we rattle along the high tracks. I close my eyes and absorb the soothing, rumbling rhythm, wondering how many times this train has traveled over these same tracks. How many different lives has it carried toward heartache, and surprise, and tragedy, and excitement?

It's been two weeks since the contest at Fever, and it feels like everything has been turned on its head and shaken up like a snow globe, then turned back over with the pieces left to settle where they will.

But at the same time I feel like my life makes sense for the first time. Like even the frayed parts are okay because I know how to deal with them now.

Lea and I are on our way to Hawk and Hogan's apartment for an early birthday dinner before they have to head to the club. Jewel invited all my friends, which was mad cool of her, plus the usual "family" of employees and regulars from Cream. I invited Lea. I wasn't sure she'd be down to start our first date hanging out with some kids from school she doesn't know and a bunch of total strangers, but it turned out she was really excited to come. I can't wait for everyone to meet.

I was fired from my job at Cream. It was inevitable. The worst part was seeing the look on Lonnie's face when he found out I'd betrayed him by lying about my age. I didn't mean any harm by it, and if I'd known I could've gotten him in big trouble and his liquor license suspended, I never would have accepted the job in the first place. Luckily he was able to keep the whole thing quiet, being that I was never on the books. But he won't talk to me anymore.

I'm starting to get offers for private-party gigs, though, thanks to all the exposure I got from the contest. I've already been hired to spin at two Friday-night parties in the next month, one of them for some kids at another fancy private school, Piedmont Academy.

But what's even bigger and more exciting than that is what's happening for Hawk. He and another DJ friend of his named Jay are working to put together their own company of several DJs for hire. They want to call themselves "Stylus" and, if it happens, I'll probably get to be a Stylus DJ and, who knows, it could end up going huge. You never can tell.

I'm back at school again, getting a chance to catch up in all my classes and bring my grades back up. I want to get back on track for college. I want to have some schools lined up. Just in case I don't get my shot in the next year at becoming an international star and traveling the world and spinning for stadiums full of people. I'm going to push for it, though, and put everything I've got into building a real career for myself as a DJ. It may be a long shot, but it isn't impossible.

And then, there's my new family. This weekend my grandmother is throwing me a second birthday party and inviting all kinds of relatives that I'll finally be getting to meet for the first time. I can't believe she only lived a half hour from us this whole time and that so many relatives are close by.

This weekend I'm also moving out of Chuckie's place and finally giving his family their spare room back. That's the part that's the best birthday present ever—I'm moving in with my grandmother. It feels too good to be true, but it is. I'll be living with her and my uncle Raul and staying in the same room Ma had growing up. My grandmother thinks my being there will be healing for all of us, and so do I.

I never thought I'd have a family again, and now I'm going to get to be a part of a big, kind, supportive one. It's like things have been so hard, but suddenly they have the potential to be really good. I turn to gaze at Lea, wanting to remember every detail, every word and touch and moment with her. I smile and she smiles back, hugging my trophy in her arms, which I got to pick up from Fever today and am bringing over to Hawk and Hogan's place to keep until this weekend.

Oh yeah. That's the other thing.

How could I forget the most important thing?

I actually won!

It's crazy really. I mean it never occurred to me I might actually win the competition. To me, the winning was in getting the opportunity to play. In fact, I left Fever right after watching the final DJ's set. Hawk and Trevor had to come outside to find me and bring me back in when my name was called. Hawk was like, "You won, you idiot," and I was like, "Won what?"

Of course, I can't collect on the real prize of landing a spot as a regular at Fever. Not after the age scandal.

I was on the front page of the entertainment section of the paper the day after the contest, holding up my trophy, with a caption under my picture that read "Marley 'Ice' Diego-Dylan Wins First Annual Fever DJ Battle, Becomes New Regular."

I bought, like, ten copies. Well, okay, I paid for one and grabbed, like, ten out of the machine when it opened, but basically I got myself a lot of them because I was so fucking excited to see my name and picture in the paper and wanted all my friends to see it too. That kind of thing doesn't happen to guys like me.

The article itself was real brief, and there wasn't anything specific about me in it that could've gotten me into trouble. I was never interviewed, being that I bailed out right after the award presentation. Mostly the article gave details of the contest itself.

But it was just my luck that someone — more than likely a certain rich senior Have from Ellington Prep — saw that article and made anonymous calls to both the newspaper and Fever, busting me out as a high school junior faking twenty-one.

I was disappointed for sure. But it's hard to feel too bad when winning was a bonus I totally hadn't expected. Even though the job ended up going to the runner up, they let me keep the trophy, which was real cool of them. And we all know who's really number one.

I've learned a lot over the past few months, but mostly I've learned that life is like music. It's all about laying out everything that happens to you like levels and seeing life as the track those levels exist to balance.

Friends, family, school, work, love, hate, past, present, future, success, disappointment...everything has its place on the scale. And without the lows, even those deep, dark, heartbreak-style lows, you can never appreciate how truly amazing the highs can be. Without the blues, you can't have the greens. Good, bad, or indifferent, you need all your levels to balance each other out if you want your track to sound tight.

Last night, I had the most incredible dream.

I dreamed I was on the highest of highs, flying just like I said I would.

I dreamed I had a family who loved me and wanted to give me a healthy home life.

I dreamed of the most elite club in the city and of a circular booth from which I had the power to free people of all their worries and replace those worries with forty-five minutes of bliss.

Last night, I dreamed of these things.

And in the morning,

when I woke from that dream,

I found out that I was, in fact,

still dreaming.

Acknowledgments

MY DEEPEST HEARTFELT THANKS TO THE FIVE people who believed in this book the most: Steve Arons; Mark McQuillen; Anthony Riva; my superstar agent, Emily Sylvan Kim; and my ever-brilliant editor, Alvina Ling. Without you, Marley would be nothing more than a dream.

Serious gratitude is also owed to the following peeps: Josefa James, DJ RasCue, Brian Furano, Charles Lawrence, DJ Iokepa, Mike and Cindy Minor, DJ Ben Seagren, Maria Elena James, Anthony Romero, Tree Kent, Kimiko Matsuda-Lawrence, Alice Allman, DJ Moses, Ann Longknife, the crew from Little, Brown Young Readers, and every other person who provided me with encouragement, feedback, support, inspiration, or really good vibes during this long, wild roller-coaster ride of a journey.

Eternal gratitude is constantly due to God for bringing me this far.

Inspired by true events, a captivating tale about two teens' paths from hate to hope.

"A must-read."
—Ellen Hopkins,
author of *Crank*, *Burned*, and *Impulse*

FREAKS AND REVELATIONS

davida wills hurwin

L B LITTLE, BROWN AND COMPANY

Discover more at www.Teen-ReadMe.com

BOB479

Love Maia

has always been a reluctant reader. She sees her writing as an opportunity to reach out to other reluctant readers and make books more enjoyable for them by combining literature and music and by creating relatable characters. In addition to writing, she enjoys underground hip-hop, kickboxing, pizza, fog, death metal, and butterflies. Her Pearl drums and her Technics also please her immensely. When not hard at work on her next book, Love can be found playing drums in an alternative rock band around San Francisco. *DJ Rising* is her debut novel.

Her website is www.lovemaia.com.